Beauty Worth Dying For . . .

Feeling old and jaded and not particularly curious, Weinstock picked up the package containing the so-called "Rembrandt." Tearing off the brown paper, he discovered that the painting was wrapped in a green plastic garbage-can liner.

Not elegant, but functional. Probably appropriate too, the art dealer thought sourly.

Weinstock extricated the painting from the bag and placed it in the middle of his desk. He settled into his chair, pulled over the lamp, and turned it on. And then he froze.

For perhaps three minutes he sat in trancelike stillness, his eyes rooted to the small, ebony-framed panel in front of him. Then he slowly realized that his hands were shaking and his mouth was dry.

Weinstock's body registered his reaction to a work of art before he was conscious of making any visual judgments, and the symptoms he felt now—the throbbing of his temples, his sharp, shallow breathing, and the tightening in his chest—were all familiar ones.

He had felt them the first time he had made love. He had also felt them, however, when the brakes gave out in his car in the middle of a steep mountain road. Weinstock wondered which was the more appropriate metaphor.

Perhaps beauty was, after all, bad for your health . . .

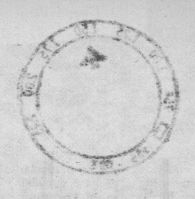

The Rembrandt Panel

Oliver Banks

PINNACLE BOOKS   NEW YORK

The lines on page 26 are from *The Iliad* by Homer, translated and with an Introduction by Richmond Lattimore, copyright 1951 by The University of Chicago. Reprinted by permission of The University of Chicago Press.

THE REMBRANDT PANEL

A Pinnacle Book, published by arrangement with Little, Brown and Company.

First printing, April 1982

ISBN: 0-523-41621-0

Cover photo by Mort Engle

Printed in the United States of America

PINNACLE BOOKS, INC.
1430 Broadway
New York, New York 10018

For Elaine

The Rembrandt Panel

1

ON A CHILL, gray November afternoon Weinstock found himself on the landing before Mrs. Caroline Emerson's apartment in Louisburg Square. He was a little surprised to be there. Although his gallery was only a few blocks away, he was hardly ever asked to examine pictures in any of the fine old Beacon Hill houses. Other people were. He had accepted this years ago as a fact of life and was not particularly bitter about it.

The door in front of him was old and ornate, with nicely carved moldings. In the middle of it was a large, equally ornate nineteenth-century brass knocker. Weinstock had to suppress a sudden childish impulse to give it a loud bang, and instead reached for the little mother-of-pearl button beside the door. He pushed it and could faintly hear a decorous tinkling sound within the apartment.

After a few moments the door opened slightly.

"I'm Samuel Weinstock. I've come about the picture."

1

"How do you do, Mr. Weinstock. Please come in. I'm Caroline Emerson."

Weinstock was a short, heavyset man with thinning black hair shot through with gray, and a round, large-featured face. He wore thick black-rimmed glasses through which he peered at the world with a perpetual myopic squint. His expression was bewildered but kindly, almost cherubic.

Caroline Emerson was several inches taller than Weinstock, a neatly dressed, rather slender woman of about thirty-eight. Her long blond hair was parted in the middle and hung straight down, and she wore no makeup but lipstick. Her features were regular and small, almost classic, but the bones in her face were a shade too angular and pronounced, giving her the slightly horsy cast favored by many Bostonians. Her figure was fashionably trim, with small hips and breasts. Her face wore an expression of ennui that Weinstock imagined was habitual.

She quickly led the dealer through the apartment. It was beautifully appointed, with high ceilings, bow windows, and a marble fireplace in the living room. The carved paneling and wainscoting looked to be fine Federal style, and the delicate stucco ceiling decoration seemed to have come from a design by Robert Adam. Among the furniture Weinstock recognized pieces by Duncan Phyfe and Hepplewhite, and they made him wonder for the second time what he was doing there.

The picture he had been asked to examine hung over a chaise in the corner. It was a large Venetian scene, half real and half fantasy. This kind of picture had become very popular in the eighteenth century, when paintings like it were sold in great numbers as souvenirs to Englishmen on the Grand Tour.

It was hung in a massive, overdecorated gilt Victorian frame. Must weigh a ton, thought Weinstock.

"May I take it down?"

2

"Of course."

Weinstock moved the chaise out of the way as delicately as he could. Then, feeling enormously clumsy and inept, he managed to lift the painting out from the wall with his right hand and, after fumbling around for a while with his left, detached the copper wire from the heavy bronze hooks which supported it and lowered it precariously to the floor. This exertion left him short of breath and slightly perspiring.

"Can I offer you something to drink?"

"Maybe coffee, if it isn't too much trouble."

In truth, he wanted her to leave so that he could examine the painting in privacy. He could feel that she was nervous and taut under the facade of boredom. She was a lady obviously used to buying things rather than selling them, and she felt humiliated by the situation in which she now found herself. The matter of the picture was merely a symptom, but Weinstock could easily diagnose the disease. Caroline Emerson needed money, probably with some urgency, and found herself barely able to face this unpleasant and novel situation.

Weinstock had sensed the anxiety beneath the surface of the elaborately casual conversation they had had over the telephone. After a long preamble, Mrs. Emerson had finally come round to mentioning "a rather fine old master painting" which had begun to seem "tiresome." Soon, no doubt, she would begin to find all the old furniture equally oppressive, and it would duly make its way to an auction house or dealer. Weinstock could easily imagine Mrs. Emerson, shortly thereafter, gaily announcing to her friends that Beacon Hill was a stuffy old bore, and that she had discovered a simply *adorable* apartment over in Charlestown or North Cambridge.

Weinstock hated these "house calls," as he referred to them, because they often reminded him that a significant part of his business was based on lives and careers

3

that were frayed or unraveling. They frequently made him feel like an intruder or, worse, a scavenger picking about among the wreckage.

He placed the painting against the wall and stepped back from it. He cupped his hands in front of his face, blocking out the frame, and scanned the composition. This trick always made Weinstock feel silly, but he nevertheless found it to be useful. If the painting were well composed the sense of depth would be vividly enhanced, and if not, it would flatten out like a pile of cards.

He walked slowly backward, stopping at different distances. Finally he squatted before the canvas and took a magnifying glass from his back pocket. It was a commercial plastic Bausch and Lomb loupe, with two lenses, three-power and six-power, and it had cost him only a few dollars. Other dealers he knew used much fancier gadgets for situations like this, but Weinstock always felt that this was just theater. If a dealer was any good he could usually find out most of what he wanted to know about style and condition with a simple loupe, and most of the time he wouldn't need that.

Weinstock didn't really need that here. A first glance had answered most of his questions. But it was important to confirm his impressions, and besides, he knew that he would probably be grilled. He leaned forward, focusing on one of the foreground figures. Then he moved back again.

The scene in the painting was recognizable as St. Mark's Square, although the artist had included a crumbling Roman arch in place of Coducci's Renaissance clock-tower. The piazza was filled with tiny little masked figures, all in comical dancelike postures.

Weinstock shifted his gaze from the figures to St. Mark's Basilica in the background. He examined the domes and the squiggles the artist used to represent the

4

four ancient bronze horses over the entrance portico.

The dealer ran his fingertips across the surface of the painting, feeling the ridges, the indentations, the changing patterns of the brushstrokes, and trying to guess the vicissitudes of the picture over the last hundred and fifty years. Then he carefully examined the craquelure, the fine mesh of lines formed by the cracking of the pigment layers. In two places the dealer could detect a bull's-eye pattern of concentric circles, like spiderwebs. These, he knew, were caused by something striking the surface of the painting. Elsewhere there was chipping and flaking, and at some point a sharp instrument had carved a jagged, two-inch furrow in the paint surface. Finally, quickly, he checked the signature. It was in the lower right-hand corner, and read *F. Guardi fecit*: "F [rancesco] Guardi made it."

He turned the canvas around to look at the back. The fabric was dirty, like the surface, and aged to a dark brown color. There were some patches that Weinstock guessed were old, and a number of stains, a few of which he could identify. The stretcher was a soft wood, perhaps pine or poplar, and looked like it might have been original. There were several inscriptions on the stretcher, including the name *Francesco Guardi* written in pencil, but these didn't help Weinstock any with the problem of who had owned the picture when.

He sighed and turned the painting around again. Then he took some cotton balls and a small bottle of turpentine out of his jacket pocket. He unscrewed the cap of the bottle, soaked a cotton ball in the turpentine, and began dabbing at one of the foreground figures with a light, circular motion.

"What are you doing?"

Weinstock had not heard Caroline Emerson come back, and he started guiltily at the sharp tone of her voice. He turned to look at her. She was standing rig-

5

idly behind him, holding a silver tea tray. He noticed that the knuckles of her hands were white, and her face looked drawn and anxious.

"Nothing to worry about, Mrs. Emerson. I'm just trying to take off some surface dirt so we can see it a little better."

Blushing hotly, Weinstock clambered to his feet and relieved Mrs. Emerson of her burden. He took the tray over to a mahogany side table. He added some cream and sugar to his coffee, which was in a demitasse, and stirred it with the smallest spoon he had ever seen. Then he sat down as gingerly as possible on the satin-covered chair next to the table.

"Turpentine won't hurt a picture if it's over a hundred years old. Just a touch, I mean; you can't drown it in the stuff. Turps wouldn't hurt the paint layer on a picture that old, in fact it probably wouldn't even disturb the top layers of the varnish."

Caroline Emerson didn't seem mollified.

"Sometimes the varnish is so strong you damn near need an acetylene torch to cut through it."

"I'm sorry if I'm being oversensitive, Mr. Weinstock. It's just that—well, a picture that old and valuable. It upsets me to see it . . . tampered with. I'm sure you understand."

Weinstock tried hard to look understanding.

"Trust me, Mrs. Emerson. Do you ever clean the painting yourself? Dust it?"

"Occasionally I go over it with a slightly damp cloth or sponge, that's all."

Weinstock considered this for a moment, while he finished his thimbleful of coffee.

"Never use water on the surface of an old picture. Water's murder. It sinks into the canvas and rots it, and that can cause flaking. Among other things. If you look at the back of the canvas, you can see several large gray or white spots. Mold. It's even worse on a panel, of

6

course, because it can cause shrinkage and splitting when it evaporates."

"Thank you for warning me."

Mrs. Emerson's voice sounded chilly and brittle. She was leaning against the mantel of the fireplace with a tall drink in her hand. Until now her manner had made Weinstock feel as if he had been summoned to fix a leaky faucet, or get rid of the roaches, and he was beginning to wish that that were the case.

"Another problem. Never rub the surface of a picture with anything. If you rub it you abrade it. A feather duster's the thing, if you can get one. It keeps the dust off and doesn't hurt the surface. Just a few light flicks once in a while, that's all. If you're in the art business awhile, though, you see everything—people who use Brillo pads, Ajax, ammonia, anything."

In the course of this speech, Weinstock could feel Mrs. Emerson covering herself back up, wrapping herself in a protective layer of bored indifference.

"I must admit that I'm not terribly interested in old pictures, Mr. Weinstock. They're pretty, of course. I'm really just interested in this Venetian scene. I know what it is, as I told you, but I'd like to have some sort of professional corroboration. About the value, and so on."

Weinstock cringed. He didn't like Mrs. Emerson very much, or for that matter her picture. She didn't like him either, and seemed to be trying to cover up her embarrassment and anxiety by treating him like something between a used-car dealer and a back-alley abortionist. He also knew that they were going to like each other even less in a few minutes.

"Well. I'd say it was a fine picture. A fine old picture."

"Thank you. Yes, it certainly is that. But I was rather wondering about its value, since I'm considering selling it."

7

Weinstock toyed with his demitasse. He found himself wishing he could quietly climb into it and hide.

"That's a little complicated, I'm afraid. I'd have to check catalogues, auction records, that sort of thing."

"Just a round figure. An approximation. You *are* a dealer, after all."

She has you there, Sammy, thought Weinstock miserably. I *am* a dealer. After all. Okay, let's get it over with.

"I could give you sixteen hundred for the picture."

Here we go, thought Weinstock, but for a moment there was no reaction at all. When Caroline Emerson finally spoke it was not to him but to herself. Her back was turned to him, and she was fingering her glass on the mantelpiece.

"Sixteen hundred dollars. I see. How nice." Her voice was venomously cheerful.

She toyed with her glass for a few seconds, then walked briskly over to where Weinstock was sitting. She held out her hand, and it took the dealer a moment to realize that he was being dismissed.

"So good of you to come, Mr. Weinstock. Thank you for your offer, but I'm afraid sixteen hundred dollars wasn't quite what I had in mind."

Taking his cue, Weinstock got up, shook her hand and walked over to get his coat. Years of experience told him to make his exit as cleanly as possible, simply to grab his hat, cut his losses, and run.

But he was getting mad. He'd missed an auction, wasted an afternoon, and was tired of Mrs. Emerson and all the other Mrs. Emersons he had had to deal with.

Halfway to the door, he stopped.

"What *did* you have in mind, Mrs. Emerson?"

She hesitated for a moment, undecided, then gave him a false, bright smile.

"Well. I believe I'll take it over to the Robinson Galleries. I know, you see, that a Guardi of this size sold at a Christie's auction last year for over one hundred and fifty thousand dollars. So your sixteen *hundred* would seem a little low."

Her smile became even brighter.

"But we all have to make a living, don't we, Mr. Weinstock?"

That tore it. Weinstock, furious, threw down his coat, picked up a chair, carried it across the room, and slammed it down in front of the picture.

"That's right, lady. We do. And mine is pictures. So sit down there—sit down and shut up and I'll tell you about yours. You want to know, I'll tell you."

"Just who do you think—"

"Shut up. I said sit down and shut up."

Looking a little frightened now, she did as she was told.

"First, I don't mind being treated like a petty trader. I come from a long line of petty traders, and I'm not proud or snotty. I happen to deal in pictures, but maybe it could have been cars or furniture or any other damn thing. And it doesn't make any difference that you think I'm stupid. Lots of people have thought I was stupid. I got a tenth-grade education at High and Latin. I've found it useful to be thought stupid, and I've probably made almost as much money by people thinking I was stupid as I have by being smart. So I don't mind that part either."

Mrs. Emerson was nervously picking at a thread on the cuff of a sleeve.

"All that's okay, fine with me. But the part about my being a crook I can't stand still for. It's bad for my reputation, bad for business. You want crooks, lady, I can give you crooks—starting with Robinson, by the way. There are plenty of crooks in this business, but don't look at me. Look at the goniffs in the silk suits with the swish manners and the Harvard backgrounds."

9

Caroline Emerson stood up suddenly. She was still clutching her glass, and some of the drink slopped over the side.

"Please leave, Mr. Weinstock."

"Like hell, Mrs. Emerson. Not until I tell you about the painting. Not unless you call the cops, and not even then. I'll be here when they come, so you better make it stick."

Mrs. Emerson sat down again. The shrill edge of hysteria was gone, replaced with a sort of theatrical languor which was, if anything, even more annoying.

"First of all, about this 'Guardi' business."

"It's clearly signed. The signature's genuine."

"No. It's old, but it's a fake. That's what's called a 'floating signature' because it's on top of the varnish layer instead of under it. Even if it weren't, I probably wouldn't believe it. I've seen a lot of Guardis, and I've never seen a genuine signature except on drawings."

He walked over to the bow window and pulled the heavy draperies together.

"What are you doing?"

Her voice was shrill again. Weinstock smiled. He could feel his anger dissipating.

"Just darkening the room a little. I want to show you something. I'm not a rapist either, so you can relax."

He went over to his jacket, which he'd thrown over a chair, and pulled a long metal object from the pocket. It was open on one side; within it were a pair of thin glass tubes, and it trailed an electric cord. When Weinstock plugged it in, the light glowed pale lavender rather than white. He knelt in front of the painting and called Caroline Emerson to come over.

"This is an ultraviolet light, called a 'black light' usually. Don't look at it, look at the picture. Look at the surface. You can see that the top of the composition is mostly a sort of milky green under the light, but many of the foreground figures and buildings are much dark-er, almost black. So is the signature, incidentally. Also, there's a large black streak up here, in the sky."

He switched off the ultraviolet light, got up, and went over to open the curtains.

"All of those dark patches are overpaint. If the painting were properly cleaned, stripped down to the original paint surface, every one of those dark patches—figures, architecture, and clouds—every one of them would melt like snow. In other words, probably half the picture would go."

"Of course the painting is very old. I mean, you wouldn't expect it to be perfect. And the signature—well, that doesn't necessarily mean anything, does it?"

"No, it doesn't. Plenty of perfectly good paintings have phony signatures. And condition doesn't have anything to do with authenticity. But then there's the business of style."

Everything else having failed, Mrs. Emerson tried sarcasm. But she was pathetic now, and Weinstock found he couldn't get angry again.

"I didn't know you were an expert on Venetian painting, Mr. Weinstock."

She sounded sullen, defeated.

"I'm not. I can give you a list of books, if you'd care to check this yourself. Giovanni Maderno's book on Guardi is pretty good, for openers. I can give you a list of other painters around Guardi, too, if you'd like: Canaletto, Bellotto, Marieschi, Giacomo Guardi, a few others. You can play with names, if you want.

"Anyway, about the style. Spotting a wrong picture is like spotting a phony at a cocktail party. It's easy. Either things fit together, or they don't. Take your painting. The figures, now, they're made up of nervous, twitching lines and little dots of light. They're all dancing up and down, hopping around, having a hell of a time. Now look at the architecture. The architecture is dull and square and geometric, as if it was done with a ruler. If

11

you want names, the architecture is probably taken from Canaletto and the figures from Guardi. They don't fit together, Mrs. Emerson, they stand there yelling at each other. Like us."

Weinstock felt himself relaxing and becoming expansive. He was beginning to enjoy his lecture. Caroline Emerson eyed him warily.

"I'm sure the painting is genuine. It's been in the family for over a hundred years."

"You're right, it's not a fake. It's a *pastiche*. Maybe a Venetian painter working around the eighteen thirties or forties, judging by the canvas. Neither Canaletto or Guardi ever made much money when they were alive, but as soon as they died their stuff became very fashionable. Tough for them, but great for the dealers. Tough for art historians, too, because pseudo-Guardis and pseudo-Canalettos were painted straight through the nineteenth century and into the twentieth. Even to-day. Right off the Piazza San Marco you can find seedy characters schlepping around pictures that look like perfectly good eighteenth-century Venetian views, but which were painted the day before yesterday."

Weinstock looked at Caroline Emerson, who was becoming interested in spite of herself. For the first time since he'd arrived, she looked as though she were beginning to relax. Weinstock felt as if he'd been talking for hours.

"Okay, so far? Now. There are several ways to go with a picture like this. If you sold it to me I wouldn't touch it, except for getting rid of the signature. It'd go on my wall as is, because it would cost me a bundle to restore it properly and it's too risky. Or you could take it to Robinson. Robinson would give it to his pet boy to do some fancy surface work, play around with the signature, slap it in a Louis Fifteenth frame, and pass it off as Guardi. Or you could go the auction route and take your chances. It could bring twenty-five hundred or five hundred, depending on who the shooters were. But you won't do better than sixteen hundred from Robinson unless he's sure he can stiff the picture as a Guardi, and maybe not even then. If I were you, I'd keep it on my wall."

By the end of this, Mrs. Emerson was almost looking contrite.

"Well, Mr. Weinstock, I guess I owe you an apology."

"Skip it. It happens."

"No, really. I was just so sure about the picture. It's been in the family for so long."

"Yeah. Look, Mrs. Emerson, this is none of my business, but you have a lot of fine furniture here. The chair you're sitting on is probably worth twice the picture, and that side table maybe much more."

"Do you deal in furniture?"

"Not now. I started out in furniture, though, and I could tell you where to go, who to see. Think about it."

"Thank you. I will. And I'll also consider your offer about the picture. I really am very sorry for speaking to you as I did. I had hoped . . ."

"Yes, I know. We both hoped. It does happen occasionally that way: an unknown, major picture suddenly discovered. But not often. I'd better go. Let me know about the picture, and if you want some advice about the furniture."

A couple of minutes later Weinstock was standing in front of the apartment house, feeling tired and depressed. It was late in November, and the weather was becoming increasingly icy, gray, and bleak. There had been freezing rain and sleet for several days running, and the city, like its inhabitants, seemed to be turning in on itself.

Weinstock gazed at the stately rows of brick houses on the square. At one time Louisburg Square had been one of the most exclusive addresses in the country: all

13

Cabots and Lowells. For all Weinstock knew, it still was. But it had changed radically during the sixties, when much of Beacon Hill had been taken over by hippies, panhandlers, junkies, and worse—what the Louisburg Square residents would doubtless call "the less desirable elements." The square itself was still elegant and picturesque. It still maintained its gaslights and cobblestones and tiny park. But it had become an embattled enclave.

Mrs. Grace, a local character who had lived here for all of her sixty-three years, had recently been mugged on her doorstep early one morning. A prominent banker had been discovered one soft summer evening lying in a pool of blood on the sidewalk, his throat neatly cut from ear to ear. People learned to move quickly, to stay away from shadowed doorways, and to jump at footsteps.

At the bottom of the Hill, Charles Street, too, had changed. Fifteen years ago it had been jammed with art and antique dealers. Now it sported a noisy discotheque, a singles bar, and a bookstore specializing in "material for the mature adult." It was becoming a place for people trying to score—money, dope, sex, or all three. And of course crime. The art dealers who remained, like Weinstock, operated their businesses from behind heavy metal grates, their doors decorated with various kinds of locks and bolts. Many added to their signs phrases like "to the trade only" and "open by appointment." Many left, unable to accommodate themselves to soaring rents, high blood pressure, and insurance premiums.

With the sudden transformation of Beacon Hill came a kind of manic, carnival atmosphere. Like Berlin during the twenties, perhaps, there was a sense of aimlessness, an aura of desperation underneath the hedonism. Weinstock guessed that the "action," the sense of excitement that lured people to Charles Street, was a thin

14

veneer masking an underlying core of emptiness and fear.

Thinking these gloomy thoughts, the dealer slowly strode away.

2

BACK AT THE GALLERY, firmly planted in his heavy oak swivel chair with a beer in his hand, Weinstock was just beginning to feel better when the phone rang.

"Samuel Weinstock Gallery. Hello, Harry, how's the boy? . . . I'm not so great at the moment. Nothing, just a rough day. What's happening? . . . A big picture? So tell me about it. If it's by Guardi, though, don't tell me about it."

As the voice on the other end of the line became more excited, Weinstock could feel the black clouds closing in again. He cradled his forehead with his right hand, massaging his throbbing temples with his thumb and middle finger.

"Okay, Harry, let me get it straight. You took it to the museum. They said it was definitely eighteenth century, and—who said, by the way—Simmons? *Ross?* Why would the director . . . oh, okay. You still think maybe it's Rembrandt?

"Rembrandt! Jesus, Harry. Okay, look, bring it around tomorrow. I can always use a good Rembrandt or two. I'll just stick it in back with the Titans and Michelangelos. . . . Sorry for the sarcasm, but stories about Rembrandts in antique stores tend to make me feel tired. . . . Look, sooner or later everybody in the trade does a Rembrandt number. I've been through this twice. Twice, yeah. If you cool off I'll tell you about it.

"First time was in fifty-nine, then again in sixty-two or three, I think it was. By that time I'd learned, and I've been clean since then. The first was a religious picture, *Christ and the Samaritan Woman*. Beautiful picture. Everything was right: crackle, canvas, brushstrokes, composition, the works. Provenance, even. Anyway, it turned out to be a student named Ferdinand Bol, complete with a preparatory drawing in Vienna. That little fantasy cost me six grand.

"The second picture was even better. A small panel, a portrait of a rabbi. . . . Yeah. Well, the experts scratched their heads a long time over that one, and finally came up with the name Barent Fabritius. . . . I know, me neither. If they'd come up with his brother *Carel* Fabritius, I still would have made a fat bundle, but 'Barent Fabritius' was the kiss of death. I've still got it, and I still like it, and I'm still out thousands of bucks on it.

"Anyway, the thing with Rembrandt is this. First of all, his students. Figure about eighty or ninety students, a lot of them not even identified yet, and you've got part of the problem. Ten, fifteen of them could come really close to Rembrandt on a good day. Then there are manner pictures, imitators, God knows how many. French, German, even Italian, especially around the beginning of the eighteenth century. Then there are the modern fakes. If you get past all that, there are the so-called experts, right? You've got six or seven characters here and in Europe who all loathe each other, so if one of them says it's right, you've got five or six others saying it's wrong. So you figure the odds."

Harry Giardino was a little easier than Caroline Emerson, but not much. Weinstock wondered if he shouldn't have gone into teaching since he seemed to spend most of his time recently giving lectures, and it was beginning to annoy him that he never got paid for any of them. Instead, he usually got yelled at. That didn't seem fair to him.

"I know you've got a good eye, Harry. . . . I'm *not* laughing—can I laugh? I've been knocked out on those things for almost ten thousand bucks. You think I'm laughing? Look, the Dutch market's booming, so if it's even close you're still safe. In fact, at what you paid, you're probably golden. Okay, tomorrow. Half-past four, I may be in Quincy before that. Ciao."

Weinstock hung up the phone feeling worse than he had after the Guardi fiasco. He liked Harry Giardino, but at the same time he felt pity and something like guilt toward him.

Harry was a runner, one of hundreds of people who carved out a nervous existence on the periphery of the art market. The term "runner" was apt. Runners scurried from dealer to dealer, buying here, selling there, always looking for the big score. Most of them lived on adrenaline and fantasies. They shared a single dream that someday, in the corner of some antique shop or gallery, they would find some priceless treasure and retire to the Côte d'Azur.

It never happened.

Most dealers treated Harry and his breed with open contempt, using them and cheating them, playing on their vulnerability and naiveté. When on occasion one of them did discover a rare or valuable object, he was usually tricked into giving it up for almost nothing by the feigned indifference of a clever dealer. Without any formal knowledge or training, generally without any academic or business background, most runners were natural victims.

19

Weinstock's fondness for Giardino and his feeling of guilt toward him came largely from empathy. Weinstock had started out as a runner himself, spending almost three years in Europe in the early fifties. He had left the States with two thousand dollars. When he returned, he had three hundred dollars and enough good paintings to ensure that he would never be a runner again.

Weinstock had started out like Giardino, but he had quickly understood some facts of life that Harry would never master. First of all, he understood—and liked—the art business in and of itself. Second, he realized very quickly that chasing great pictures was an extremely dangerous way to make a living. Instead he concentrated on artists of the second and third rank, and artists that were currently unfashionable. When the French *salon* painters returned to favor in the sixties, for example, Weinstock had several small Gérômes, a Couture, and a large Bouguereau which had cost him very little and which he sold at immense profit. He also developed a subtle instinct for minor American painters of the nineteenth century, as well as for American folk art. When these areas skyrocketed, Weinstock found himself very nearly a rich man.

He had taught himself a great deal along the way. He had read extensively in history as well as art history, so that his natural instincts were usually reinforced by knowledge.

He also had very few illusions about himself.

He had grown up in a part of town where you had to be tough and street-wise to survive. His father had owned an antique store in South Boston, dealing mainly in used furniture, bric-a-brac, and plain junk, and had barely survived the Depression. Weinstock, by observing his father, developed a shrewd business sense and an exact, predictive understanding of human psychology. He also developed a rigorously unsentimental view of his profession. In a business dominated by snobbery and social posturing, he preferred to think of himself simply as a petty trader in secondhand articles.

Partly for this reason, his store looked less like a conventional art gallery than an overgrown pawnshop. Pictures, objets d'art, ceramics, furniture, sculpture, books, magazines—everything lay heaped about in a mad clutter. It often seemed to Weinstock that he spent half his time looking for horizontal surfaces on which to put things, and the other half looking for whatever it was he had put on them.

Paperwork defeated him utterly. The top of his desk was at present awash in a sea of paper, including memos, bills, letters, phone numbers, important notes, unimportant notes, and catalogues. Contemplating this chaos of paper, Weinstock decided to procrastinate. In three days Sheila Woods would return from the Cape, and then she could get his life in order.

Sheila had started out as a glorified secretary but had quickly become his researcher, confidante, salesperson, and general factotum. By now, Weinstock realized, he needed Sheila to tell him the shape of his finances, remind him of deals and dates, keep track of his voluminous stock—damn near tie his shoelaces for him, he thought with a touch of self-pity. Mainly, however, he missed her wisecracking, high-spirited presence.

Deciding to call Micheline, the other woman in his life, he reached for the phone.

"Hello, Miche? Sammy."

"Oooh, Sah*meee,* you son of a *beetch,* you 'ave not called me in _weeks_!"

"One week, Miche. A bad week. Want to come over? Look, I've got a fat steak and some real pâté. We could make *tournedos Rossini.* You could do a nice salad, I'll bust open the Chambertin, and maybe we could mix up a good dessert—chocolate mousse, something like that—"

21

"Sah*mee*, you will make me fat and ugly."

"—and then we'll tell each other stories, and screw like rabbits until dawn—"

"Oooh, Sah*mee*!"

"—which won't make you fat, and certainly not ugly."

"Sahmee, you are a bad man."

"Right."

"A very bad man. Give me 'alf an hour."

"Right."

3

THE MOMENT Weinstock hung up the phone another man, not five miles away, was confronting a desperate decision.

He did not look desperate. Encountering him casually, a stranger might have interpreted his expression as one of boredom, or even mild amusement.

Elton Ross was a tall, distinguished-looking man in his late forties. His dark hair, just graying at the temples, was still full. His clear blue eyes were deeply set under prominent brows, so that overhead lights often cloaked them in pools of shadow. His nose was long and fine, and the planes of his face from the pronounced cheekbones to the strong chin were angular, sharp, and clean.

Close approximations of Elton Ross could be found half a dozen times in any copy of any large-circulation magazine in the United States. He was the man with the glass of twelve-year-old Scotch, the figure holding the door of the sky-blue luxury sedan for the spectacular blond vision. He was the man used to illustrate the

proposition that the only obstacle between the reader
and the presidency of General Motors was the lack of a
particular pinstripe suit.

Like most men of his kind, Ross was not a woman's
fantasy but a man's fantasy of a woman's fantasy. The
women who had frequent contact with Ross more often
than not became guarded and wary around him, instinctively sensing not so much danger as contempt. Beyond that, there was something narcissistic and slightly
sardonic in his manner. Most of all, women intuitively
understood that virility so assertive was probably on
some level equivocal.

If the mask of Elton Ross's face held any clue, it was
in his smile. Ross seldom frowned, and when he did it
was a token of bafflement rather than anger. His habitual expression was a smile; he was, in Yeats's phrase, a
"smiling public man."

His public smile, which could be seen frequently in
the society section of the Boston newspapers, was open
and amiable and projected the illusion of warmth. Ross
had found it a most useful tool in the museum world.
At the beginning of his career his superiors had interpreted it as friendly and ingratiating. The smile of an
acolyte, or perhaps a sycophant. Later, when he had
achieved his goal of the directorship, this amiable
weapon was largely utilized as a means of expanding
the Museum's endowment. It also served as useful cam-
ouflage, disguising qualities of ruthlessness, ambition,
and calculation that few suspected.

Ross had many other smiles that people seldom
saw—smiles of mockery, of lechery and greed and
triumph. An arsenal of smiles. One in particular, a tight
smile with white lips drawn slowly back, the nostrils
slightly flared and eyes hooded, indicated a pathologi-
cal rage that was almost bottomless.

It didn't seem to bother many people in the Museum
that no one appeared to know Ross really well. He

24

came from an impeccable Boston family, held a doctorate from Harvard, and had continued his studies in Bonn, Athens, and Paris. He had proved himself to be a brilliant and wide-ranging scholar as well as an able administrator. His wife, Vassar graduate, was attractive and aristocratic if somewhat cool, and they had two beautiful children. Ross's elevation to the directorship of the Museum three years ago had been virtually unopposed and was hailed by many as a superb choice.

It was early in the evening now. Ross was sitting in a black leather and chrome chair designed by Mies van der Rohe, behind a large mahogany desk also lined in black leather. The top of the desk was bare except for a beige manila folder.

The director's office was the antithesis of Weinstock's gallery. It was spare, almost Spartan, and could have belonged to a corporation president as easily as to a museum director. The walls held only three paintings: a fourteenth-century Madonna and Child by Lippo Memmi, a late Cézanne watercolor view of Mont Sainte-Victoire, and an oil sketch by Picasso for *Les Demoiselles d'Avignon.*

Across from the desk where Ross was sitting was a massive Renaissance table with elaborate designs of cut semiprecious stones. Sitting on top of the table, riveting his attention, was a Greek vase.

The vase was about eighteen inches tall, and was of a type known as a calyx krater. It was made of terracotta fired to a deep reddish orange. It was decorated with friezes of figures in black slip, accentuated with lines incised into the clay, and the friezes were enclosed within rich ornamental borders of stylized linear designs.

It had a heavy base from which the body of the vessel projected out in a sharp curve. About a quarter of the way up the body of the pot two handles were attached which were bent upward to form convex curves

25

balancing the concave curves just below them. The broad body of the pot above the handles flared out in a subtle, elegant, concave form like the floral calyx from which the vase derived its name. The top of the krater was articulated by two circular bands which together made up the lip of the vessel.

Like many of the best Greek pots, the shape of this work was as exquisitely refined and perfectly proportioned as a great piece of sculpture.

The scene painted on the side of the vase facing Ross was composed of only three figures. Two warriors carrying spears and shields confronted each other in battle over the body of a third, which lay on the ground between them. Ross examined the figures from across the room, savoring the spare, controlled lines, the superb discipline and balance of the composition.

It was the most perfect example Ross had ever seen of the austere, heroic style of Greek painting in the sixth century B.C. He recalled fragments of the Homeric verse telling of the encounter between two warriors, Menelaus and Euphorbus, over the body of the slain Patroclus:

> Son of Atreus, Menelaus, illustrious, leader of armies:
> Give way, let the bloody spoils be, get back from this body,
> Since before me no one of the Trojans, or renowned companions,
> Struck Patroclus down with the spear in the strong encounter.
> Thereby let me win this great glory among the Trojans
> Before I hit you and strip the sweetness of life away from you.

Ross repeated the last line aloud, slowly, and stared at the formalized ritual of battle on the vase, wondering at its mute eloquence.

Two men, in strict profile, locked in a deadly pas de deux.

Ross smiled to himself.

Elton Ross had seen the vase for the first time only three months before. He had found it sitting in a wooden crate on his desk one morning with a brief, cryptic note attached:

My dear Elton,
    I thought you might want to see this.
                                        Sarkes
P.S. I shall return Thursday week.

Sarkes Manoukian was a familiar figure to Ross. Indeed, he was a familiar figure to museum directors throughout Europe and America. He was a short, thickset, swarthy man of a physical type that Ross found particularly repellent.

His face was sensual, even carnal, with a wide mouth, bulbous nose, flaccid cheeks, and a pendulous double chin. His eyes, small black beads, were set beneath comically large and bushy black eyebrows that made him resemble a bloated Groucho Marx. His sparse black hair was slicked back, and he wore a heavy scent that always reminded Ross of Shakespeare's line about lilies that fester.

Perhaps because of his aura of reptilian depravity Manoukian seemed ageless, although he might have been in his mid-fifties. No one knew much of anything about him, although legends and rumors abounded. Some thought that he was a Greek; others that he was a Cypriot or Turk. It was also rumored that the police in several countries were anxious to discuss some small matters with him.

None of Manoukian's detractors, however, disputed

his intelligence. He spoke several languages fluently and was familiar with the entire body of archaeological literature, starting with Winckelmann. He was reputed never to have lied about the condition or authenticity of a piece he handled, and only once had he sold a work of art that had been seriously questioned.

This was a small, insignificant terra-cotta figurine that he had placed in a museum. He had listened in silence to the argument of the curator, and, without saying a word, immediately made out a check for the full amount that the museum had paid him. He had handed it to the curator and picked up the statuette. He carefully examined it with a magnifying glass, then, eyes closed, with his fingertips. Still without a word, he smashed it to the floor. Then he bent over, picked up one of the fragments, and scrutinized it meticulously. Beaming from ear to ear, he announced to the startled curatorial staff: "Ah, gentlemen, I was right. It is perfectly genuine." Then he turned on his heel and left the room triumphantly, leaving the others to wonder whether Manoukian had really discovered something, or whether it was all pure bluff.

As scrupulous as the dealer was about the work of art itself—this was, after all, virtually a religious matter with him—he was equally unscrupulous about where he acquired his goods, and under what circumstances. Part of the Manoukian mythology involved speculations about smuggled and/or stolen antiquities crossing Europe along mazelike routes of Byzantine complexity.

Carrying art across the Italian border into Switzerland was no longer easy and safe. Now it was sometimes necessary to go south to Sicily, cross by boat to North Africa—Tunis and Algiers—then to Spain and France, finally crossing over the Franco-Swiss border. This was a tedious and demeaning process, and one which made dealers like Manoukian sometimes feel like common narcotics peddlers. There were also rumors that Manoukian's pots were not always empty when they entered the States.

Precisely a week after the mysterious appearance of the calyx krater Manoukian himself appeared, equally mysteriously. When Ross arrived at his office at half-past eight, Sarkes was already there. He barely moved when Ross entered the room. Half-seated, half-sprawled in his Barcelona lounge-chair, the dealer looked to Ross like some corrupt pasha. When he turned his face to Ross his eyes were half-closed, his mouth wetly smiling. For a second it seemed to Ross as though his office, the Museum, perhaps Boston itself, were Manoukian's property, his sheikdom, and Ross himself merely some minion, petitioner, or bumbling intruder.

"My dear Ross, so good to see you. Pity you weren't here twenty, even fifteen minutes ago. There was such a lovely view across the park. It had a soft gray mist. Very Impressionist. I thought, Monet—but then, no, not Monet, softer. And then I thought, not French, something American."

Manoukian smiled dreamily for a moment before continuing.

"Whistler. That's what it was, a Whistler, all grays and silvers. The colors were delicate, like washes, and all the forms across the park—trees, bridges, buildings—they all looked like ghosts. I never understood your Whistler until this morning and then, when I look out your window, I understand him."

Ross laughed.

"Sarkes, you always astonish me. I came in this morning expecting to talk with you about Greek pots, and it turns out you're flogging Whistlers instead. The pot was just a ploy. I'll bet you have three paintings of the Thames by moonlight rolled up in your briefcase."

Sarkes Manoukian giggled, then roared with laughter, his whole frame shaking. Finally composing him-

29

self, dabbing at his eyes with a large monogrammed handkerchief, he turned back to Ross.

All trace of levity was gone. In its place was a deadly seriousness. Very quietly, almost in a whisper, Manoukian said to the director: "Yes, let us discuss the pot."

The game was started.

4

NOW, THREE MONTHS LATER, Elton Ross tried to reconstruct the game. Seated at his desk, staring across the room at the small clay object that now threatened to destroy him, Ross recalled the contest point by point in a furious, futile effort to discover the exact moment in which he had lost not only the game but quite possibly his reputation and career. The manila folder on the desk in front of him held most of the evidence. He opened it and shook the contents out on the desk top.

The first piece of evidence was a small stack of black-and-white photographs which had already been compiled before Sarkes appeared at the Museum for the second time. The ones on the top of the stack contained three views of the vase across the room, and Ross spread them out in front of him. Underneath these three, the director placed twelve photos like playing cards in a game of solitaire. Each of them was of a vase similar either in shape or in style of painting to the Manoukian vase in the three photographs above them.

He knew each work in every detail, knew every comparable feature by heart, yet he reviewed them one more time, searching for a mistake or a weakness in logic. There was none, as far as he could see.

The vessel on the table and in the three photographs on Ross's desk was by Exekias, the most famous of all Greek vase painters. There could be no doubt. This fact in itself made the piece fabulously rare and valuable. Moreover, it was signed by Exekias both as painter *and* potter, which made it yet rarer. Finally, the shape—the calyx-krater type—had in all probability been invented by Exekias himself. A comparison of the Manoukian vase with several pots in the photographs on Ross's desk supported the hypothesis that this vase was the earliest known of its type and, indeed, perhaps the first ever made. This made it more than rare; it made it unique.

Equally remarkable were the quality of the piece and its condition. It had been broken, but cleanly. The joins were almost invisible.

Slowly, line by line, Ross had compared the Manoukian vase with the greatest known works by Exekias, such as the famous Dionysus cup in Munich and the Achilles amphora in the Vatican. Then he judged it against the best works of the other great black-figure painters: Psiax, the Amasis Painter, and so on. Next he had compared it with other painters, other styles: Euthymides, the Brygos Painter, the Berlin Painter, and the Achilles Painter. At last the comparison had been narrowed to twelve works, the twelve masterpieces whose images now lay on the table in front of him.

And then finally to one, the Euphronius krater. The Euphronius krater, for which the Metropolitan Museum had given away over a million dollars as well as a large number of valuable Greek coins. The Euphronius krater, bought under circumstances questionable enough to threaten the jobs of both the curator of antiquities and the director of the museum itself. This was the work which Metropolitan officials proclaimed as the greatest Greek vase in the world—a meaningless hyperbole which had annoyed Ross at the time.

He recalled one official announcing, with a combination of childish enthusiam and fatuous pomposity, that the history of art would "have to be rewritten." He also recalled, with some bitterness, the public spectacle, the promotion, the vulgar excesses which had accompanied this acquisition. And, in all honesty, the galling sense of jealousy and defeat he had felt when this latest trophy was triumphantly displayed. Ross had flinched at the news-shots of a credulous public, as awed by money and spectacle as it was different to art, voraciously pressing its collective nose against the protective Plexiglas hood at the museum.

The three photographs remaining in the folder were all of the New York krater. Ross removed the bottom line of twelve photographs from his desk, replacing them with the three from the folder, and repeated once more the arguments for and against the two works.

The scene on the obverse, or front, of the New York krater—the death of Sarpedon—was indeed the equal of the obverse of the Manoukian krater, the battle over the body of Patroclus. However, the scene on the reverse of the New York vase was startlingly weaker than the scene on the front of the same vase, or the analogous scene on the back of the Exekias krater. Where Euphronius had casually strung a random group of warriors in rather awkward poses, the Exekias exhibited a superb chariot group.

The third photograph in each row showed the side views, allowing Ross to compare the forceful outline and exquisite proportions of the Exekias vase to the looser, fuller profile of the Euphronius krater. Even in the shapes of the two works one felt the greater sense of discipline, of tension, in the piece now sitting across the room.

"It is better," Manoukian had said, "better and more important than the New York Euphronius."

Ross had laughed at the time, saying that the two were incommensurable. But this was just hair-splitting. Manoukian was right, and Ross knew it.

The comparisons between the two works would inevitably be made, probably by every significant scholar in the field. So the matter of the vase concerned not only money but scholarly reputations as well.

How Greek, how Homeric, Ross remembered thinking to himself. Vast phalanxes of spear-laden, sword-wielding troops, their armor glinting in the sun, spread out on the field of battle. But instead of handsome, Praxitelian youths there would be fat, balding curators, enraged German archaeologists, and febrile museum directors. It would have been a splendid scholarly blood-bath. This prospect was, as Manoukian had doubtless foreseen, irresistible to Ross.

The director put the photographs aside and turned to the documents in the file. The first was a rather brief, notarized letter to Sarkes Manoukian in French. It authorized him to act as agent in the private sale of a vase, which was described in detail in an attached memo. The letter specified that the sale should be made expeditiously, and that the name of the owner should be divulged only, and in the strictest confidence, to the principal in the sale. The letter was signed by the Baronne de R_____.

The fact that the name at the bottom of the letter was that of one of the oldest and richest families in Europe was reassuring to Ross at the time, and in retrospect it seemed to him a bold stroke. The notoriety of the name explained, to a degree, the insistence on anonymity and the curious willingness of the owner to give Sarkes Manoukian virtual carte blanche in the disposition of the pot. By making Manoukian, in effect, sole proprietor, the letter also implied that he should be

34

solely liable should he be caught in the illegal exportation or clandestine sale of the work.

The second document, a restoration report from the Laboratoire Nationale d'Archéologie just outside Paris, dated 1947, described the condition of the pot, an analysis of clay samples, and the removal of calcium deposits on the foot, as well as a small repair near the lip. This had, of course, been checked against similar documents from the Laboratoire in the files of the Museum, although Ross had decided against a direct inquiry in regard to the Baroness's desire for absolute anonymity.

The next document was certainly genuine. It was a small pamphlet printed on embossed linen, the catalogue of a small exhibition of masterpieces from the collection of the Baron and Baronne de R————. The exhibition, held late in 1947, had taken place in a small and obscure gallery in the rue Bonaparte in the Latin Quarter of Paris. It was a charitable event organized to raise money for the restoration of war-damaged monuments, and the gallery charged a rather steep admission fee. Apparently few people had attended, which seemed to Ross a pity since the exhibition had included major Renaissance and Impressionist paintings that had never been publicly exhibited before and might never be again.

The note on page 3 was curt:

No. 73: Vase Grec, attribné à Exékias: Scène de Bataille

Beneath were listed the measurements of the pot.

Apparently this was the only published reference to the vase. This fact had bothered Ross a good deal, although it was well known that the Baron and Baronne de R———— were extremely careful of their privacy, and allowed access to their collection only to a handful of distinguished scholars. Further, their taste and acquisitions were strongly oriented toward the rococo and Impressionism, not antiquities.

35

Ross recalled a parallel case in England. It concerned a large Ming vase. Its owner, a connoisseur of paintings, had had absolutely no idea what it was, or even that it was valuable. It had been in the family for generations and had apparently always been used simply as an umbrella stand. A friend noticed it one day and suggested that the owner check it out at one of the London auction houses. Shortly thereafter the vase was sold for approximately a half million dollars. In what dingy corner of what estate, Ross had wondered, had the Exekias been hidden? Was it a centerpiece for the table, or locked in a cabinet, or did it sit on a mantel filled with flowers? Who had bought it, when, and why? There were no answers to these questions from Manoukian, and the stipulation of anonymity had barred Ross from futher inquiries.

To this point Ross was guilty of only one major oversight, and Manoukian had taken only one major risk. The catalogue of the small exhibition in Paris was unillustrated, and the description of the vase was worthless, but it did include a record of the measurements. Incredibly, Ross had neglected to convert the centimeters in the catalogue into inches and check the height of the vase against the one on the table. Had he done so, he would have found a discrepancy of nearly an inch and a half. Would this have warned him, or would he have simply rationalized it to himself? This was one of the questions that tormented him now.

The next document in the folder was small, short, and to the point. Like the note the foreman of the jury hands to the judge, Ross thought bitterly. It was Ross's personal check, backed by the Museum's money, to Sarkes Manoukian. A canceled check, made out in the amount of seven hundred and fifty thousand dollars, no cents.

It was a small, nondescript rectangle of paper, no different from the kind that Ross received in stacks every month from his bank: Fred's Groceries, $20.75; Dr. William Schonstein, $42.50; Brooks Brothers, $82.50; Sarkes Manoukian, $750,000.00.

All things are relative, even money. As Ross reminded himself, seven hundred and fifty thousand dollars was only ("only!") three quarters of a million dollars. One had to consider the context. The Washington Leonardo had cost more than five million; Rembrandt's *Aristotle Contemplating the Bust of Homer* more than two million; and the Velázquez *Juan de Pareja* was reputed to have cost six million. More to the point, the Euphronius krater had cost (counting the Greek coins) in the neighborhood of one and a half million dollars, at a conservative estimate.

Yet the Exekias had been just three quarters of a million, a mere fraction. It was all just a matter of perspective. Ross smiled. Cheap at twice the price, he thought to himself. Hardly been driven. Buy two, we throw in another pair of pants. Get it while it's hot. Hot, indeed.

The next piece of evidence in the folder was likewise short and to the point. It was a brief letter, signed by the chairman of the Board of Trustees of the Museum, agreeing to allow Ross discretionary use of certain funds to the amount of one million dollars.

The document, accompanied by a letter of credit, recorded an extraordinary triumph which Ross had worked long and hard to achieve. For it had been his goal not merely to obtain the vase, but to do so entirely under his own auspices, bypassing both the Department of Antiquities and the Board of Trustees itself.

In arguing his brief before the trustees Ross had given a superb performance. The transaction must be completed immediately, he had told them. It could not wait. And it must take place in total secrecy. Even the board itself could not be informed of the nature of the acquisition until it was unveiled. Again and again, Ross had repeated his theme: the object was bigger, more important, more significant than the Metropolitan's Euphronius. It would push Boston to the forefront of the museum world.

It was a unique work, a great work. Attendance would double. The history of art would have to be rewritten, he had told them shamelessly. He had appealed, again and again, to their instincts of greed, acquisitiveness, and jealousy, his manner alternately wheedling and imploring, or bullying and imperious. In the end they had given in, authorizing the director to spend hundreds of thousands of dollars for a work of art about which they knew literally nothing. Ross knew that at that moment he had acquired not merely a Greek vase, but virtually monolithic control of the Museum.

The final document in the file was a letter which Ross had received only ten days before. It was written by Roberto Anselmo, chief of police in charge of the security of Italian art in the Province of Latium.

In rather stilted formal prose Anselmo begged to inform the *illustrissimo signore* that an important work of art had recently been stolen. A Greek vase. Seven months ago, a group of thieves had raided an Etruscan tomb site currently being excavated near Cerveteri, just north of Rome. Most of the stolen objects were insignificant. One vase, of which there was an enclosed photograph, was, however, of the greatest importance. The decision had been made not to publicize the theft immediately in the hope that the *tombaroli*, unaware of the significance of their prize, might try to dispose of their spoils locally and thus alert the authorities. With the passage of time, this hope had had to be abandoned. It was Anselmo's assumption that the vase was now either in the possession of a private collector, or possibly on the international art market.

A full-scale investigation had been authorized. Copies of the letter were being sent to all major Western museums, and Interpol was fully apprised of the situation. Anselmo closed by begging any director of any museum contacted concerning a Greek vase of uncertain origin or provenance to alert the police immediately, and to contact the nearest Italian embassy.

The appended photograph was grainy and somewhat blurred, but it was clear enough to dispel any doubt. It was the vase on the table in front of Ross.

Ross closed the file. It had been, he had to admit, a very pretty job. The Baronne de R_____ still had her vase—a charming amphora, it turned out, probably painted by a minor artist known as the Phrynos Painter, and worth at the most sixty thousand dollars. Sarkes Manoukian, perhaps retired or traveling incognito under a false passport, had presumably strengthened his friendship with the officials of a small Swiss bank. Ross, on the other hand, had a great Greek vase which he alone would ever be able to see, and a canceled check for three quarters of a million dollars.

In the near future Ross would also have a meeting with the Museum's Board of Trustees, which he anticipated with no pleasure at all.

Until the day before yesterday Ross had maintained a kind of fatalistic serenity in the knowledge that his situation was completely hopeless. That day, though, his stoic acceptance of the inevitable had been shattered when a disheveled middle-aged man stumbled by accident into his office carrying an old painting in a paper bag wrapped with twine. A glance at the painting, a glib lie, and a night spent in concentrated research had convinced Ross that perhaps, just possibly, he could escape.

Ross placed all the material on the desk back in the folder, put the folder in a manila envelope, and unlocked the bottom drawer of his desk. He pulled out the drawer and replaced the envelope, then reached into the back of the drawer and withdrew a small automatic pistol wrapped in a handkerchief. He unwrapped it, placed it on the table, and stared at it.

He had bought it years ago in Germany when, as an assistant curator, he had had to act as a courier transporting valuable works of art to and from Europe. He had specified to the gunsmith that he wanted a pistol small enough to be easily concealed and powerful enough to kill a man at close range.

The German had smiled at this and said: *"Ach, eine Totschlägerwaffe!"* A killer's weapon. Ross had explained rather stiffly that he was not a killer but a curator, and that he wanted the pistol merely for protection. The German had seemed unconvinced. It had unnerved Ross to be thought capable of killing a man, but at the same time he could remember feeling a slight *frisson*.

Now, perhaps, he would see if the German had been right about him.

Ross smiled.

"Vita brevis est, ars longa. Life is short and art is long, like the man said."

Trying to recall whether the quotation came from Cicero or Seneca, Ross wrapped the pistol up again in the handkerchief and put it into his jacket pocket.

5

AT FOUR O'CLOCK the following afternoon Samuel Weinstock leaned back in his chair, feeling extremely pleased with himself. He had sold a painting, which brought him a couple of weeks of relatively guilt-free inactivity, and the evening with Micheline had left him giddily euphoric. It had worked out just as planned: a marvelous meal, wonderful stories about an antique fair at Brussels that Micheline had just attended, and, at the end of it, a long period of languorous, luxurious sex.

With her exaggerated and improbable accent, her flair for melodrama, and her unique blend of aristocratic refinement and peasant vulgarity, Miche was undoubtedly Weinstock's woman. But just as certainly she would never be his wife, or anyone's.

Since arriving in the States just after the war with little English and less money, Micheline Duvet had managed to build up an impressive antique business that now occupied two stories of a building only a block away from Weinstock's. Two businesses, really. The first, on the ground floor, was filled with furniture, bric-a-brac, decorative arts, and various kinds of jewelry. She referred to this part of her operation cheerfully as "my *merde*." The second floor, visited by only a select handful of customers, contained a small collection of French, German, and Italian rococo masterpieces: ornate mirrors, escritoires with elaborate inlaid wood and mother-of-pearl designs, fragile, delicate terra-cottas, and a small number of paintings, oil sketches, and decorative panels by artists like Boucher, Tiepolo, and Pellegrini, all of them superbly chosen.

As prices had skyrocketed, Micheline's tactics for acquiring important pieces had become increasingly complex and subtle. Most of recent acquisitions were the product of detailed campaigns of a military sort with long sieges, lightning raids, and wars of attrition. Her latest expedition to Brussels and Vienna had produced only two second-floor works: a small Meissen figurine and an elaborate ormolu candlestick. Once Miche could have bought both of them relatively cheaply, but now, as she told Weinstock, "Ooh la la, I will have to sell very much *merde*."

For years Weinstock had tried without success to convince her to give up one operation or the other so that they could get married. However, Miche wanted, indeed needed, both the downstairs junk, which amused her, and the superb objets d'art upstairs, which enthralled her. Her shop was in fact a perfect expression of Micheline herself. As she told Weinstock, she had her salon above and her whorehouse below; why should she give either of them up? Besides, as she explained periodically, while she had extraordinary talents as a mistress, she thought she would have none at all as a wife or mother. So the status of their relationship, formed many years ago, remained quo. Weinstock had gradually become resigned to it.

The doorbell rang, pulling Weinstock from his reverie. He went to the door, peered through the peephole, undid the chain and dead-bolt locks, and opened the heavy oak door.

On the other side of it, Harry Giardino was flapping his arms and hopping up and down to keep warm. Tall and gaunt, he looked like a nervous stork. It had begun to snow. Harry bounded into the shop, stuck the bundle he was carrying onto an already precarious tower of magazines, and tossed his cap neatly onto a nearby bronze statuette of a dancing nymph.

"How's the boy, Harry?" It occurred to Weinstock that he'd never seen Giardino when he didn't look breathless.

"Okay, Sam. In fact, good. Things're beginning to break. If the weather doesn't screw me up—hey, look at it out there. Goddamn snow. I got to get to Keene on Thursday—the Mallory sale. You goin'?"

"Not me, Harry."

"No? Look, Sammy, there's this painting. Let me show you . . . it's here someplace . . ."

Giardino began frantically to empty his coat pockets, dropping facial tissues, gum wrappers, paper clips, and other flotsam and finally locating a thin, rolled pamphlet illustrating some of the glories of an upcoming sale in a small New Hampshire auction gallery. Harry opened it quickly to a dog-eared page with a halftone illustration showing a portrait of a rather dyspeptic-looking Colonial officer. It had been circled twice with a red felt-tipped pen. The caption underneath read: "Portrait of an officer. School of Trumbull."

Weinstock looked at it for a moment.

"So what?"

"Swear to me, Sammy, you won't tell anyone. Nobody. Especially that bastard Robinson. If he goes, I'm screwed; if he doesn't I got a good shot. Look, the estimate is one-fifty to three and I figure if I've got five hundred, I'll take it."

"What's the big deal, Harry?" Weinstock was beginning to get a signal that made him nervous.

"Don't you see?"

Harry moved closer to Weinstock, looked conspiratorially to the right and left like a character in a class B spy movie, and said: "Stuart."

" 'Stuart,' Harry?"

"*Gilbert Stuart.* I swear to God. Look, Sam, I've read all the books, done all the work. It's Gilbert Stuart. You'n' me are the only ones who know."

"Christ. First Rembrandt, now Gilbert Stuart. Some guys have all the luck."

"Hell, Sammy, you do pretty good yourself."

Basking in his latest discovery, Giardino was oblivious to the sarcasm. "The thing is, it's about the five C's."

"I kind of thought it would be." Weinstock had been expecting this from the moment Giardino pulled out the catalogue.

"What I figured was, I'd give you half-shares on the Rembrandt. Half-shares, only five hundred bucks. Nothing. But I figure, what the hell, Sam's been a friend. Also, you can handle it for me."

"Yeah. However. Five hundred bucks, at the moment, is quite a lot of—"

"Sammy!" Harry's face became grim. "Don't forget the Muriel, Sammy."

"*Murillo,* dammit."

But Weinstock already knew he was beaten. The Spanish baroque painting the runner had sold him years ago had been paid for many times over, but he had never discovered an antidote to the particular whipped-dog expression that Harry produced on these occasions. With a sigh, Weinstock gingerly extricated a check from his wallet, made it out to Giardino, handed it over to him, and silently, wistfully, bade his money good-bye.

"Aren't you going to look at the Rembrandt? It's

great, Sammy, really great." Giardino waved the check a couple of times, then casually stuffed it in his hip pocket without looking at it. *Sic transit,* thought Weinstock.

"I'm sure it's great, Harry. But I'm damned if I'll look at anything with you hanging over my shoulder. Give me a couple of days, then call me, okay?"

Harry was already pulling on his cap and grabbing his coat. A runner is a runner is a runner, thought Weinstock to himself.

"Thanks. I'll call you when I get back, right? I won't forget this, Sammy. I'm cutting you in on the Stuart." In a swirl of movement, Harry was across the room and out the door.

The "Rembrandt," a soggy, nondescript package in a brown paper bag, was already sinking below the horizon of Harry Giardino's consciousness, becoming lost in the blinding aura of the great, undiscovered masterpiece by Gilbert Stuart.

Feeling old and jaded and not particularly curious, Weinstock picked the package up off the top of the stack of magazines and carried it over to his desk. Cutting the heavy twine with a knife and tearing off the wet brown paper, he discovered that the painting was wrapped in a green plastic garbage-can liner. At least it wouldn't be wet.

Very good, Harry. Not elegant, but functional. Probably appropriate too, the dealer thought sourly.

Weinstock extricated the painting from the green bag and placed it in the middle of his desk. He settled into his chair, pulled over the gooseneck lamp, and turned it on. And then he froze.

6

FOR PERHAPS THREE MINUTES he sat in trancelike stillness, his eyes rooted to the small, ebony-framed panel in front of him.

Then he got up and quickly walked over to the window at the front of the store. He took the last cigarette from a pack in his pocket, lit it, crushed the empty pack into a ball, and dropped it absentmindedly on the floor. He noticed that his hands were shaking and his mouth was dry.

Weinstock's body registered his reaction to a work of art before he was conscious of making any visual judgments, and the symptoms he felt now—the throbbing of his temples, his sharp, shallow breathing, and the tightening in his chest—were all familiar ones.

He had felt them the first time he had made love. He had also felt them, however, when the brakes gave out in his car in the middle of a steep mountain road. Standing now by the window, watching the snow drifting down on a miserable November afternoon, he wondered which was the more appropriate metaphor.

Perhaps beauty was, after all, bad for your health, and great works of art should bear warnings from the Surgeon General. Perhaps it was a disguised blessing that Weinstock found most of the "art" perpetrated in the last fifty years unbearably ugly, or just drab and pretentious.

He dropped the cigarette butt on the floor, stepped on it, and went back to his desk. He felt suddenly oppressed by the clutter of papers and magazines, so after putting the painting under the desk he cleared the top by the simple expedient of making two wide semicircular arcs with his arms and sweeping everything to the floor.

Sheila would kill me, he thought sheepishly.

Retrieving the painting and placing it in the middle of the desk, again adjusting the lamp and taking his telephone off the hook, Weinstock settled down in his chair for an operation he suspected would take hours: the long, brutal, concentrated discipline necessary for looking at something and actually seeing it, correctly and completely.

Weinstock guessed that in this case it would demand most of what he knew about paintings. This was the easy part. It would also demand much of what he knew about himself, which was the hard part. To be able to see, he had to separate himself from all the distractions of greed and ambition, all the big-name, big-score fantasies of the Harry Giardinos of the world. He had to allow the painting its discrete identity, its otherness, and guard against its becoming a distorted projection of Weinstock himself.

There was nothing complicated or oblique in the image before him. It was simply a picture of a woman standing at an open door. A woman, not a girl; she seemed to Weinstock to be in her late thirties, or perhaps older.

She stood at a Dutch door. Dutch doors are split in

48

half, and each half opens separately. In this case only the top half was open, forming a kind of frame-within-a-frame, a common convention in Dutch seventeenth-century painting.

The woman leaned forward slightly, supporting herself with one hand on the sill, and her other hand resting on the closed half-door near the bottom of the painting. She was dressed in a plain, loose-fitting white shift over which a heavy brownish-yellow garment, perhaps a robe, hung down in broad folds.

She wore several pieces of jewelry: a golden brooch or clasp in the simple linen cap, a modest piece of ribbon around her neck from which a gold ring was suspended, pearl earrings, and a ruby ring.

She stared directly out at the dealer.

Her eyes were large, heavy-lidded, and dark, her mouth slightly open but unsmiling. Her face was not in any conventional sense beautiful. Nothing playful or coquettish was reflected in her features, and Weinstock felt a slight discomfort in the frankness of her gaze.

Her face and pose suggested exhaustion or resignation. Illness, perhaps. Yet there was something else, more troubling and difficult to define.

Weinstock felt himself being pulled in, mesmerized and controlled by the presence in the painting. Forcing himself to break free of the grip of the image, he turned the painting over and began to examine it as a physical object. An hour later, he had the following facts:

The painting was fairly small, but not unusually so, measuring twelve by eleven and a quarter inches. It was on a single oak panel which was slightly warped, bowed out in the middle, but not in any danger of splitting. The four edges of the back of the panel were sharply beveled, which was common, and the oak had aged to form a dark brown patina, also common.

What was unusual was that the frame seemed to be original. It was a heavy frame with an ebony veneer, and it was decorated with carved patterns of waves and chevrons in a manner typical of Netherlandish frames in the baroque period. Its only sharply distinctive characteristic was a curious herringbone shape to the mortices in the corners of the back.

What was even more extraordinary was that the panel seemed never to have been taken from its frame. Extraordinary, almost incredible, because the first thing any dealer would do would be to remove it. Likewise, of course, any restorer.

Carefully extracting the four small triangular wedges of oak which held the panel in place, Weinstock was amazed to discover that the wood underneath was dark yellow rather than brown, indicating that they had never been taken out before. Then when he removed the panel itself he found that the operation demanded equal parts of strength and delicacy, since time and dirt had almost frozen the panel to its frame.

More facts. A blood-red wax seal on the frame, cracked, which showed in relief a crowned double-headed eagle, over a row of stars. This was presumably the personal emblem of a former owner, perhaps a clue. There was also an inscription on the frame. With a magnifying glass Weinstock could barely decipher an ink scrawl, which read "Henriette," perhaps another clue.

Weinstock got up, took the frame over to the bin in the corner where a number of frames were already stacked, and returned to the panel. He turned it over and resumed his examination.

The surface of the panel seemed to be bathed in a soft amber light which the dealer recognized as the famous "golden glow" tradition ascribed to Rembrandt. This was just romantic nonsense, of course, simply the fortuitous effect caused by the progressive discoloration of the varnish layers. Every baroque painting that had not been thoroughly cleaned was bound to have the same "golden glow." A half century ago, a restorer at a major museum finally had worked up the courage to clean a Rembrandt properly, to remove the muddy varnish and accumulated grime of centuries and disclose it in its original brilliant colors. The predictable result was shock and outrage, not merely from the public but also from scholars who could not accept the idea of a Rembrandt without murk. In the uproar, both the restorer and the director of the gallery lost their jobs.

For Weinstock, though, the dingy varnish on the panel was a hopeful sign. It meant that the painting had not been restored, stripped, or tampered with. The ultraviolet light revealed no overpaint. An infrared light allowed Weinstock to see some of the underpainting and the preliminary drawing on the panel itself, and both of them appeared powerful and assured. A raking light—the gooseneck lamp held at an acute angle to the panel's surface—revealed the complex texture of the paint surface.

Part of the painting seemed flat, indicating relatively thin areas of pigment. In some places the paint was built up with heavy ridges and streaks, almost like a piece of relief sculpture, and in other parts it was pocked and pitted like a lunar landscape. This was another cause for optimism, because most copies and fakes betray themselves immediately in the thin, dull, even paint surface.

This painting, however, revealed signs of struggle. Weinstock could see places where the artist had changed his mind, and sharp alterations of tempo in the passage of the brush over the wooden support. He could sense that the image of the woman had grown and metamorphosed like a living being.

Finally Weinstock examined the craquelure. It was even and fine, like the pattern of cracks in the vitreous glaze of some old porcelains.

These were the physical facts. A laboratory could

make X-rays and run pigment analysis tests, but all that might add nothing to the little that Weinstock already knew.

The panel was in all likelihood painted in the seventeenth century in Holland. It was most probably an original rather than a copy. However, the possibility of forgery could not be entirely discounted. Since the nineteen thirties and forties, when a failed and embittered Dutch artist named Hans van Meegeren had foisted a number of fakes on the art world as lost Vermeers, dealers had learned not to be too quick or categorical on the matter of authenticity in Dutch paintings. Van Meegeren had taught many people humility.

Except in obvious cases like the "Guardi," Weinstock's method of examining was formalized. He asked himself a number of questions that followed a standard progression as ritualistic as a litany: first, physical evidence; second, formal analysis; third, style.

Most of his major mistakes, he had found, had been the result of neglecting the first two categories in favor of the third. For style, the most important matter, was also the most treacherous. Style was the main interest, sometimes the sole interest, of the forger. Through bitter experience, Weinstock had learned that it was necessary to establish whether a picture was well painted in a formal sense before trying to pin a name on it.

He looked again at the figure in the doorway. Using his eyes almost as a tactile sense, he examined the planes of the face and the way the eyes were sunk in their sockets. Then the critical junctures of the body—the transitions between the neck, shoulders, and head, the articulations of hand and wrist, the subtle indications of the body under the drapery.

Then he sought the artist's understanding of the delicate muscular shifts and balances necessitated by the simple mechanical act of standing erect. Sharpening his attention, Weinstock tried to imagine the exact arrangement of the woman's lower body, which was masked by the closed half-door. He found that this was possible. In a lesser artist, a weaker artist, there would be an awkward abruptness and sense of truncation.

He scrutinized each brushstroke looking for a slip, an ambiguity, a moment of hesitation or indecision. He couldn't find any.

Okay so far, thought Weinstock. You've passed your physical. Now just one more little question, please. Who painted you?

Weinstock got a fresh pack of cigarettes and went back over to the window. The world outside was now covered by a thin layer of snow which looked unreal in the lamp light, like Styrofoam. There were fewer cars and pedestrians now, and the street outside seemed quiet and almost peaceful. The dealer noticed that his hands were steady again.

When he returned to his desk Weinstock was carrying a big folio volume entitled *Rembrandt's Paintings*. It had been published in the early fifties, and had a number of faithful halftone reproductions as well as a useful catalogue of the works.

Half an hour later he had a list. Paintings in Vienna, London, Stockholm, Berlin, and Chicago. All were half-length portraits of women framed in doorways, windows, or niches. All were vaguely similar in style, composition, and mood.

Weinstock found his attention suddenly caught by the Chicago picture. Superficially, the painting was close to his panel. A girl, shown half-length, was depicted standing in a doorway. Her pose was simple and frontal. Her hands were resting on the half-door, her head was tilted slightly, and her glance was directed obliquely downward. Her face, bathed in a gentle light, was soft, dreamy, smiling.

Yet as he stared at it, the dealer became increasingly aware that something was wrong. First he noticed a certain woodenness and awkwardness in the pose. Where there should have been tension and movement the figure was static, doll-like. Something was also off in the relationship between the head and shoulders. That was it: the neck was too short. And the eyes weren't aligned quite correctly: they were tilted a bit at the corners, giving the face a slightly feline cast.

Something's funny about the left hand, too, thought Weinstock. The expression, the mood—queer. There seemed to be an almost sneaky quality in the girl's expression, like someone hiding something. The more Weinstock looked at it, the more the picture seemed to disintegrate before his eyes.

He got up and went over to a rickety-looking bookcase in the corner, rummaged around, located what he wanted, and went back to the desk. A paperback this time, the book was the latest compilation of Rembrandt's accepted works. The plates were terrible, but the information in the text was invaluable.

He quickly found what he was looking for. The book's author, a noted Dutch scholar, strongly doubted the authenticity of the Chicago picture. Weinstock, feeling vindicated, heaved a sigh of relief.

Sorry, lady. You're quite beautiful, but you're not a Rembrandt.

Slowly going down the list of the other comparable works, the dealer finally came to the Berlin picture. It was a portrait of Hendrickje Stoffels, Rembrandt's common-law wife after the death of his wife Saskia. It was painted around 1658 or 1659.

The face, slightly altered, was the face in the panel on the desk.

Weinstock examined the plate in the book carefully, and then skimmed several pages of the text. Armed with this knowledge, he turned back to the panel, comparing it slowly, feature by feature and passage by passage, with the plate in the book. For the first time, he allowed himself to succumb to the mood of the painting.

Both the panel and the Berlin canvas reflected the breadth and power of Rembrandt's late style and had the same rough, almost encrusted paint surface. The effects one could see in the panel could be felt as well in the Berlin picture, even in a black-and-white reproduction: a mysterious luminosity, a shimmering, palpitant inner light.

The poses and expressions in the two works were so similar that Weinstock realized only gradually how great a gulf separated the two.

As the dealer examined it, the Berlin picture increasingly struck him as a marvelous combination of the spiritual and the sensual. In the full curves of Hendrickje's body, clearly legible under the drapery, in the half-smile and the almost sultry, heavy-lidded eyes, Weinstock could feel a powerful sexual impulse. The gesture of the right hand, apparently opening the top of the split doors to the viewer, added to the mood of erotic invitation. Weinstock was reminded of the Venuses of Titian and the nudes of Rubens.

In the panel this erotic dimension was gone. The arm leaning on the top of the half-door was no longer relaxed, and the right hand was now used as a strut or support, as if the body could sustain its own weight only with difficulty. The smile of the Berlin picture had faded, and the face in the panel confronted the viewer with grave solemnity.

The model seemed older and thinner. Her head was more vertical and frontal, no longer tilted seductively, and her mouth was almost closed. By means of barely perceptible adjustments of pose the artist suggested a quality of enervation, a hint of serious physical decline.

Weinstock checked the book. Hendrickje had died in 1662 after a long wasting illness.

He turned back to the painting. He noted that the

55

closed half-door served not merely as a framing device and support, but also as a barrier. The figure in the panel seemed to communicate a sense of withdrawal and isolation. Weinstock suddenly remembered his own father at the end, his body ravaged by disease, all his physical resources spent. He remembered how he had withdrawn, confronting his own mortality, beyond human solace and human needs.

The background of the painting was entirely shrouded in shadow, and the surrounding gloom seemed to encroach on the figure of Hendrickje and intensify the mood of tragic premonition. If the Berlin picture was a love poem, the small panel was an elegy. Weinstock marveled that such a depth of sentiment could be expressed without sentimentality.

My God. Could it be? Could the thing be a Rembrandt?

Weinstock went over again to the window. As he lit his third cigarette he noticed that his hands were shaking again.

7

TWO HOURS AFTER Weinstock finished his cigarette, Elton Ross entered the vestibule of an apartment building six blocks away.

The building was about fifty years old and still retained a sort of threadbare dignity, but it had long since begun to lose its battle with neglect, vandalism, and indifference. The vestibule was small and nondescript: intercom on one side, letterboxes on the other, and a glass door leading into a hallway with an elevator painted a bilious shade of green.

A quick glance assured Ross that no one else was in the hall. He punched the button next to the piece of tape marked "Giardino, H." There was a click, then a raucous squawk barely identifiable as a human voice.

"Hello? Who'zat?"

"Mr. Giardino? This is Elton Ross, from the Museum."

"Ross?" Giardino's voice sounded quizzical, but not suspicious.

"Yes. I've made a rather exciting discovery about

that little painting of yours. I wonder if I might come up and speak to you."

"What? Up here? Well, sure, I guess, come on up. Sixth floor, number six-o-seven. Great to see you."

There was a buzzing sound from the door. Ross opened it and went quickly to the elevator.

He was dressed in black shoes and a dark gray over-coat with the collar turned up. The only unusual part of his costume was a fairly silly-looking beret he had bought years ago in Spain, and then in a more sober moment relegated to the bottom drawer of his bureau. He'd never worn it before, but he hoped it gave him a slightly shabby appearance appropriate to the setting.

In the elevator he placed his hand over the gun in his pocket. He checked the safety catch and ran his finger along the magazine in the butt of the pistol. Then he put on gloves.

Halfway to the sixth floor fear hit him like a fist. He staggered against the wall of the elevator overcome with dread, and for a second or two felt as though he were suffocating. The claustrophobia quickly became so intense that he wanted to scream.

The psychic storm passed as suddenly as it had come. When the elevator stopped at Giardino's floor Ross felt slightly weak and light-headed and discovered that his body was drenched with sweat, but he had regained control of himself. When the door to 607 opened and Harry Giardino breathlessly ushered him into the drab, uninviting little apartment, Ross felt a resurgent sense of his own superiority and mastery.

The gun slid easily from his pocket, and Ross was pleased to find that the hand that held it was steady. He was also reassured to find that the expression of shock and disbelief on Giardino's face struck him as comical rather than horrifying.

"I really apologize, Mr. Giardino. But, you see, I *must* have that painting." His voice, too, was calm.

58

* * *

When Ross left the apartment three quarters of an hour later he was quivering with rage rather than fear. But he was apparently capable of yet another transformation, because when he emerged from the elevator in the hallway he appeared totally self-composed.

Anyone seeing him leave the apartment building might have described him simply as an attractive, middle-aged man with a funny sort of foreign-looking hat. Beyond that they might have noticed his smile, the smile of someone remembering a private joke.

But no one saw him come, and no one saw him go.

8

AT TEN the following morning Captain Michael O'Rourke, Homicide, Seventh Precinct, was standing next to Harry Giardino's bed. Giardino's corpse lay in the middle of it.

O'Rourke said, "Jesus, Mary, and Joseph," quietly to himself. He had been staring at the corpse for several minutes. This was the first thing he had said since entering the room.

His second remark was to the man standing next to him, Lieutenant Leo Callahan.

"Leo, how many people been through here? The usual crowd, like Grand Central at rush hour, right? Look, I want them all the hell out. Now. All I want here is—let's see. I want the examiner, the best lab men. Get Derringer and Henckel. And a photographer. I want photos of everything. And I don't want nobody touching anything. No press. I want a tight lock on this, and that means no *Globe,* no *Herald,* no CBS or WBZ or anybody else. Set up interviews with all the people on floors one, five, six, seven. Everyone on those floors stays put, and anybody else who leaves, find out first if they heard any noises, saw any strangers, you know the drill. I want the manager to stay in his office—get Jenson to baby-sit him—and also get the guy who reported the noise. I'll start with them."

During this monologue O'Rourke's eyes had not left the corpse.

Ungainly in life, Harry Giardino looked grotesque in death. He was lying backward on the bed, his arms flung out to the side and his legs awkwardly bent back with his feet pinned underneath his buttocks. There was a gaping hole at the base of his neck marked by thick gouts of blood, another, equally gory, in the middle of his chest, and a third, somewhat cleaner wound in the area of his stomach.

Giardino's clothes, the sheets and blankets, and the wall behind him were all saturated with blood.

Several small details were somehow almost more horrible. Eight scarlet crescents in his hands, where Harry, before he died, had driven his nails into his own palms, and a jagged wound that indicated where he had bitten through his lower lip. Wide, staring eyes, and the salt tracks of dried tears down his cheeks.

Harry Giardino's body was a hieroglyph of terror.

"Jesus." O'Rourke, suddenly furious, spat the word through clenched teeth.

He turned away from the figure on the bed and slowly made a tour of the room. The other members of the squad had left to conduct interviews, leaving Callahan in awkward attendance. The lieutenant stood in the middle of the room, trying hard to avoid looking at the figure on the bed. For no ostensible reason he held a small spiral notebook open in his hand. O'Rourke went over to him.

"Say, Leo, you mind waiting outside? I'd like a few minutes to look around before the professors get here and screw everything up." Captain O'Rourke, profoundly skeptical of scientific criminology, referred to everyone who didn't carry a gun as a "professor."

"Sure, Mike." Relieved, Callahan made his escape.

Giardino's apartment was sparsely furnished. The tiny bedroom held only a chest of drawers surmounted by a small mirror, a closet, and a small portable stereo set, which sat on the floor in the corner. Other than this there was only the bed, a metal cot with its head set against the wall. Next to it was a window, curtainless, with the shade drawn.

The decorations consisted of a sentimental, nineteenth-century painting of Christ and a number of cheap prints.

The print over the bed showed several nude women by a pond. O'Rourke went over to it and idly read the caption beneath: "Frolicking Bathers—A Masterpiece by RENOIR."

The bather in the middle did not seem to mind the bullet hole through her leg. Someone had drawn a circle around it in yellow chalk, which reminded O'Rourke to call in Ballistics.

The closet door was partly open. Wrapping his fingers in tissue, the policeman opened it farther. The clothes on the hangers had been pushed over to one side.

The bottom of the closet was a tangle of shoes, dirty clothes, and boxes of papers. There were several stacks of catalogues on the shelf above the rack, and one of them had been taken down and left on the floor of the closet. The rest of the stacks seemed to have been recently shoved around.

Someone had apparently been looking for something. O'Rourke hoped to God it had been either the killer or his victim rather than another cop. It seemed to O'Rourke that it had not really been a serious search, just someone like him poking around.

The captain moved the door back to the angle at

which he had found it and went over to the bureau. The drawers were slightly ajar. When he opened them, he again had the feeling that a rather desultory search had taken place. In all four drawers the clothes were pushed over to one side or another. Whoever had done this had apparently felt no need to pull the drawers out entirely and empty them on the floor.

O'Rourke felt puzzled, and it took him a moment to realize why. This was another thing that didn't fit the usual pattern.

He had seen corpses like Giardino's before. He had seen mob slayings where the object had been the total savaging of a human being. He had also seen theft-related homicides in which the murderer, driven by rage or desperation, had turned from his victim to the house or apartment with the same violent impulse, trashing both.

But this was different. The brutality of the murder had a totally different quality, even tempo, from the casual, almost fastidious search of the apartment. O'Rourke found that he could not associate the two acts with the same person.

He went over to the stereo set. It had been on when the landlord had entered the apartment, spinning aimlessly on the last groove. At first the landlord had thought that the monotonous, dull clicks were drops of blood dripping from the bed. It had shaken him.

O'Rourke bent down and read the print on the label of the record carefully. Then he turned to the metal rack beside it. Each record was in its jacket, and each jacket had a small gummed label with a number.

O'Rourke riffled through them, again covering his hands with tissue, until he came to the empty sleeve. He pulled it out.

He recognized the cover immediately. It was an album of the Benny Goodman jazz concert in Carnegie Hall in 1938. He removed the cover from the rack and

64

placed it against the wall, carefully avoiding touching it with his fingers.

Bemused, he returned to the rack. All the records were jazz or rock. Some names he recognized—Mingus, Coltrane, Coleman. Most of them were rock stars—the Beatles, the Rolling Stones, and many others that O'Rourke had never heard of before. Could there really be a group called the Jefferson Airplane? The Goodman record was the oldest in the collection. O'Rourke thought it showed taste.

The search of the rest of the apartment was disappointing. The living room was dotted with magazines, more catalogues, and several articles of soiled clothing. It contained a large, blocky, bright blue couch. O'Rourke pulled it away from the wall. Behind it were several canvases, out of their frames, leaning against one another. O'Rourke thought some of the paintings looked quite old. Bending down, he discovered that the frames were neatly stacked under the couch.

He wondered if any of the paintings were missing.

The magazines in the living room were a mixed assortment, most of them being either glossy, expensive art periodicals with names like *Apollo* and *Connoisseur* or girlie magazines of the sub-*Penthouse* variety.

On an end table O'Rourke found Giardino's wallet in a mare's nest of notes and papers. Checking it, he found two twenty-dollar bills, a ten, and two fives. He decided to save the notes and papers for the station house. They were never as important as they looked, and O'Rourke was in no mood for disappointments.

This left the bathroom and kitchenette, neither one of which contained anything that particularly interested the detective. Perhaps he was getting old and sloppy, but he had lost his faith in cryptic messages stuck in toothpaste tubes and keys taped to the bottoms of chairs. Let the lab men look for the fatal strand of hair or grain of pollen that would clinch the case.

So far there wasn't any case. Just a body that had once been a man, lying in a blood-soaked bed.

When Leo and the rest returned five minutes later, they found Captain O'Rourke on the couch looking like a parody of the proverbial burly Irish cop. Red-faced and sweating, O'Rourke was sitting slouched forward, his huge arms hanging like dead weights from his shoulders and his knuckles almost touching the floor. He was chewing a piece of gum with his mouth open, making a monotonous smacking sound painfully familiar to everyone who worked with him, and roundly disliked by all.

His face had the appearance of total vacuity, a kind of simian stupidity that Callahan recognized from experience as the ironic corollary of furious concentration. O'Rourke was the smartest cop Callahan knew.

He blinked, sat up, spat the gum into a piece of paper, and turned to Lieutenant Callahan. Callahan's notebook was already open.

"Okay, Leo, here's what I want. The wallet and papers on that table go in a plastic envelope. I'm taking them to the station. I want the record-player in the bedroom dusted for prints, also the record jacket leaning against the wall as well as the record on the turntable. Get the lab boys to do a thorough number on the closet, the chest of drawers, any other surfaces that might take prints."

O'Rourke paused to let Callahan catch up with him.

"There are some paintings behind the couch. I want to find out what they are, anything I can about their value. Call—hell, I don't know, call the Museum. Take them over there as soon as possible. Get Ballistics working on the slugs, and tell the medical examiner's office that I want the report as soon as possible. Sooner."

O'Rourke stopped, took a deep breath, and sighed.

"I don't know what it is, Leo, but this one spooks me. Too ugly, too psycho, too hot and cold. Something about it. Okay, let's go down and see the manager and the guy upstairs."

9

AT FOUR O'CLOCK that afternoon Weinstock was standing in the middle of his gallery, hands on hips, feeling smug. Repressing his desire to start the research campaign on the painting immediately, he had decided to spend several hours cleaning up the gallery before Sheila's return the next day.

He pivoted around, surveying the results with undisguised self-satisfaction. By Weinstock's standards, the place was immaculate. The books were back in the bookcase, the papers, magazines, and notes were, if not exactly organized, at least segregated into their own quanta of space. Empty cans and bottles, Q-Tips, half-eaten sandwices, plastic cups, Kleenex, rags, empty cartons, bits and pieces of cardboard, old newspapers, and a mound of soiled puffs of cotton had all been thrown out.

Disregarding the temperature outside, Weinstock had thrown open a window, and after half an hour or so the place smelled less like a chemical warehouse and more like a gallery. Sheila had always been nervous about the oil, varnish, and turpentine-soaked rags, and neither one of them was sure why they had never ignited and burned the place to the ground. Weinstock had tried without success to convince them both that spontaneous combustion was a scientific fallacy.

He was surprised by the sound of the doorbell, and even more surprised when he looked through the peep-hole and saw who was there. The dealer immediately recognized the tall, distinguished figure who was smiling amicably at the top of the stoop.

"Elton Ross, from the Museum. I hope I'm not bothering you."

"Not at all, I'm generally open on Sunday. Samuel Weinstock. Come on in."

As Weinstock helped the director off with his coat, he couldn't help wondering to himself what a man like Ross was doing in a shop like his. He had the same sense of slight disorientation he had felt in Caroline Emerson's apartment.

"I'm on a bit of a busman's holiday, actually. Seems to me a bit silly that the people at the Museum always know what's going on in London and Paris and Madison Avenue, and yet we never take the time to find out what's in our own backyard. So I decided to spend the day on Charles Street and Newbury Street mending some fences."

True enough, thought Weinstock. Occasionally when he got a major work he would send a photograph to the Museum. Lately he'd stopped doing that. The photographs were usually returned with a chilly note from an assistant curator to the effect that the Museum did not find the work sufficiently "significant" or "outstanding," and at other times, he never got the photograph back at all.

"But I believe we got those two marvelous Morans from you several years ago."

"Right. Two small beach scenes."

70

The dealer was tempted to correct Ross, but decided against it. He still had a bad taste about the Moran deal. One of them had indeed been a beautiful painting, but the other one was so riddled with overpaint that the dealer did not feel he could confidently attribute it. The curator of American paintings, however, had been insistent. She had wanted them both, to hang as a pair. Disregarding the dealer's warnings, the Museum had acquired them together.

When scientific examination proved Weinstock's suspicions to have been well founded, the Museum sent him a nasty letter implicitly accusing the dealer of misrepresentation. The good picture was now relegated to a dark corner of a small gallery, as if in penance, and the bad one was consigned to the merciful oblivion of the storage area.

"I see you're not a specialist, Mr. Weinstock. You deal in everything."

"Anything I can find a market for, and a few things, maybe too many, that I can't."

Weinstock could sense that the casual conversation was only a pretext. Ross was looking, and looking hard. He seemed to stalk through the gallery, nervously touching the objects on the tables.

He stopped at a heavy, vaguely Art Nouveau candlestick and picked it up. The base was an abstract composition of free-form curves, like a stylized lily pad. Emerging out of the base was a vertical stem that metamorphosed into a seminude woman. Her position was reminiscent of the Statue of Liberty, but instead of a torch she held an elaborate candleholder.

"Charming. Is it French?"

"God, no, don't I wish. It's upstate New York, and about twenty years too late."

But before Weinstock had finished Ross had already put it down and resumed his pacing. Touching things, picking up small objects and replacing them without looking at them, his eyes nervously darting, searching. Like a hunting animal, thought Weinstock, who felt himself come alert.

"I must admit my ulterior motive. My wife's birthday is coming up. Fortunately, she prefers art to jewelry or clothes." Ross's laugh sounded fake. "She likes small, precious things. Small paintings, bronzes, netsuke, that sort of thing. Miniaturistic works of art. A woman's taste, very Madame de Pompadour. Cabinet pieces. Something rather like this."

Ross lifted a small painting from its hook and carried it over to a lamp. It was an oil sketch, predominantly brown in color, which showed a feverish-looking monk kneeling in a cave.

"Magnasco?"

"School of, probably. Magnasco's a little like Guardi. If he'd painted with both hands for two hundred years, he couldn't have done half the stuff that's been attributed to him. But that's at least close, and period, and it has a school price."

Ross had moved over to the desk and picked up the Dutch panel.

"Sorry, that's not for sale. I'm still working on it."

Ross turned on the gooseneck lamp, tilted the panel at different angles to the light, and squinted at it.

"A charming painting. I've always admired the eighteenth-century Rembrandtistes, haven't you? Nobody much buys this kind of thing today. . . . Let me see, this would be Grimou perhaps, maybe Dietriche, someone like that."

Games, thought Weinstock. You shouldn't play games with dealers. They know all the games, all the moves. The feigned indifference, the veiled and not so veiled insults, the elaborate boredom which customers and other dealers affected toward some work they in fact desperately coveted. He also knew all the lines by heart. Lines like "Oh, by the way, that little thing over there in the corner" or "Of course it's only a copy, but . . ." or "Believe it or not, I have a customer who's mad for this kind of crap." Dealers who referred to any still life they didn't own as "a pretty bit of decoration." Any gambit that could be used to discredit a work they wanted, and to chisel the price down.

"Yes, I really rather fancy this little panel. It would be perfect for Jean's mantel . . ."

"It's not for sale."

"I'll give you six—no, even seven hundred dollars—"

"I repeat, Mr. Ross, it's not for sale. I never sell anything until I've studied it thoroughly."

So that's why you're here, thought Weinstock. He remembered what Harry Giardino had told him. Ross and the panel were old friends.

Well, now.

"It's bad business practice to have pictures in the gallery you won't sell. I should think that a serious customer, even a potentially serious customer, would be granted certain considerations—"

Noting the expression on the dealer's face, Ross stopped short. He laid the panel carefully on the desk.

"Of course, I don't want to push you into anything. If you don't want to sell it yet, you have a perfect right not to. I might leave you my telephone number in case you change your mind. Let me look around some more. Perhaps I'll find something I like better."

Weinstock sensed that when Ross resumed his tour of the gallery his mood had changed. He was no longer stalking, but merely wandering around. He also seemed more relaxed, affable, and chatty.

"We're always looking for American Impressionists. Do you have anything in that line? Hassam, Prendergast, anybody like that? That's a lovely Bierstadt sketch, by the way. Pity we already have so many. . . . We're already strong in major figures, Copley and Innes and Homer and all those, but if you

73

move into the minor artists you can spot the holes. . . . Nice Doughty you've got there. . . . America's not my field of course, but when you work at the Museum you pick it up . . ."

During this soliloquy Ross threaded his way through the gallery, squatting periodically to run through rows of canvases leaning against one another like oversized dominoes. Finally he came to the front of the shop again.

He turned to Weinstock, smiling.

"Well. I'm afraid I must be going. Sorry to rush through like this, but I have to stop back at the Museum this afternoon. Perhaps next week I could make an appointment to visit your fine gallery at a more leisurely pace."

"Sure, any time. If you call my secretary, Miss Woods, she'll give you my schedule."

Ross retrieved his coat and scarf, put them on, and walked to the back of the gallery where Weinstock was still seated at his desk. He shook the dealer's hand warmly, thanked him for the visit, and began to leave the store.

When Ross was halfway to the door, Weinstock heard a sharp crack and a muffled "Damn!" The director stopped and knelt down next to a rack of framed canvases.

"How stupid. I seemed to have knocked the corner off one of your frames."

Weinstock went over and knelt next to Ross. The director was holding a small ornamental plaster shell which he had kicked off the corner of a reproduction rococo frame.

The dealer went over to his desk, rummaged around, and came up with a small tube of plastic cement.

"No problem. I do it myself all the time. It's easy to fix. Besides, it was just a Madison Avenue fake. This just 'antiques' it a little more."

He knelt down, covered the broken piece with glue, and fitted it against the jagged surface of plaster. Intent on this small chore, he wasn't aware of Ross standing behind and over him. He never noticed Ross's movements. He was just about to remind the director to leave his telephone number when the heavy base of the Art Nouveau candlestick, swung savagely in a flat, diagonal arc, stove in the back of his head.

For a moment the candlestick remained embedded in the dealer's skull, caught on a spur of bone, and for the same fraction of a second the dealer's body maintained its absurd kneeling position, like a Buddhist monk in prayer. Then it collapsed of its own weight, slumping to the side in a spreading pool of blood. The weapon clattered on the hardwood floor.

Ross stood over Weinstock's body, transfixed, his heart pounding and his breath coming in short gasps. As before, he recognized in himself horror, blind fear, and some other emotion that he dared not name. He was swaying slightly, and had to reach out to a table to steady himself. He found that he had to fight back successive waves of nausea which seemed synchronized to the throbbing he half-heard, half-felt in his own skull. It took him a full minute before he felt sufficiently recovered to move.

When he did move, his actions were precise, calculated, and methodical. He went through the store quickly, wiping with a handkerchief each object he could remember touching. He wrapped the panel in a newspaper, and put the newspaper into the same green plastic bag it had come in. Then he left.

Again there were no witnesses. No one came forward later, no one remembered seeing the tall figure with a small green parcel stepping out of the shadowed doorway into the cold, gray Boston evening.

10

AT THE MOMENT the second murder was committed, Captain O'Rourke was sitting in his office at the station house worrying about the first murder.

"I don't like it. I didn't like it when I first saw it. Now I've had a chance to think about it, I fucking hate it."

This remark was addressed to his partner, Callahan, and it worried him mildly, first because O'Rourke obviously saw something Callahan didn't, and second because O'Rourke was seldom known to swear.

Around the station O'Rourke and Callahan were known as the Irish Odd Couple. Like many successful partners, they were a study in contrasts. O'Rourke was big and beefy and looked dumb and lethargic, though in fact he was neither. Callahan was shorter, thin and wiry, and had the kind of brooding, intense expression that women find hard to resist. His face didn't reflect his nature any more than O'Rourke's did, though, since Callahan was actually easygoing, generally cheerful, and not particularly bright.

Callahan was devoted to O'Rourke, who treated him

with a kindly, avuncular protectiveness although he was only eight years Callahan's senior. Callahan was forty-two, O'Rourke fifty.

At present the two men were sitting in O'Rourke's office. It was a tiny cubicle which held an old hat-rack, a bulletin board, two straight-backed chairs, a swivel chair, and a big oak table that served O'Rourke as a desk. Aside from two wire-mesh racks filled with forms and data sheets the entire surface of the table was covered with material from the Giardino killing.

O'Rourke leaned back in the swivel chair, put his hands behind his head, and closed his eyes. Then he opened them, blinked, and turned to Callahan.

"Tell me what you think. You were there. You saw the photos, the ballistics stuff, so you tell me what happened. Professional or amateur? Then I'll tell you what I think."

Leo pursed his lips and knitted his brows in a caricature of profound concentration.

"What I think is, it's professional. Gotta be professional. Too neat. No struggle, no fight, no clues, nothing. The guy just sets him up against the wall and shoots him. Maybe one guy, maybe more, but one could've done it. Maybe he's after a picture, maybe money, maybe the reason is a woman, a grudge, anything. Who knows? This Giardino's a seedy-looking dude. He makes out, barely, but it's always on the fringes, never big time. But it's gotta be a professional hit, because it's too clean and too smart. The music, for instance. He turns the record up loud to cover the shots, a pro's trick. Also, nobody saw nothing. If the guy upstairs hadn't phoned the manager the next morning to bitch about the noise, Giardino'd probably be lying there a week.

"And the shooting. Three shots, high caliber, no mistakes. Whoever it was wanted this Giardino dead and knew what he was doing. I make it a professional job."

78

O'Rourke nodded, leaned forward in his chair, and took the gum he was chewing out of his mouth. He wrapped it carefully in tissue and dropped it in the waste-paper basket. Then he looked sadly at Callahan. "Yeah, that's the way I figured it. At first. That's the way I figured it when I first saw it."

Callahan's face fell. Meetings with O'Rourke generally ran this way. O'Rourke would ask Callahan for his theories, listen politely, and then tear them apart. This was another reason the two men were partners. Nobody but Callahan could stand working with O'Rourke.

This time, however, when O'Rourke began to speak his voice held none of its usual bravado. There was no aura of condescension. Instead the captain sounded grave and worried, and Callahan sometimes had the feeling that O'Rourke was unaware of his presence.

"Look, Leo, I don't know who did it or why, but I have a theory about how. That's what spooks me. First let's go through the actual killing, then discuss the business about the record.

"You've seen the medical examiner's report, the corpse, the photos. Three shots, two entering from the back, one from the front. Thirty-eight caliber pistol, some kind of heavy-duty foreign make. No silencer."

"How do we know about 'no silencer'?"

"We don't know, we guess. Heavy powder burns around all three wounds. Presumably the murderer was not just close, he was right against him with the gun pushed into him. He used Giardino's body as a silencer."

"Jesus."

"Yeah. Not exactly squeamish, considering the caliber and considering the effect. Giardino was kneeling at the head of the bed, his forehead leaning against the wall. Pieces of him are probably still there.

"Three bullets. The first entered at the base of the neck. According to the report, it did the job. Traveling at a forty-five-degree angle, it cut the cervical vertebra, severed a carotid artery, and exited at the base of the chin. At that point, Giardino was dead twice over.

"Ever see a chicken decapitated, Leo? It's a real lesson. Teaches you all you ever want to know about blood pressure. It also teaches you to stay away from knife fights. Anyway, the carotid artery means business. If it's cut you don't just bleed, you spurt blood in a pulsing stream. Remember the wall behind Giardino, and the bed.

"That was probably shot number one. For shot number two, the killer was probably propping Giardino up with his hand. How many people could've stuck around for that second shot? You, me, probably even the goddamned medical examiner would've been puking our guts out.

"Anyway. He holds him and shoots him again. Bullet number two enters between the seventh and eighth ribs, pierces the left auricle of the heart, and exits through the sternum. So Giardino's dead a third time. Give the killer points for thoroughness.

"Giardino falls back on the bed, arms out, like we found him. The killer sticks around for a third shot, and this time he does it looking at Harry Giardino's face. He isn't a pretty sight by now, but still the killer doesn't chuck his cookies. He puts the gun against Giardino's belly and pulls the trigger. Third slug misses the main organs, pierces the intestines, passes through the mattress, and winds up buried in the floor. It also doesn't make any sense, except it tells us it's not a professional job."

"I don't follow that."

"The third shot is nerves. A pro wouldn't gut-shoot a corpse. A pro would know he'd done it with the first slug. Why stick around? And if it was a message killing or a revenge killing it still wouldn't be three slugs, it'd be eight or ten, close-spaced, through the head. This guy wasn't leaving a message, he was just making sure. In other words, *he didn't know*. Amateur."

"Jesus Christ."

"Yeah. The physical part's pretty bad, but it gets worse. If I'm right, much worse."

At this point O'Rourke sat up, mopped his brow with a handkerchief, lit a cigarette, and eased back into his chair.

"Remember the interview with the super and the guy upstairs? The guy upstairs can't stand Giardino's stereo. Giardino loves it, plays it all the time, so they have a fight. Giardino makes a deal: no music after nine o'clock. The guy upstairs hears music last night around ten o'clock, steams around for a while, and at ten-thirty calls Giardino. No answer. Next morning he's still mad, so he calls the super. The super decides to confront Giardino. He goes up and knocks on the door; still no answer. So the super decides to leave a note, enters the apartment with his passkey looking for paper, finds Giardino, calls us. So far so good.

"Remember what the guy upstairs says about the music? It wasn't the volume, it was the time that pissed him off. It was supposed to be quiet hour. Remember, when I questioned him about it he said that the music was soft, briefly got quite loud, then soft again. He didn't think it lasted more than half or three quarters of an hour at most. Let's say, leaving a margin for error, that the music was playing sometime between ten and eleven—that is, about the time Harry Giardino is supposed to have been killed. So let's assume we're right that the record was used to cover the shots. This gives us the approximate time of the murder, for what that's worth. Know anything about jazz, Leo? I mean, the early stuff?"

Callahan shook his head. O'Rourke stubbed out his cigarette and picked up a record jacket that was leaning against the desk.

"This is the record he used. Benny Goodman, the Carnegie Hall concert of 1938. My old man was a jazz buff. I grew up on it. I knew this record backwards and forwards, since the time I was a kid. It was a historic concert, the first time anyone ever played jazz in Carnegie Hall. The Goodman Band had all the greats— Harry James, Gene Krupa, Ziggy Elmán; God, look at the names.

"This is what spooks me, or part of it. The killer wanted a record, some noise, something to cover the sound of the shots. But he didn't pick any record. Most of Giardino's records are rock or electric rock—loud stuff, crazy stuff, stuff that would have served the same function better.

"By this time he probably has his gun out, and Giardino's probably against the wall. He takes his time, looks at all the records, and picks the only classic among them. Picks it why? He picks it because he likes it, no other reason.

"Now, most of the Carnegie concert is just songs— great songs. Great numbers, sure, but nothing unbelievable. But there's one number that stopped the show cold. There's never been anything like it, before or since. It's called 'Sing, Sing, Sing.' It's almost fifteen minutes long; I timed it last night. Give you an idea about 'Sing, Sing, Sing': there was a piano solo in it by a guy named Jess Stacy. Stacy's solo is maybe three to five minutes long, that's all. But you ask anyone who knows anything about jazz piano, he'll know about Jess Stacy, if just for that short bit in 'Sing, Sing, Sing.'

"Near the end of the piece, Gene Krupa cuts loose on the drums. This is even shorter, maybe a minute. But even on medium volume it would be loud enough and strong enough to cover the shots. After Krupa, the band quiets down a bit."

O'Rourke was getting hoarse. He drank some water out of a paper cup on his desk, and lit another cigarette.

"So this is how I see it. I may be crazy, but it fits with what the guy upstairs said: soft, then loud, then soft.

"This is the thing that really spooks me. The killer puts on the record, side two, 'Sing, Sing, Sing,' from the beginning. It starts soft, then builds up. About thirteen minutes, remember, to Krupa's solo. Giardino must have either known or sensed what was happening, what they were waiting for. That must have been when he bit through his lip.

"Thirteen minutes is a long time, waiting to die. I wonder what he thought about. More, I wonder what the guy with the gun thought about. I wonder what he said to Giardino. And most of all, I wonder what kind of person kills like that."

O'Rourke stopped, stubbing out his latest cigarette. Callahan's face was hot and angry.

"Yeah, maybe. But a psycho under control. A sadist."

O'Rourke began picking up the photographs on the desk.

"Oh, and one other thing. I think he was looking for something. You ever watch the cop shows on the tube, Leo? There's one line, you hear it again and again. There's a murder, see, the cops bust in, sniff around, and one cop says to another cop—very serious—'Find out if there's anything missing.' I must've heard that line thirty or forty times, and nobody ever laughs at it but me. I almost caught myself saying it yesterday.

"So anyway. Whatever the bastard was looking for, I sure hope he found it."

11

IT WAS NINE-THIRTY the next morning when Callahan and O'Rourke got the call at the station house.

It was another bleak, gray November day. The night before had been typical, with freezing rain turning to sleet and then to light snow. The next morning the rush-hour traffic was reduced to a crawl.

Callahan drove. He liked the siren, the flashing light, the sense of melodrama and swagger. He liked to watch the other cars creeping timidly over the side as he roared by. In truth, he also enjoyed scaring O'Rourke silly and got a fatuous pleasure from noticing his partner hunched over and cowering in the corner of the seat. O'Rourke particularly dreaded calls like this one that gave Leo an opportunity to cross Beacon Hill, because the Hill was really very steep in spots and it gave Leo the chance to do what his partner called "the San Francisco chase scene."

In clear weather, on a flat road, the San Francisco chase scene was dangerous. On Beacon Hill, in winter, it seemed to O'Rourke suicidal. As Leo always pointed out, they had never had a serious accident. As O'Rourke always pointed out, they had never actually chased anybody, either. So, O'Rourke wanted to know, why the hell didn't Leo get out of Homicide and into Traffic Control if he wanted to be "some goddamn Mario Andretti"? This hurt Leo's feelings, so O'Rourke always let him drive.

The cruiser had two plastic statuettes of Saint Christopher, a medallion of the Virgin, and a copper plaque with a prayer dedicated to Our Lady of the Highways. O'Rourke hoped it was enough.

When the car slowed to a stop in front of the Samuel Weinstock Gallery, the area around the stoop had already been cordoned off. As always, fifteen or twenty people were hanging around, small knots of figures talking to each other in conspiratorial whispers. Again as always, there was nothing to see.

A young policeman whom O'Rourke recognized but didn't really know had been diverted from traffic duty and stationed behind the police sawhorses to keep the crowds back. Since there weren't any crowds, he had nothing to do. Occasionally he muttered things like "Okay, everyone, nothing to see, just keep moving, please." Nobody paid any attention to him.

Callahan and O'Rourke showed him their badges, stepped around the barricade, and went up the stairs.

The scene of the murder was anticlimactic, like the scene of a big fire the day afterward. The three officers who were standing around looked self-conscious and uneasy, as if embarrassed to be there so long after they could have done any good.

The coroner, a fussy little man named Burdock, was squatting next to the corpse. O'Rourke went over to him.

"Want to make an estimate of the time of death? Just approximate."

"Just approximate, twelve to twenty-four hours. I

can't get much closer than that before the autopsy. Not a great deal of mystery about how he died, though. Look at this."

He pulled back a corner of the sheet covering Weinstock's body, exposing what was left of the back of the dealer's head as well as the bloody candelabrum lying next to it.

"Holy Mother. No, I see what you mean. No mystery at all."

He clambered to his feet.

"Anybody in charge? Okay, then I am. DiStefano, call the precinct and get the technicians. See if you can get everybody that's involved in the Giardino case. Tell them not to give the press anything more than they have to. Get rid of the barricade out front and tell the guy standing there to go back to his beat. There isn't anything to protect, and he's just causing trouble."

Then he noticed the girl in the corner.

O'Rourke grabbed DiStefano's arm before the policeman had a chance to go to the phone, and spoke to him in a low voice.

"Who's that?"

DiStefano looked down at a pocket note-pad.

"Says her name's Sheila Woods. Says she works for him." He hesitated, looking shamefaced. "She found him."

"Oh, great. Marvelous."

O'Rourke went over to Callahan, who was trying to peer over Burdock's shoulder at the body, and said a few words to him. Then he moved to the back of the gallery.

She was seated on the floor, her back against the wall, her legs drawn up against her body. She was rather thin and fine-boned, with pale skin and long, straight, copper-colored hair. She was simply dressed in corduroy pants and a plain white blouse with a green sweater thrown over it. O'Rourke noticed that the sweater was decorated across the shoulders with a band of small pink and white flowers. She looked very young to him.

She was weeping softly, openly. Her eyes looked straight ahead but didn't seem focused anywhere, and her expression appeared to O'Rourke to be part desperation, part exhaustion.

He shook her gently by the shoulder.

"Miss. Excuse me, Ma'am. It's all right. Everything's going to be okay." Whatever that means, he thought.

"I wish I could believe that."

Her voice was surprisingly steady. She turned to look at O'Rourke, and he could sense the effort it cost her to contain her feelings of fear and shock.

"I'm Captain Michael O'Rourke, Homicide. I'm afraid I must ask you some questions. But perhaps they can wait—"

"No. Better now than later."

Again O'Rourke was impressed. Her voice showed a fierce determination which belied her appearance of fragile vulnerability. She was holding herself together, and would continue to as long as necessary.

"I suppose you want to know who I am."

"Sheila Woods, is it?"

"Yes. I've been Sam Weinstock's secretary and assistant for about five years now. I was down at the Cape for ten days. I returned this morning at nine, quarter of nine, something like that . . ."

"Was the door open?"

"The knob-lock was secure, but the two dead-bolts were open. I thought that was strange, but I assumed Sam had just got here himself. I came in, I saw him, I think I screamed and sort of fainted for a moment."

"And then you called the police?"

"Yes. When I'd recovered."

"Did you go near the body?"

"No. There was no reason to. I mean, you could see."

O'Rourke noticed Sheila stiffen, as she fought off the memory.

"I understand. Please. Just two more questions. Is there anyone you know—anyone who comes directly to mind—who might have wanted to do this? Anyone with a personal motive, any violent hatreds?"

"No. Nobody that I know, I'm quite certain. He had enemies, of course. But everyone respected Sam, nearly everyone, and most people liked him. His enemies were other dealers, but that was just professional rivalry. Rivals, not monsters."

She glanced at the inert form in the middle of the floor, and seemed to shiver momentarily before continuing her thought.

"The man who did that was a monster."

"I agree. One final question. Does anything appear to have been stolen?"

Sheila smiled wanly. "It would probably take days to check the whole inventory, but offhand I don't see anything. The important pictures were mainly on the walls, and they seem to be where they should be." She reflected for a moment. "It's funny. When I first walked in the place looked strange. Bare, somehow. Then I realized that Sam had cleaned it up, I guess to surprise me. Poor Sam."

"I see. Thank you, Miss Woods. We'll probably have more questions for you later, but now Lieutenant Callahan will take you home."

O'Rourke handed her a Kleenex. She stared at it curiously for a moment, then blew her nose. He helped her get unsteadily to her feet.

"I'm all right. My apartment's only three blocks away, on the Hill."

"Lieutenant Callahan will go with you. There may be some people outside."

Bastards, he thought.

He helped her over to Callahan, who draped her coat

over her shoulders, kept his arm there for support, and guided her toward the door. O'Rourke trusted his partner. implicitly in situations like this, which demanded an instinctive delicacy and tact that few people possessed, O'Rourke included. He knew that Callahan could take her home, pour her a stiff drink, give her a sedative, and even put her to bed without intruding on her grief or invading her privacy in any way.

After they left, O'Rourke felt angry and depleted, but at the same time he was glad to be able to concentrate on the crime without the distraction of its human ramifications. O'Rourke wanted to consider Weinstock not as a man but as a corpse, a body, a physical fact without identity, mind, or soul: a passive datum, a cipher, a thing on the floor that had to be analyzed and observed.

Later, by the curiously inverted process required in a police investigation, Weinstock would begin to live, grow, and take on a particular personality in O'Rourke's mind. For the moment, however, the captain was interested only in a form under a sheet.

When Callahan returned to the gallery, everyone seemed to be busy but O'Rourke. The captain sat slumped in Weinstock's oak swivel chair. His jaw was working up and down in its usual maddening rhythm, and the rest of his face reflected the slack, Neanderthal vacuity that Callahan recognized and understood. O'Rourke had already examined the body, noting the chips of gilt-covered plaster still clutched in the hand, the frame with its broken corner, and the crumpled tube of glue next to the corpse.

Everyone else looked briskly efficient. The medical examiner was kneeling next to the body, examining the wound with an instrument that looked like a pair of calipers. All vitreous and metallic surfaces were being dusted for prints. Two high-intensity lamps were positioned on either side of the body, flooding it with a brilliant white light, while the photographer scrambled about taking shots from different angles. The crowded room seemed tawdry and unreal, like a movie set.

In twenty-nine years on the force, O'Rourke had yet to see a murder case where fingerprints were the primary evidence. He had only once seen a case where the medical examiner's testimony was the central element in a successful conviction. Still, people had to do something.

Callahan threaded his way over to the captain.

"Get her back okay?"

"Okay. There was a photographer out front, of course. He got a great shot of us: her trying to cover her face, me looking mad as hell. Which I was. Sadistic cop, innocent victim. Ought to sell a lot of papers."

"The creeps. Is she all right?"

"Pretty steady, considering what happened."

"She's a lot tougher than she looks. Smart, too. She'd obviously been asking herself all the right questions. Pity she didn't have any more answers to them, but what the hell."

O'Rourke looked around briefly, sighed, and suggested to Callahan that they get back to the station. Then he got up and went over to a tall, lanky policeman with a large Adam's apple standing at the front of the gallery directing the operations around the body. Leo saw the cop's head bob up and down, and heard his partner telling him not to touch anything around the desk, that he'd be back in the afternoon for that.

At the door, O'Rourke turned, calling back to the policeman he'd just spoken to: "Oh, one more thing. Find out if there's anything missing."

The cop nodded again. Callahan, uncertain whether or not to laugh, decided against it.

A couple of minutes later, in the car, O'Rourke broke the silence.

"So, what do you think? Think it's the same guy that iced Giardino?"

"I don't know, Mike. I mean, it's different MO and all."

"MO? What's MO? For Christ's sake, Leo, MO's a laxative!"

This outburst was unusual.

"So what do *you* think? You think it's the same guy?"

"Yes."

"How do you know? What makes you so damn sure?"

"How the hell do I know how I know? I know, is all."

With this, O'Rourke lapsed back into moody silence until the police cruiser pulled up in front of the station.

12

THREE DAYS LATER, Callahan and O'Rourke were sitting in O'Rourke's office. O'Rourke was flipping through a folder. His desk top was awash with folders, memos, reports, and transcripts of interviews. The investigations of both murders were by now top priority. Both detectives had spent hours talking to Micheline Duvet, Sheila Woods, and a number of art dealers, collectors, and teachers in the greater Boston area.

The problem with the Giardino case was that nobody seemed to know the victim intimately. His life, in reconstruction, seemed arbitrary and aimless, without any strong attachments. With Weinstock, there was almost a super-abundance of friends, acquaintances, partners, and associates. Yet somehow this investigation, like the Giardino case, had also failed to produce a clear form or direction.

O'Rourke was beginning to get edgy. Callahan knew the characteristics: fits of manic silliness alternating with bleak, brooding silences. O'Rourke was now in one of his black-humor phases.

"Isn't science wonderful? Listen to this. This is the report from the coroner's office: 'The victim was struck once from behind with a heavy, blunt object. The body showed an irregular penetration of the cranium approximately two and one quarter inches wide and two inches deep along the posterior quadrant of the parietal suture. Passing through the cranium, the weapon ruptured the meningeal membranes and, in combination with fragments of bone, caused massive cerebral trauma in both the menencephalic and rhombencephalic regions . . .'

"Blah, blah, blah. I wish to God just once in a while these things told us something interesting that we didn't know. I want one that goes: 'Careful examination of the wound suggests that it was caused by an ax-wielding, three-hundred-pound albino midget with *Mother* tattooed on his left thigh.' Something spicy, like that."

"Lucky we have that report, though, Captain. Some joker like me might've thought it was simply some guy bashing another over the head with a candlestick. I never figured on this 'cerebral trauma' stuff. Puts the case in a whole new light."

"You missed it again, Callahan. It's the 'parietal suture.' That's what we've been looking for. I remember a case just like it back in aught-twenty-five in Cody, Wyoming. Caught the bastard red-handed. The parietal sutures were still in his saddlebags. That was the case that made me famous."

"See, you should've been a police surgeon. 'Doc O'Rourke of the Seventh Precinct.' You could've been even more famous—TV shows, the works. Fame, money, broads, parietal sutures—"

"Instead of which, I'm cooped up in a stuffy office with a baboon for a partner and two homicides I can't solve."

"Right. You blew it, Mike. But don't say I didn't warn you."

O'Rourke closed the file and tossed it on a pile of others in the middle of his desk. Then he put his elbows on the table, rested his chin on his massive fists, and stared past his partner into space. Callahan guessed that the break was over.

"Let's run through it one more time. What we know, what we guess, what we don't know but damn well should. When I get through tell me what hits you. What I'm missing, where I'm being stupid. I must be being stupid as hell about something.

"We have the memo from Weinstock's desk: 'Harry, Saturday at 4:30.' Harry Giardino died that night. Which is enough connection for me, until we get something better. Why was Weinstock meeting Giardino? Answer that, we could probably break the case.

"What we know about Giardino is more or less as follows. Like you said, Harry Giardino is strictly small-time, a fringe operator, a guy who runs around here and there trying to scare up enough action on the art scene to keep himself going. Harry comes across as reasonably honest and not very bright. Let's assume he was killed for something he did, something he knew, or something he had.

"Let's take something he did, first. Motive, revenge. This seems to me to be the least likely possibility, given what we know about Harry. Not smart enough to be that sneaky, not enough financial leverage to screw anybody badly enough to warrant getting himself killed. Talking to the dealers, talking to Sheila Woods, Harry Giardino comes across as somebody nobody takes all that seriously. No sexual motive either. Harry's straight, but his sex life seems to be mostly Mary Five-fingers.

"I like the second possibility better, but not much. Something he knew. Motive, blackmail, or silence. Talking to dealers, I get the feeling that the art dodge is a whole world of secrets: big ones, little ones, nasty ones, and maybe a few that are worth a heap of money.

But I don't see anybody telling Harry Giardino any of the big ones, and I don't see Harry figuring them out on his own. Plus, I don't see Harry as a blackmailer, although it's possible.

"So that leaves something he had. Or didn't have. Something he discovered, maybe, and took to Weinstock. Whoever kills him comes looking for it, can't find it, kills him anyway. Then he goes after Weinstock. I like that one best. So what do you think, Leo?"

"Makes sense, Captain. I've been thinking about the killer. Couple of things. First, they both know him—or at least knew of him. They both let him in. This day and age, if you've got valuable things hanging all over the walls, you've got to be nervous. But they both invited him in like an old friend, and Weinstock even kneels down and turns his back and makes it a piece of cake. So neither one was even a little bit suspicious.

"Second, the killer has to be both smart and lucky. Probably looks respectable. He knows about a jazz concert in 1938, which could make him older rather than younger. And if he's after art he must know something about it, maybe a hell of a lot if he's willing to kill twice for it. What's worth a double murder rap?"

"What do you know about art, Leo?"

At this Callahan frowned, concentrated, and finally glared suspiciously at O'Rourke. He suspected a trap.

"I know what I like."

O'Rourke laughed.

"Okay, so what do you like?"

"I like traditional stuff. You know. Pictures that look like things. Nude women, landscapes. I like Impressionism."

"Yeah, me too. I like Renoir, Wyeth."

O'Rourke was silent for a moment.

"I don't know anything about it either, Leo, so stop looking at me like that. I used to know something about

96

crime, but I'm beginning to think maybe I've forgotten it. What we need is some kind of art expert, some damn professor or something. I spoke to a guy at Harvard. He gave me a name. Look at this."

O'Rourke pulled a telegram out from under a stack of papers and tossed it across the desk to Callahan. Callahan noticed that it had been sent from England. It read:

Informed of homicides. Will be in Boston Friday. Hope I can help.

Amos Hatcher

"Who is he?"

"Sort of a private dick, on permanent retainer to some international group of dealers. He also works with Interpol. He did a job two years ago for Harvard when somebody stole a little ivory doodad worth a fortune. Hatcher apparently got him. It turned out to be a seventeen-year-old kid from Belmont, totally an impulse theft. They finally found him in his old man's garage with the thing in his pocket, cold, hungry and scared stiff. Anyway, they're big on Hatcher at Harvard."

"I don't know, Mike. Sounds like another professor. You want a professor screwing around in a murder case?"

"Hell, no. But we need somebody who can get us a fix on the whole art scene, someone who knows the moves. You talked to the dealers, you saw the tricks and games, you think we can go up against that cold? If he can't do anything else, at least he can interpret the goddamn tapes for us."

"He'll muddy the waters."

"You kidding? You seen anything but mud since last Sunday? Besides, if we don't like him, we can can him.

He doesn't need us; he's working on something else in Europe anyway. It's worth a shot, Leo."

"Balls."

O'Rourke detected a note of profound conviction in Leo's remark.

13

"ART INVESTIGATOR, MY BUTT. Probably some aging fairy dressed up like Sherlock Holmes. The Drag Queen of the Art Scene."

O'Rourke knew that Callahan's invective was largely a smoke screen. It wasn't that Leo hated homosexuals. He hated anybody he thought was interfering in one of his and O'Rourke's cases. "We don't need no third parties" was one of his themes. O'Rourke understood that this was part pride and part loyalty, so he didn't try too hard to placate Callahan on the way over to meet Hatcher.

"Gotta be a queen. You ever hear of a white man named Amos before?"

"Enough, Leo. Maybe we can use him. So don't get surly. Just don't sit there staring at his wrist for an hour and a half, is all I ask. Give him a small break."

It had been Hatcher's suggestion that they meet him at his room at the Holiday Inn rather than at the station house. As he'd said to O'Rourke, the fewer people who knew about it the better. He wanted to move freely, and anonymously, as long as possible.

O'Rourke had mixed feelings about this. On the one hand, he was impressed with Hatcher's professionalism. On the other, he didn't like the fact that Hatcher was making O'Rourke and Callahan come to him.

The man who answered the door looked virile enough, which reassured Callahan, and slightly seedy, which reassured O'Rourke. He was tall and loose-jointed, his body maintaining the look of the long-distance runner Hatcher had been in his college days. His face, equally bony, culminated in a towering cranium. Hatcher's sandy hair, which had largely abandoned the broad, spherical plane of his forehead, was now fighting a doomed holding action around his ears and the back of his head, where a few locks curved down like tendrils over his collar. His eyes were blue, deep-set, and overhung by craggy brows which gave him a look of habitual concentration similar to Callahan's.

There was something a little odd about Hatcher which took strangers a while to identify. In a face and body mostly composed of angles, none of the angles seemed quite to fit. No two planes were exactly parallel or perpendicular to each other. His nose was slightly crooked, one eyebrow was more sharply arched than the other, and both his smile and his shoulders were distinctly lopsided. The cumulative effect of all these slight distortions was that although Hatcher was graceful, even athletic, he projected a misleading aura of adolescent gawkiness. The fact that women found him attractive was usually attributed by other men to female perversity.

He looked, to O'Rourke, to be in his early or midforties. His rumpled clothes gave him the appearance of being either a successful academic or a failed businessman.

"Come on in. Glad to see you, Captain O'Rourke,

Lieutenant Callahan. I'm Amos Hatcher. Partly, anyway. I feel like most of my brain and a large chunk of my digestive system is still on some damn plane or other. Probably lost someplace over the North Atlantic. Why don't you two take the chairs? I can sit on the bed. Also, there's coffee on that tray if you'd like some. Then you could tell me about the murders, or I could tell you about me, whichever you prefer."

"Why don't you tell us a little about yourself, Mr. Hatcher? About what you do."

This came from Callahan. O'Rourke was pleased to notice that the undertones of hostile skepticism were scarcely perceptible.

Hatcher took a long yellow legal pad from the table, went over to the bed, stuck the pillow against the headboard, and sat down. Then he swung his right leg onto the bed, cocked it as a support for the pad, and put his hands behind his head. He looked comfortable.

"I work for the IAAD, the International Association of Art Dealers. A consortium of dealers, but very loosely organized. My association with them is also very loosely organized. Once a year I send them an elaborate report; once a year they pay me. My job is to work as a liaison with the police to solve art crimes. It's as simple as that."

"Who picks the jobs, you or them?"

"I do. That's a key clause in my contract."

"On what basis?" O'Rourke was becoming interested.

"Several bases. Sometimes a theft is important because it involves a great work of art, sometimes because it's beautifully executed, sometimes because of the ramifications. A crime ring, for example."

"Why are you interested in our case?"

Hatcher hesitated for a moment.

"I suppose because it seemed complicated. Also very nasty. Murder doesn't often happen in the art world,

101

and when it does, it's usually spur of the moment. Fear or panic. From the clippings I read, these were premeditated, which makes it an important case automatically."

Hatcher hesitated again, glanced at the impassive faces across the room, and then added, almost as an afterthought: "A second factor, I suppose, was that the case I was on in Europe didn't seem to be going anywhere."

"A failure?" Callahan was becoming interested.

Hatcher smiled. "Not a failure, just a dormant phase. Nothing happens. I wait, he waits. I can afford to wait. Years, if necessary. That's why I'm paid on an annual retainer, by the way, rather than case by case. If I were paid by the case, I probably couldn't eat."

"You can't wait with a murder case, Mr. Hatcher."

"I know. That's why I flew back as soon as I got the news. Oh, one more thing about the way I work. I call myself a private investigator, but this isn't really accurate. The IAAD is only indirectly my client. My real client, on a case like this, is you. There's no one I'm protecting, no one to cover up for, no one to withhold information for, so there's no reason to treat me the way private investigators usually get treated by the police. I will give you everything I can find that you need or can use. On the other hand, I have to have everything that you have: ballistics reports, medical reports, witnesses, all the details.

"The police sometimes have the happy idea of letting me worry about the art while they worry about the crime, thinking that it will all somehow come together at the end. I've almost been killed twice that way, when people didn't tell me what I needed to know. So I don't merely ask for trust; I demand it. I've got a pretty good record, as it happens. There's a dossier here someplace . . ."

Hatcher swung himself off the bed and went over to the suitcase lying next to the wall. After rummaging about for a moment he emerged from the suitcase holding a ragged-looking black notebook which he handed to O'Rourke.

"You can check through this, talk it over, see what you think. Meanwhile, why don't I go downstairs to the cafeteria and get some breakfast? I could be back in about three quarters of an hour. Okay?"

When Hatcher returned later, he found the two policemen sitting rigidly where he had left them. The black notebook lay closed in the middle of the table. After a few seconds of awkward silence, O'Rourke coughed and cleared his throat.

"We've decided maybe we can use you."

"Fine," Hatcher said amicably. Then he ambled over to the bed, dropped back onto it, and propped the legal pad against his knee.

Two hours later, O'Rourke got up, stretched, and glanced over at Hatcher. The investigator had covered seven sheets of paper with a small, crabbed script, and was flexing his right hand to get rid of a cramp. Callahan looked bored.

"There are a couple of other questions, just small details, and maybe I should hold off on them until after I speak to Sheila Woods. This will keep me for a while, anyway. And if you could send over some copies of the reports, it would be a great help. Especially the coroner's report. Oh, and if you have it, the key to Weinstock's gallery. I'll want to go through it with her tomorrow. And a list of Boston art dealers, if you have that. Some of them I already know, of course, and if you don't have a list I can use the telephone directory."

Hatcher dropped the pad on the bed and got up.

"I have the feeling nothing about this is going to be easy."

O'Rourke grinned. "I know. Welcome to the force."

Later, in the car, Callahan said to O'Rourke: "I still don't like the son of a bitch."

"Then why don't you leave him to me? I sort of do."

14

IT WAS SEVEN-THIRTY that night when Hatcher reached
Sheila Woods's apartment at the top of Pinckney Street
on Beacon Hill. A narrow brick building, the house was
a late, ersatz version of the bowfronts a block away in
Louisburg Square. To reach her apartment, Hatcher
had to climb three flights of narrow stairs and walk
down to the end of an equally narrow hall garishly illuminated by a naked bulb. Hatcher wondered why the
building wasn't in better condition, given its choice lo-
cation.

He located Sheila Woods's name on the door and
knocked. The door opened a crack.

"Yes?"

"Miss Woods? I'm Amos Hatcher."

"Yes. Captain O'Rourke phoned me. Come in.
There's someone here." The voice sounded very tired.

In sharp contrast to the hall outside, Sheila Woods's
apartment was extremely dark and murky. The only
light he could see was a small lamp with a stained-glass
shade. As his hostess retreated back into the room,

Hatcher was somewhat surprised to discover that the "someone" with her, now coming toward him out of the gloom, was also a woman.

She walked straight up to Hatcher, grabbed him by the arm, and stared at his face for a long moment. As she grasped him, she stepped into a beam of light from the half-opened door behind him. She looked, to Hatcher, like the wreck of a beautiful woman. Her black eyes were red-rimmed and sunk in dark pits, her iron-gray hair was tangled and matted, her lipstick smeared. She looked wild and feral and not quite sane; when she spoke her voice was hoarse and gasping.

"You must find him. The *cochon*, the filthy bastard, the *salaud*. Find him and kill him."

The woman didn't wait for a response, which she apparently didn't expect anyway, but dropped Hatcher's arm and went to the door.

"Sheila. *Chère fille*. I must go, I must sleep. I will telephone tomorrow, eh? You are my rock."

After the woman had left, Sheila went over to where Hatcher was standing and took his coat.

"That was Micheline Duvet, Sammy's lover, if you're curious. A rather informal introduction, I'm afraid. What you saw was just a little denouement. The heavy scenes were much earlier. I've had three hours of Micheline tonight, which is way over my limit. I had two hours of O'Rourke this morning and three hours of Miche tonight, and after you leave I plan to stand in the middle of this room and scream for a long, long time."

"I'll try to speak very softly."

"Yes. Thank you. But don't carry a big stick."

While Sheila hung up his coat, Hatcher remembered O'Rourke's description: "Skinny, but sort of cute." Sheila Woods was slight and graceful in her movements, and her face was fine-boned and extremely pretty, almost beautiful, like a Florentine Madonna.

Her copper hair seemed very fine. It was long and hung straight down. Although O'Rourke had mentioned to Hatcher that she was twenty-eight, she looked much younger than her age, as people with red hair so often do. She was dressed in a simple white cotton blouse, black corduroy slacks, and slippers.

Her apartment was very small. Her bed occupied a corner of the living room, and the tiny kitchenette looked like a slot in the wall. But in compensation for the size, there was a stunning view out the window across the Beacon Hill skyline to the Charles River. There were several potted plants growing on the sill, and a spectacular spider plant hanging next to the window. An oak drop-leaf table was placed under the window and supported the lamp that Hatcher had noticed earlier and that, on closer inspection, seemed to him to be a genuine Tiffany rather than one of the myriad reproductions.

Two simple wooden chairs were set next to the table, and two sling chairs with brightly colored canvas seats were placed in the middle of the room near a low coffee table. Two things offset the austerity of the apartment. One was a cinderblock bookcase that occupied an entire wall, floor to ceiling. Hatcher noted approvingly that here there was no sacrifice: sets of art books, many of them old and rare, stretched from one end of the room to the other. The second was a selection of framed Renaissance prints which included a number of the great German and Italian graphic artists. All the prints were small, some hardly bigger than postage stamps, and they were hung one above the other over the bed.

"I've got some good ones. Dürer, the Behams, Altdorfer, Jacopo de' Barbari. No Schongauer, but I'm working on it. You know prints?"

"Pretty well. I knew them better ten years ago, when I could afford them."

"I know. I do a lot of poking around. Working for a dealer makes it easier, of course. Can I get you a drink?"

"Just ginger ale or Fresca, if you have it."

"Sure. Come into the kitchen while I get it. You can start asking questions. Not too many, though, and make them easy ones. O'Rourke said you specialized in art. Are you a cop, by the way?"

"No, I'm just sort of an investigator."

"Good. I don't understand cops very well, or they don't understand me. I made some bad mistakes with those two. First mistake, I blurted out to the other cop that I loved Sammy Weinstock. That meant, of course, that I was sleeping with him. I told him no, I wasn't sleeping with him. I think Sammy would have been shocked at that idea—which is pretty odd, if you know anything about art dealers—but he couldn't accept both ideas. That I loved him, that I wasn't sleeping with him and didn't want to. The confusion got worse, of course, when Micheline showed up. Now, I think, he's off composing some kind of crazy ménage à trois."

"What other mistakes did you make?"

"The other big mistake was when they asked me if I knew anyone who hated Sammy. I said sure, lots of people. In the art business, everybody hates everybody. It's routine. Everyone Sammy's ever outsmarted, everyone who's ever been at an auction where Sammy walked off with the bacon while they were staring at their feet, every dealer Sammy exposed as a fraud or a poseur—it adds up. This has nothing to do with murder, of course. Still, I'm afraid I put the whole art business under collective suspicion."

"I've thought about that. I agree with you. I've seen dealers set out to ruin or humiliate or destroy one another, but murder is in a different category. Murdering a rival dealer would be a Pyrrhic victory. Fratricide."

"Exactly. The art business is, in a funny way, a kind of brotherhood. Sometimes I'm not even sure whether the art is really the central issue, or whether it's the game. Killing another dealer would be like going to the racetrack, placing a bet, and then shooting all the other horses once the race had started. From one point of view it makes sense, but from another, it makes no sense at all."

Hatcher drained his glass, put it on the counter, and walked into the living room. When Sheila joined him, Hatcher was frowning.

"You mentioned questions before. I have two hard ones, I suppose, and I might as well ask them now. First, do you want to be involved in finding Weinstock's killer, and, if so, how much? This doesn't have to be answered tonight."

"That's not really hard. The answer's yes, of course. I'm already involved. I found the body. I owe Sammy that, at least. I'd be grateful to do anything you or O'Rourke want."

"The second question, then, is will you go back with me to the gallery tomorrow? I hate to ask you, and I didn't mean to trap you. O'Rourke has been through Weinstock's apartment from top to bottom. None of the police reports have given him anything. So far it's a dead end. There must be something at the gallery, some slight alteration, some incongruity, something misplaced, perhaps. Any small change, any broken pattern . . ."

Hatcher could feel her stiffen.

"I went through it once, with O'Rourke."

"I know. I'm sorry."

Hatcher could feel himself blushing. He hesitated. "O'Rourke said . . . well, he thought you might have missed something."

Sheila Woods exploded. "Jesus Christ, what do you

expect? What do you think? I was in shock. I passed out cold the moment I walked through the door. Don't you understand? *I was the one who found him!*"

Her head in her hands, Sheila bent over the table and wept convulsively. Feeling dreadful, Hatcher got up, poked around, and finally returned with a box of tissues. Her weeping had stopped, but she looked tired and completely drained.

"Isn't there someplace else we could go? How about Paul Revere's house or Faneuil Hall? I could show you the South End . . ."

"Sheila. He's not there now, you know."

"The hell he's not."

15

WHEN HATCHER ARRIVED at the Weinstock Gallery the next morning, he found that Sheila was already there. Apparently he had the only set of keys, for she was huddled up on the stoop trying to stay warm. The weather, which had been oscillating between late autumn and early winter, had turned sharply colder.

Inside the gallery Sheila tossed her coat on a chair in the corner and immediately set to work. As on the night before, she was simply dressed: Levi's, a white turtleneck, and sneakers. She looked slightly drawn and pinched to Hatcher, but she also seemed determined.

"I went over the stuff on the desk pretty carefully with O'Rourke. There was a note about Harry Giardino which O'Rourke took. He thinks it may be an important link. But the rest of it didn't seem to mean much. Most of it was mine anyway, since I handle the bookkeeping. There was something else; I can't quite remember it."

"Is there any formal inventory?"

"O'Rourke has it. I don't need it; I'm sure I'd recognize it if something important were missing. We completed it just before I left, so that whatever Sam did during the last week or so wouldn't be there anyway. He was pretty sloppy about records."

"Can I help?"

"Yes. Just by standing around and being someone to talk to. Later maybe you can rub my back, or pound a few disks back into place."

Hatcher weighed this remark for sexual innuendo and decided that there wasn't any.

Two walls of the gallery had linoleum-topped counters running their entire lengths, perhaps sixty feet in all. Pictures, separated by sheets of cardboard, were racked against one another under the counters. To check them all, Sheila would have to spend an hour or so bent over or kneeling down.

"I kidded Sammy that he should give up running a delicatessen and turn this into a classy establishment. Ten or twelve absolutely first-rate pictures a year displayed in an elegant Empire drawing room, with an androgynous young man to coo over the customers."

"What did he say to that?"

"He laughed. He said he liked delicatessens, and besides, if he'd wanted a classy establishment he'd have to fire me. On some emotional level, though, I think he needed this kind of inventory—the sheer numbers. And I think he was just as happy buying a painting for a hundred dollars that he knew he could sell for two as he was closing a deal for a major picture."

"He liked the business part."

"Exactly. He loved to deal."

Quickly Sheila worked her way down the left-hand rack. Periodically she would stop, pull out a picture, and frown at it. At one point she pulled out a large still life in a frilly Victorian frame. Hatcher walked over and looked at it with her.

"Genoa or Naples, I would say. Late seventeenth."

"I think it's Neapolitan. The sale was a week before I left and we had a fight about it. Sammy said that any floral, even a mediocre one, was money in the bank. I said I thought it was rubbish and he should leave it to the interior desecrators."

Hatcher laughed. "I take it he won."

"He won that one. I pouted around for a while, and he called me 'the Duchess' for a day or so before things got back to normal."

"Did you ever win?"

"Oh, yes. Sometimes he let me win. There's a beautifully painted Italian baroque martyrdom around here someplace. I think it's Saint Erasmus. I lobbied for months for it. When we got it, he smugly informed me that it was a drug on the market and that we would have great difficulty giving it away. 'Sheila, you're a nice kid, but you got no commercial sense.' I can hear him saying that. He was right, of course."

A little later, Sheila found another painting. This was slightly smaller, a landscape in a plain mahogany frame.

"I'll be damned. He finally got it."

Hatcher squinted at it. "Italianate Dutch, it looks to me. Somewhere around Berchem."

"You're right, or very close. It came from Robinson's. There's someone Sam really hated, by the way, Robinson. Robinson's a snooty fraud. Anyway, Sammy's been after this picture for about three years. He worked on Robinson slowly. Very slowly. I knew he'd get it sooner or later. He was playing Robinson like a fish."

"Who painted it?"

"The picture's by Herman van Swanevelt. Robinson didn't know it, the Rijksbureau in Holland didn't know it; no one had the right name but Sam. Robinson called it School of Cuyp. Sam recognized it as the pendant to a signed picture he'd seen at auction years ago."

113

Sheila straightened up, rubbing her back.

"Sam had an extraordinary visual memory. On the other hand, he was skeptical about books and hated libraries. He was ambivalent about academic art history in general. A little envy, a little contempt. Mainly, I think, he hated frauds."

"Dealers in general are ambivalent about academics. Quite rightly, for the most part. Many art historians—even famous ones—are rotten connoisseurs. One man I know at Harvard practically needs a Seeing Eye dog to get through a lecture."

"I think I know who you mean. Another thing, I find most academics treat dealers with condescension. I gather they see themselves as standing above the vulgar, corrupting world of commerce. The funny thing is that teachers are often such voracious, grasping people. Since coming here I've met plenty of generous dealers, but I can't think of many generous art historians."

Sheila sighed, slid the picture back into its slot, and started to walk across to the other rank of pictures. Turning the corner around Weinstock's desk, she stopped.

"That's funny."

"What is?"

"That frame. That frame wasn't there before."

She was looking at an ebony frame lying on the top of a pile of frames in a bin. She was walking over to pick it up when Hatcher grabbed her arm.

"No. Don't touch it."

"What?"

"Just don't. Look at it carefully. Are you sure that it wasn't there before?"

"Yes. Of course. I cleaned that bin up just before I left. It wasn't there."

"How well do you know frames? What would you say about that one?"

114

"I know frames. That was one of the first things Sam taught me. That one's good. Without turning it over I can't be sure, but I'd say it's period. Dutch or Flemish, early or mid-seventeenth-century."

Hatcher was alert now. His face was stern, his eyes intent. For the first time since Sheila had met him, he looked like her image of a detective.

"Good. Why 'early or mid'? Why not late?"

"You're grilling me?"

"Good. Why 'early or mid'? Why not late?"

Sheila concentrated.

"The paintings within paintings. Dutch genre interiors, the cabinet pictures of Teniers and the other Flemings. Anyway, in the framed pictures that are represented in painted interiors, the frames are almost always ebony, like this, until about 1650 or sixty. Then they are usually gilt."

"And is this frame valuable?"

"God, yes, if it's original. And if it's a copy it still must have cost hundreds."

"You are absolutely certain you haven't seen this before?"

"Yes. I would have remembered it."

"Good! Don't touch it."

Hatcher took a slip of paper from his wallet, went over to the phone, and dialed a number.

"O'Rourke? Hatcher. I'm at Weinstock's gallery. I think I have something. Can you get over here quickly, with a photographer and a fingerprint kit? Good. I'll be here."

He hung up the phone and went back to where Sheila was standing.

"One more question. Do you have any ideas how that could have got here?"

"Must have come from a painting. It was on the top of the pile, so it must have just come in. That was the

115

first thing Sammy did when he got a new picture—almost a ritual. He'd grab a hammer, give me a big grin, and say, 'Let's whack it out of the frame.' "

"Always?"

"Always. He wanted to find out immediately if it was relined, if it was a canvas, or whether it was cut down, if it was a panel. If the picture was important, that is. If he left it in the frame it meant he wasn't particularly interested in it."

"So. There was a picture in a frame. Now there's a frame. No picture. Could it have been sent out for restoration?"

"Not without the frame. If he wanted it cleaned, he would have put it back in its frame for protection. But I could call the restorer's."

"Please."

"You think it's important."

"It may be."

Sheila was just hanging up the phone when they heard the keening of the police-car siren. It grew briefly louder, then stopped with a petulant growl, which was followed by a sharp crack and a clatter that sounded like someone dropping a metal plate on a linoleum floor. A minute later O'Rourke and Callahan burst through the door, red-faced and shouting.

"If you'd got the brakes adjus—"

"The *brakes*! Will you stop with this 'the brakes,' for God's sake? You were doing twenty, you slam on the brakes in the middle of an ice patch, what the hell you think's gonna happen? Jesus, Mary, and Joseph."

"Hey, c'mon, Mike."

"Mario Andretti, here. He just knocked over the goddamn No Parking sign out front."

"Well, I was parking, wasn't I?" Leo giggled.

"Now that's funny. That's extremely funny. Funniest thing I ever heard."

Callahan continued to giggle.

"Okay, Leo, I'm taking your license."

Leo stopped giggling.

"You can't."

"I can. There's gotta be a way. There are about a million regulations; there's gotta be one in there somewhere. If I can find it, I'm grounding you."

O'Rourke dropped into a chair. His face was cherry red and he was sweating profusely. Callahan, looking sheepish, went over to the corner to sulk.

O'Rourke stuck a piece of gum in his mouth, mopped his forehead with a large, none-too-clean handkerchief, lumbered to his feet, and went over to Hatcher.

"What've you got?"

"Sheila found an empty frame that wasn't here when she left."

"Yeah, good. Let's see it."

"It's that one. Do you think it might take prints?"

"If the wood is smooth enough, if it's been waxed or varnished recently, maybe. Why not?"

Taking a Kleenex from a box on one of the counters, O'Rourke carried the frame over to the desk.

"This could be a clue. A real clue, just like in the books; wouldn't that be nice? Two murders, one clue. I'm not asking for too much, am I?"

Hatcher took a leather-covered magnifying glass from his pocket, sat down, and began inspecting the frame in detail. Sheila had gone over to the other rack and was continuing her search through the paintings. Callahan went over to her.

Nodding his head sideways in the general direction of Hatcher, he said to Sheila in a low voice: "Has that guy been giving you any trouble?"

"No. Why would he?"

"Well, if he does, call me. Any trouble at all."

"I will. Thank you, Lieutenant."

"Glad to help."

117

Callahan went outside to see if either the sign or the right headlight of the car could be salvaged. Sheila finished her inventory, while Hatcher and O'Rourke remained riveted to the frame on the desk. At the end of fifteen minutes Hatcher had half a page of short notes, most of them ending in question marks.

"I want to take it back to the lab. I want it gone over thoroughly."

"Can I have it back when you're through?"

"I don't know. It may be evidence."

"Not without the picture that went in it. That's what I'm going after, and I'll need the frame."

"You think you can use the frame to find the painting? Isn't that a little like trying to figure out from looking at a chair who's been sitting in it?"

Hatcher smiled. "A little. But there are chairs and chairs. It helps, of course, if the chair happens to be a throne."

"I can see. Still, it sounds to me a bit like Cinderella and the glass slipper."

"It is. Oh, one more thing. Better not let it out to anyone that we have the frame."

"No. If the killer knew that, he'd destroy the painting, or alter it, and we'd still have nothing. I figured it this way, Hatcher. I mean, an art theft. This is at least a start."

Later, when the two policemen climbed into the cruiser, O'Rourke was in the driver's seat. He rested his massive arms on the wheel and stared straight ahead for a moment, his jaw working up and down.

"I'll be damned," he finally said to Callahan.

"What?"

"Hatcher found something that was missing. I'm gonna have to stop laughing at that line from now on."

16

WHEN THEY LOCKED UP the store two hours later, Sheila and Hatcher had not succeeded in finding anything else of value.

"What do you think of the Keystone Kops?" Sheila's mood, which had been steadily improving, was now downright cheerful.

"O'Rourke knows his job, but I can't say I'm too impressed with the other one."

Sheila made a face.

"O'Rourke's just a cop. Callahan's sweet, though. He was the one who took me home. He's very chivalrous. I think he has a crush on me."

Hatcher snorted.

"He thinks you have evil designs on me."

"When I first met him, he acted like I had evil designs on him."

Sheila laughed.

"Will you come with me? Every day I get some rolls at the bakery, take them down to the Charles, and feed the ducks."

"Even in November? God, Sheila, it's cold out here."

"I know. For them, too. I do it every day I can. It's more fun in the spring, of course, and the early summer, with the broods of ducklings, but I almost never miss a day. They expect me. Do you know, ducks have very distinctive personalities?"

"I've never noticed."

"They do, though. Some of them are very shy and just sort of hang around the outside of the pack. Some are greedy and aggressive, and don't want the others to get anything. If you toss a piece of bread at one of the shy ones, one of the pushy ones will attack it and drive it away. Nice guys finish last. That seems to be one of nature's laws."

"The big fish eat the little fish."

"Yes. Some day I want to get ahold of Brueghel's print of that."

At the bakery, Sheila turned serious.

"It was good for me to go back there. So much of Sammy is in that gallery that it's hard to imagine that he's dead. No, that's not quite it. I mean that in a sense he's still alive. I hope Micheline gets it; she'd keep it going as the Weinstock Gallery."

Later, they stood leaning against a guardrail, crumbling up the rolls and dropping the pellets in the river. A small group of ducks had gathered and others were flapping across the water, drawn by the quacks.

"You'd think they'd shut up about it, wouldn't you? They set up a big racket, letting everybody else know where the action is. You start with three or four, then you get fifteen, then it's 'there goes the neighborhood.' I'm always out of bread by the time the big crowd gets here, though."

She dropped the last bits in the water and slapped her sleeves to get rid of the crumbs.

"I guess ducks aren't very bright. They're pretty, though, not like pigeons. I've always thought that pigeons look dirty and stupid. I've never understood why anyone would care about them. Let's go get some coffee."

Before they left, Ṣheila tugged at Hatcher's sleeve and pointed to the west. The sun was just beginning to go down, and it made a shimmering golden track across the river.

"I love the Charles. It's pretty much an industrial sewer now, of course, but plenty of people remember when you could swim in it. And it's still beautiful if you don't get too close. Over there, you see where the boats are moored, you can rent a dinghy and sail up through Cambridge and Watertown. Miles and miles. Some hardy souls even take them out in the winter. Frostbite sailing, it's called."

"Do you sail?"

"Only in the spring and summer. My hardiness is distinctly limited."

Warming up over a cup of coffee at a café on a corner of Charles Street, Hatcher asked Sheila how she'd come to work for Weinstock. She stirred her coffee, reflecting for a moment.

"That's a funny story. It was late in the spring, I think, five years ago now. I'd just finished my master's degree, and was looking for an apartment on the Hill. I was also looking for a summer job.

"I was walking along Charles Street, minding my own business, when I saw a man sitting on a stoop with a picture. It was Sam. The picture was an oval portrait, and he was dabbing at it with some cotton soaked in turpentine to take off the surface dirt. He preferred to do that outside in the sunshine where he could see better, and where the fumes wouldn't bother him.

"The first thing he said to me, when he noticed me, was, 'So what is it—French or English?' Without thinking, I said, 'French.' He asked me why. I said I didn't know, it just seemed more like Fragonard or Boucher

121

than it did Gainsborough or Hogarth. I had the feeling that if the girl in the painting spoke, she'd be speaking French. He invited me into the gallery, showed me a number of pictures, and two hours later offered me a job."

"How did he know you knew anything about art?"

"That's the funny part. I have no idea, and neither did he. I asked him about it later, and he said he didn't know. He had amazing instincts about people. He was almost never wrong about them."

"He was wrong about the man who killed him."

"I know. That's what frightens me."

"Me too. Tell me some more about him."

"No. No more questions, unless you take me out to dinner like a proper gentleman."

"That's a lovely idea."

"I'm glad you think so. I'm famished, and I haven't had a chance to shop, so there's nothing in the apartment. If you'd said no, I would have had to call Lieutenant Callahan."

"To report me?"

"Of course. I would have told him you were no gentleman, and he would have thrown you in the jug."

"You're a dangerous woman, Sheila."

"Only when I'm hungry. We have to go back to my apartment first, though, so I can change. How do you like Italian food?"

"Better than French, even."

"*Benissimo. Andiamo.* There's a nice little place on the other side of the Hill."

Later, at the restaurant, Hatcher decided that Sheila was a woman of excellent taste. Her artistic taste he already knew from her books and the prints on her wall. Her culinary taste, if this restaurant was any indication, was also exemplary. They had had a marvelous *lasagne verdi* with homemade noodles, followed by *co-*

tolette alla Bolognese made with real Italian prosciutto, and were just finishing off a bottle of memorable Chianti.

"It's strange. When I met Sammy, I was fully expecting to begin doctoral studies in the fall. I'd been accepted at Harvard, I had a tuition fellowship, and everything was set."

"What happened?"

"I don't entirely know. I think I realized that summer that I was crazy about art—and, at the same time, that I didn't know a damn thing about it. I knew a good bit about art history. I knew about scholarship and books and articles and slides; I could identify a hell of a lot of monuments, but I didn't know the first thing about the object itself. How to look at it, analyze, evaluate quality and condition—these were the things Sam Weinstock taught me. It took one year to feel comfortable just looking at a work of art without wanting to grab some damn book or other."

"And the two of you got on pretty well?"

"Like the proverbial house afire, whatever that means. We fought a lot, of course, but we basically liked each other enormously. We fit together very well. He concentrated on American paintings, which comprised most of the business, and I concentrated on Old Masters, did research at the libraries, dealt with customers, and handled the clerical and financial end. Also, he spent a lot of time on the road and needed someone to tend the store."

"Have you ever felt like going back for your doctorate?"

"I get twinges. Sometimes Sam would get it into his head that a doctorate would be good for my character, make me an honest woman or something. And Tom was adamant about it."

"Tom?"

"My late, unlamented fiancé. He was after me for years to go back. I finally figured out that it had nothing to do with me, though. It was simply his fantasy about me as his wife. My-wife-the-doctor. I think the idea was that I hang my diploma in the living room over the couch and then get back to doing the floors."

"Is that how he became an ex-fiancé?"

"One of the ways. As for me, I don't know if I could go back to school now. I think that that life would feel very gray and flat. I have a lot of connections with the academic world, of course, but it all seems pretty alien to me.

"Can we continue this conversation back at my apartment? It's after ten, and I think our waiter's gaze is getting clammier by the minute. Besides, I have espresso and Strega, and I'm afraid I've already cost you too much."

When they got back to the apartment, Sheila busied herself with the espresso while Hatcher undertook a closer examination of her collection of prints on the wall. When she returned, he was peering closely at a charming little genre scene bearing the well-known monogram of Albrecht Dürer.

"That's a copy."

"Oh? I was wondering if it were a late impression."

"Nope. Fake. If you compare the monogram with an original, you can see that the lines of the A are tilted slightly differently. When I found it, the dealer was asking two hundred dollars for it. When I proved to him it was a forgery, the price came down to twenty-five."

"That was a bargain."

"Yes. I'm afraid I may have forgotten to mention to him, though, that the forgery was made by Raphael's engraver Marcantonio Raimondi only a few years after the original, and that it's probably much rarer than the Dürer."

Hatcher laughed. "Is that another thing you learned from Weinstock?"

124

"Sure. Dealer against dealer, it's every man for himself. Or woman."

Sheila carried the tray over to the table. Hatcher was pleased to see that she had a little aluminum Italian pot made for espresso. She poured the dark, steaming coffee into two demitasses, handed one to Hatcher, sat down across the table from him, and smiled.

"Well, this has been very nice. My ego hasn't had such a lovely time in years. But I still don't know anything about you, and I was brought up to be suspicious of strange men."

"I should apologize. I've really been very rude. I suppose I'm rather in the habit of interrogating people, and you've been so enjoyable to listen to. Also, it occurs to me that we seem to have asked ourselves many of the same questions, so that much of what you've been saying has a familiar ring."

"About what?"

"About the art world, about academe. I stuck it out longer than you did. I got the Ph.D., for what that's worth, and I even taught for six years. I had a wife, and tenure, and a vague image of growing older and wiser surrounded by doting students."

"What happened?"

Hatcher knitted his brows and stirred his coffee absentmindedly.

"I don't know exactly. I think a lot of things. Partly, I realized at some point that while I was growing older, I certainly wasn't growing any wiser. In some fundamental sense, I had a feeling I was dying. I remember one episode vividly. I was teaching Michelangelo's *David*. There are certain things you have to say about the *David*—the story of the block, the original placement on the Cathedral, the anecdote about how the arm got smashed—and so on and so forth. I was saying all these things. In the middle of this, I had a sudden,

125

blinding insight. I had the feeling—I don't know if it was true—that everything I was saying I had said, exactly the same way, several times before. The same words, the same phrases, even the same intonation.

"I began to feel faint, so I dismissed the class. I sat in the back of the room for fifteen minutes staring, staring at the slide of Michelangelo's sculpture and during that whole time I felt nothing. Absolutely nothing. I could remember words, phrases, bits and pieces of articles, theories, but I still couldn't feel anything. I remember I went home in a daze, and for the only time in my life I got blind, stone drunk in the middle of the afternoon."

"Did you tell your wife what had happened?"

"Not immediately. I tried to pull myself together, as they say. For my wife's sake I began to see a psychiatrist. But at the same time, I made a decision. I decided I would not teach any work of art that I couldn't intensely, passionately respond to."

"That must have created some interesting classroom situations."

"It did. My students that year spent three hours looking at a six-inch-high panel by Carlo Crivelli, I remember, but they never saw the Sistine ceiling at all."

"I think I would have enjoyed that class."

Hatcher laughed.

"Would you? My wife, my shrink, my colleagues, and many of my students thought I was crazy. But I came to some decisions about art, art history, and the academic world that I still consider eminently sane."

"Tell me about them."

"First, that all great art is essentially mysterious, and that the fundamental element of beauty is passion. I think the great art historians—Wölfflin, Burckhardt, Panofsky, Friedländer—all of them—felt and communicated that passion, even if they transposed it to an intellectual sphere. I have a notion that the great age of art history is over, that it died with them. What you

126

find today are narrow intellectual technicians—what the Germans call *Fachidioten*: technical idiots. People pawing through documents in archives or trying to push data around like pieces on a chessboard. But the great discoveries, and the great imaginative syntheses, are over."

"What happened then?"

"Briefly, I left the groves of academe, and my wife left me. Quite justifiably, I might add. As she pointed out at the time, she knew exactly what she wanted and I, quite clearly, no longer had any idea what I wanted. She married a mathematician eight months later. We still exchange Christmas cards."

"How did you get into what you're doing now?"

"Art detection? More or less accidentally. One summer, when I was still teaching, I was doing some research on a minor Sienese *quattrocento* painter named Domenico di Bartolo. One of his key works was missing, stolen during the war. I decided to trace it. I finally found it, in a crate in a storage warehouse in Bayonne, New Jersey. Five people wound up going to jail, and I became something of a minor celebrity."

"How did you find it?"

"Oh, that's a long story. Anyway, the history of how the Domenico di Bartolo wound up in Bayonne turned out to be much more interesting than the Domenico di Bartolo, even to me. At that time, the international traffic in stolen art was reaching major dimensions and the art dealers decided they needed a person full time. Someone who would be based in the States, but could travel easily in Europe. After I left teaching, I contacted them."

"Will you tell me the Domenico di Bartolo story someday?"

"Sure."

"Will you rub my back now? I think I dislocated it this morning. Or maybe just plain broke it."

She went over and lay down on her bed, which was simply a mattress on top of a box spring on the floor. Hatcher knelt down by the bed and placed his hands on her shoulders. He felt a sudden sharp sexual pang, which surprised him with its force, and which he gamely attempted to suppress. Trying to act the role of a professional masseur, he worked his way slowly down her back. Her breathing became heavier and more regular, and when he reached the small of her back he stopped, thinking she was asleep. Wordlessly, she rolled over slowly and, eyes still closed, put her arms around his neck.

17

THE NEXT MORNING Hatcher woke up slowly. He felt slightly disembodied, like a patient coming out from under anesthesia. For a moment he lay on his back, wondering how the delicate stucco decoration over his head had wound up on the ceiling of a room in the Holiday Inn, and also wondering why he didn't seem to be wearing pajamas. Then he heard Sheila humming to herself.

With a Herculean effort, he turned his head to look at her. She was wearing a big, floppy, striped terrycloth bathrobe and slippers, and was engaged in straightening up the room. She looked very pretty.

"My God, Sheila. What happened?"

"Morning, Lover. I don't know—what did?"

"I remember supper, and espresso. And then I was giving you a friendly, innocent back rub. And then someone came up behind me and dropped the Bunker Hill monument on my head."

"They say the earth is supposed to move."

"Move, yes—not fall on you."

"Funny, I seem to remember the same thing. Do you suppose it was something in the espresso?"

"Espresso, nothing. I told you I thought you were a dangerous woman."

"And I told you, only when I'm hungry. Speaking of which, how do you like your eggs?"

While Hatcher showered and dressed and tried to make himself as presentable as his rumpled clothes and one-day growth of beard would allow, Sheila rattled around in the kitchen preparing things. Hatcher, catching sight of her out of the corner of his eye, felt the powerful tug of domesticity.

Still humming, Sheila emerged from the kitchen moments later, bearing a tray laden with orange juice, eggs, bacon, sausages, and toast. She put it down, placed the food on the table, and turned to Hatcher. Hatcher was frowning.

"Well?"

"Mmmm. I don't know, Sheila. Going on this way—aimlessly—year after year. Maybe we should get married."

"I thought you'd never ask."

"Well, we're not getting any younger, you know."

"Maybe you aren't. I definitely am. I felt about a hundred and twelve yesterday. Now I'm somewhere in my mid-thirties, and tomorrow I expect to be pre-pubescent."

"I don't think I'd like that."

"Oh, I don't know. It's supposed to be the coming thing. Twelve-year-olds."

Cleaning up the dishes later, Sheila became serious.

"I think I'd better get back to Miche. I'm afraid she's still pretty shattered. It's hard to know what to do, exactly. Sam didn't have any living relatives, so most of what has to be done will be up to us. Sam and Miche weren't technically married, but in every real sense they were. They go back a long time—twenty years or so."

"Miche didn't have any ideas about the crime, about who killed him?"

"God, no. If she had, little pieces of the murderer would be scattered all over New England by now. Miche came from Paris, but temperamentally she is pure Corsican. I don't think they actually knew much about each other's business. I think that was an unwritten law between them. They'd give each other tips, of course."

"I take it there was never any jealousy between you and Miche?"

"No. Why would there be? They were both very parental about me. They called me 'the Kid.' Also, they were both completely monogamous. Sammy called Miche his 'old lady,' and Miche referred to Sammy, with much flaring of nostrils, as *'mon homme.'* And I've always got along with Miche pretty well, except when she becomes a little too maternal, or too Corsican."

"What will you do?"

"I think just hang around. The burial was last week. As a Jew, Sam had to be buried immediately after the autopsy. I believe Miche was trying to arrange a memorial service somewhere. And she's also been receiving friends at Sammy's apartment—'sitting shivah,' I think it's called."

"Was Weinstock very religious?"

"Not really, which makes it a little awkward. I think Sam was very proud of being Jewish and fascinated by Jewish history; and most of the dealers he worked with were Jewish. But he didn't have any interest in the religion per se. Miche is a lapsed Catholic—very lapsed. But she got interested in Judaism through Sammy. They were both more or less Zionists."

"I suppose there are also business arrangements to be made."

"That's the part I'm trying to forget. Lawyers, assessors, accountants, God knows what all. I think they're hunting around for a will. I guess it's up to me to take care of all that. If we don't see each other for a year or so, I want you to know it was a lovely date."

"Mmm. It was, wasn't it? I suppose I'd better get back to work too. I'm supposed to be some kind of detective. I'd better go detect something."

"I've been thinking about that. I mean you, as a detective. We're going to have to clean up your act. Amos—what kind of a name for a detective is Amos? You should have a name like Lance, or Spike. Something macho."

"The only Lance I know is gay. The only Spike I know is a woman."

"Hmm. How about Rocco?"

"Rocco Hatcher. I sort of like that. But that macho stuff, that's the old-style detective. I'm a new-style detective."

"Oh?"

"Yes. Undercover man."

"I know." Sheila leered at Hatcher.

Returning to the Holiday Inn, Hatcher shaved, changed his clothes, had a second cup of coffee, and called O'Rourke.

"Hatcher, where the hell have you been? I've been trying to call you."

"Here and there."

"Oh." O'Rourke sounded icy. "Well, just don't tell Callahan."

"That's what Sheila said."

"Anyway, why I called is, we got the frame back from the lab. They got three clear prints off it and several partials. Enough. One of the prints was Weinstock's, and another was Giardino's. So that's the link I've been looking for. If you want, I'll drop it off. I'd like to talk to you anyway."

"Fine. Why don't I stay here and wait for you?"

When O'Rourke walked into Hatcher's room, he was carrying the frame in a shopping bag. His jaw was working furiously up and down. He was red-faced and sweating, which Hatcher had begun to recognize as O'Rourke's natural condition. Hatcher was impressed that O'Rourke could walk two blocks through a gray, freezing, mid-November Boston day and still be perspiring at the end of it.

The policeman dropped the bag casually on the bed, sat down on the overstuffed chair, stuck one massive foot on the coffee table, and removed his gum, which he fastidiously wrapped in tissue before dropping in the wastepaper basket.

"Ho, for the soft life of the private dick. Well, should I tell you what I've been doing, or should I embarrass you by asking you what you've been doing?"

"Why don't you tell me what you've been doing? I've been waiting for the frame."

"Ah, yes, the frame. Well, like I say, we got two big, beautiful prints that match Giardino and Weinstock, but that was all. There were some more that apparently belonged to a woman, who knows who, and the rest were smudges. Anyway, it made me feel good for a whole two hours. You know how often it is prints make any difference to anything? Practically never."

"So then?"

"So then I call this guy at Harvard, the guy who recommended you."

"Sabin?"

"Yeah. I couldn't get you. I wanted to find out about this frame, so I called Sabin. Sabin tells me the frame is definitely from someplace in northern Europe, he thinks Holland, and that it was made in the seventeenth century."

"That's what I told you."

"Yeah. I like to get it from two sources, though. I

133

mean, I don't know too much about art. Sabin called it 'broke.' "

"Baroque. With an 'a.' "

"Yeah. I thought about that for a while. I'll tell you what I thought, you'll tell me where I'm being stupid."

Hatcher smiled. By now he was used to O'Rourke's big-dumb-Irish-cop act and understood it well enough to know that the dumber O'Rourke seemed, the more carefully Hatcher would have to watch and listen.

"What I'm thinking is, what we got now is a stolen painting. One stolen painting. If it belongs in that frame, it's a seventeenth-century painting from maybe Holland or Belgium. So I figure, whoever does this must know something about pictures—particularly seventeenth-century pictures from northern Europe—"

"Baroque."

"Yeah, baroque pictures. He must know all about them, and he must see something in this one that makes it pretty valuable. You don't kill two people because you got an empty spot on the wall over the sofa."

"No, you don't."

"So, point one, it's got to be something important. Vermeer, Rubens, Rembrandt, someone like that."

Hatcher grinned broadly. O'Rourke turned scarlet.

"So what. I did a little reading up, is all."

"I didn't say a word. What's point two?"

"Point two is, how many people would even recognize a painting like that—not just what it is, but how valuable? Now comes a guess, and here the ice gets a little thin. The guess is, whoever did this is local. Not necessarily Boston, but New England."

"I hope you're right. But why?"

"Giardino. Giardino's a local operator, and he seems to have stuck pretty close to home. My guess is that he would have been eaten alive in New York, and probably knew it. I think the picture came from around here, I think the killer came from around here."

134

"I tend to agree. I hope this isn't just wishful thinking."

"I do too, otherwise it gets complicated as all hell. Anyway, assuming the painting wasn't lifted out of a museum—you don't have to remind me, by the way, how often I've been using the word 'assuming' lately—and, assuming that the picture was that big a deal, how many people could have spotted it? Not just guessed, but known, been sure enough of their judgment to take that big a risk. Sabin says this kind of thing is tricky. There are copies, fakes, all kinds of three-dollar bills floating around."

"There are. What do you think of Sabin, by the way?"

"I think he's a pretty sharp old coot."

"He is. What did he say?"

"We spent a lot of time on that. He made us up a list. He figures maybe twenty people or so in the greater Boston area could have spotted a picture like that absolutely cold. Like to see the list?"

"Sure."

"Keep this. I got a Xerox."

O'Rourke reached in his back pocket, pulled out a single sheet of paper that was folded several times, and flipped it over to Hatcher. Hatcher unfolded it and read it, whistling several times.

"Know most of the names?"

"Maybe three quarters, the professors and dealers mainly, some of the curators and maybe a couple of collectors. I take it these are just people who could have spotted it, forgetting motive, means, and all the rest of it?"

"Yup. Just spotted it."

"Mary Craig? Mary Craig is a little old lady about seventy-five years old."

"Yup. She could have a ne'er-do-well nephew in hock to a bookie. Who knows?"

"Elton Ross? The head of the Boston Museum?"

"Sabin said he'd messed around in that neck of the woods. Wrote a master's thesis on Dutch paintings."

"I see Sabin put himself on the list."

"He said he didn't do it. Said it might have crossed his mind, though, if it was the right kind of picture. Can you think of anyone he left off?"

"Not offhand. If any names come to me, I'll let you know. What are you going to do with this list, by the way?"

"Oh, the usual sneaky, covert things that cops do. Spy on people, cause trouble, violate human rights, and commit public and private nuisances, for starters. What are you going to do with that frame?"

"Try to figure out what went in it."

"I've decided I like that idea. Don't lose it, though."

"Can I keep the keys to the Weinstock Gallery? I want to go back and look for something."

"Okay with me. Don't solve the crimes until we have a chance to check some of the people on the list, though, or you'll hurt Sabin's feelings."

"That I can promise."

"Good. See you, Hatcher. And if you come across any human rights we've neglected to violate recently, don't hesitate to call the station."

Captain O'Rourke buttoned his coat and walked out the door, leaving Hatcher to his own devices.

18

THE WEINSTOCK GALLERY was empty when Hatcher arrived there. The cardboard sign announcing that the premises were closed by order of the Boston Police Department was still nailed to the door, but no policemen were enforcing it. Nor was Sheila at the gallery. Hatcher had no real reason to expect her; she was probably at Micheline's shop down the street. But he felt a slight twinge of disappointment nonetheless.

It took him only twenty minutes to find what he was looking for. It was a small plain white envelope rolled up and secured with a rubber band; Hatcher found it jammed into the bottom drawer of Weinstock's desk. He opened it up, looked inside, and shook the contents out on the desk top. There were twelve nails and four triangular wooden wedges about two inches long. Hatcher was pleased and rather surprised with his discovery.

He picked up one of the wedges and fitted it to the long light patches on the back of the frame. One of them fit it exactly. Just to make sure, he continued the process with the three other wedges. Then he picked up the nails and examined them. One of them had snapped off in the middle. After testing several of the holes in the frame, Hatcher discovered the one where the tip of the nail had snapped off. Then he carefully scrutinzed one of the nails with a lens. It was old and rusted to a dark brown, almost black, color, and both the head and shaft looked as though they were forged with a hammer rather than simply cast. Instead of being round, the nail was square in section.

He considered the situation. Somewhere, doubtless, there was someone who knew everything there was to know about nails. The Nail King. Probably a little old geezer about ninety-three years old. If he could find the Nail King, one glance would tell him everything he needed to know. Hmmm. I'd say it was made in May 1636, in Delft, Holland, by Frits Langendijk. Got any others to show me, Sonny?

However, Hatcher decided it would probably take him eight years to locate the Nail King. He would arrive at an adobe hut in the middle of southwestern New Mexico to find that the Nail King had died the week before, taking his encyclopedic lore about the subject with him. To hell with experts, thought Hatcher.

Nevertheless, the pile of objects on the table told Hatcher something important. It told him that Weinstock had asked himself the same question: the question of whether the nails and little wooden splints were original. The question, in fact, whether the picture had ever been out of the frame. Otherwise, there was no reason why Weinstock would have kept them in a rolled-up envelope. As far as Weinstock had known or been able to tell, the painting might have been in the original frame, which implied to Hatcher that whatever he could deduce about the frame would at least tell him something about the picture as well.

He could also assume, by the angles at which the

nails had been set in the frame, that the missing picture was a wooden panel. If it had been a canvas in a stretcher, the nails would have had to be much longer and set much farther back along the ledge of the frame.

Hatcher put the nails and pieces of wood back in the envelope, replaced the rubber band, and stuck it in his pocket.

Before leaving, Hatcher decided to look around the gallery a little more. Squatting along the row of pictures lined up against the wall, he pulled fifteen or twenty of them out at random. Most of them were by Americans—minor artists, as far as Hatcher could tell. None of the signatures were more than vaguely familiar to him. American impressionists, minor Hudson River painters, a few primitive portraits. Along with the American pictures, Hatcher discovered a few Old Masters. Like the Americans, the Old Masters were entirely minor artists or anonymous. But, again, like the other pictures, each one seemed to reflect a subtlety of discernment. The pictures at Weinstock's gallery were by no means major works, but each one seemed to have some particular excellence: design, color, a witty or charming subject, some unique quality of appeal. Weinstock, Hatcher concluded, had had a large measure of that curious and indefinable substance called taste.

He slid the pictures back, stood up, winced, and wondered if Sheila would give *him* a back rub later on. Then he carefully locked both the inner and outer doors and headed for the Charles Street subway station. The weather was still bitter, and a sharp wind increased the chill factor. Hatcher pulled up the collar of his coat and cursed himself for not owning a scarf.

After muddling about for a while in Harvard Square, Hatcher finally found his way to the Fogg Art Museum and the adjacent library. The lady in charge of the art history library was attractive, pleasant, and helpful, all of which contradicted Hatcher's ingrained prejudices

139

about librarians, but she directed him to a prissy, scrawny specimen at Widener—Harvard's main library—who just as quickly reaffirmed all of them. After a certain amount of running back and forth, Hatcher obtained, at the cost of a substantial sum of money and after proffering a vast amount of documentation in the form of references, credit cards, and various forms of identification, a small card. The card gave him access to the hermetic, cavernous reaches of the fine arts library and would allow him to take out books for a period of two weeks. By the time he had procured the card Hatcher was exhausted, both physically and mentally.

The stacks of the library itself quickly revived him. Where an average university library might have two or three books on the subject that concerned him, the Fogg Library had three shelves, certainly the most comprehensive selection he could have found in the United States. He pulled out eleven of the books and took them over to an empty carrel, turned on the desk lamp, and began to read.

An hour later, he returned seven of the books to the shelves and carted the remaining four up to the desk. He took them out on his temporary loan card, put them in the shopping bag with the frame, which he had checked at the desk, and went off to find the Romance Languages Department. This errand turned out to be easier. He was quickly directed to the relevant scholar, an elderly man who answered his questions with exquisite old-world courtesy and modesty. Hatcher thanked him warmly and returned to the subway station in Harvard Square.

It was quarter past four in the afternoon when Hatcher slipped off onto the Charles Street platform. He hurried through the turnstile and raced along the narrow overpass leading from the elevated station across to the banks of the Charles River. He walked along the embankment for a few minutes until he spied a figure in a heavy, navy-blue coat, red knitted wool cap, and mittens leaning over the railing.

"Hi."

"Hi, there. I was afraid you wouldn't come. I saved a roll for you, here. Don't toss any to that big dark one, though. His name is Peking Duck. He's a real sneaky type. A thug."

"Do you play favorites?"

"Of course. Only the ones I like get any. I specialize in the ones that are either very small or very stupid. See that one there? That's Duck Soup. A real ignoramus. I tossed pieces of bread at him for ten minutes, and he never got anything. The bread kept bouncing off the top of his bill. My theory is that they're mostly pretty dumb. Have to be to stay in Boston in late November. What's in the bag?"

"Some books, plus the frame you found. Would you like to come over to my hotel, warm up with some coffee and a drink, and listen to some of my theories?"

"I'd love to. I don't have too much time, though. I promised I'd be back at Miche's by seven-thirty. She's invited a number of Sammy's friends tonight for food, drinks, and an evening of boozy reminiscences. I gather it's to be a sort of Franco-Jewish version of an Irish wake."

"Sounds like a nice idea."

"It is. I wish we could spend the evening together, though. I'm in the mood for another back rub."

"Me too. Nice to discover you have a talent you didn't know about before."

"Oh, you have a talent, all right."

When they got back to the Holiday Inn, they went to the coffee shop and sat in a booth exchanging news about their respective day's activities. Then they

141

quickly went to Hatcher's room where, as soon as the door was closed, Hatcher grabbed Shelia's arm, spun her around, and gave her a warm, slow kiss.

"Hello again."

"Hello yourself. I clean forgot that this morning, and I missed it all day."

"So, tell me your theories, Mr. New-Style Detective. One more kiss like that and this whole conversation is likely to go right down the drain."

After they had dropped their coats on one of the twin beds and Hatcher had had a chance to pour both of them drinks, he got the frame from the shopping bag and handed it to Sheila.

"Here's a lens. I'll tell you my theories, and you tell me where you think I'm being dumb."

"That sounds like one of O'Rourke's lines."

"It is. But he only uses it when he's being smug."

Hatcher reached in his pocket, withdrew the envelope he'd found at the gallery, and emptied the contents on the coffee table.

"I found these this morning in Weinstock's desk. My guess is that he was interested in finding out whether they were original, which would be an incredible piece of luck. I can tell from the position of the nails that the picture was a panel. Now, see the inscription near the bottom of the frame? Can you read what it says?"

"Let me see. It's—wait—Henri-something. Henriette. Henriette, with a small 'h.' "

"Right. I showed that to a professor of French literature at Harvard who does a good deal of archival work with manuscripts. He told me that the calligraphy is definitely French rather than Flemish, and probably dates from the late seventeenth or early eighteenth centru. Let's assume, then, that at the time it was written the picture was in a French gallery or private collection. Now."

142

Hatcher got a book from the bag, flipped through it, found what he was looking for, and handed it to Sheila. Sheila opened it to a large color plate.

The plate reproduced a baroque portrait. A magnificently attired and very beautiful young woman was shown standing, in three-quarters view, smiling down at the viewer. Her complexion was milky white, which set off the soft pink glow of her rouged cheeks and the scarlet of her sensual mouth, with its artistocratic and perhaps slightly ironic smile. Her eyes were large and dark and seemed to dance and gleam with a marvelous vivacity. Her hair was a mass of tight dark curls that swirled about her face like tiny rivulets. Her taffeta gown was shot through with blazing lights and lent animation to the cool, regal figure wearing it.

Sheila whistled softly.

"My God, she looks like a queen. Van Dyck?"

"Van Dyck. And she was a queen. Henrietta Maria, wife of Charles the First and Queen of England from 1625 until her husband's execution by the Puritans in 1649."

"Henriette—Henrietta. That would do it, wouldn't it?"

"I'm hoping. Van Dyck was court portraitist to King Charles from his return to England in 1632 until his own death in 1641, and he did a large number of portraits of the queen during that time. After the Revolution, many of the arsitocratic collections were broken up, sold, and dispersed. Many of the greatest of Van Dyck's English portraits wound up in France. The most famous of all, *Portrait of Charles the First Hunting,* is now in the Louvre, for example."

"That would explain the French form of the name, and the reason the picture was in France."

"Yes. Another thing. Henrietta Maria was herself French. 'Henriette Marie' was her real name. She was the daughter of Henry the Fourth of France and his consort, Maria de' Medici, who was one of the last important figures of the great Florentine family."

"Was she really this beautiful?"

"Is anyone ever as beautiful as Van Dyck's women? According to witnesses she was rather small—she looks six feet tall here—and rather plain. She seems to have been a witty and charming woman, however, so at least that part is true."

"What a magical image. I suppose a Van Dyck portrait of Henrietta Maria would be very valuable, even a small one?"

"I think very. First of all, because it would be extremely rare. Most of Van Dyck's portraits wound up in royal collections pretty early in the game."

"What is the wax seal on the frame?"

"The emblem? I haven't checked it out, but the *impresa* of the double-headed eagle was one of the Hapsburg emblems. This would fit nicely too, since Flanders was still under Hapsburg rule in the seventeenth century, as was Spain. Royal portraits were of course frequently diplomatic gifts."

"Clever Amos. You *are* a detective, aren't you. I think it's a lovely theory."

"That's all it is, right now. As you can imagine, I have a lot of research to do, and maybe tomorrow I'll discover it's all a lot of rot. I never trust myself when things look easy and I'm beginning to feel smart as hell. Never. In fact, I'm already looking for one of life's little banana peels."

"Nuts. I don't believe it. This is really getting fascinating. God, I wish I could stay here and work with you instead of holding Miche's hand. However, I'd better go. If we don't get in touch tomorrow morning, will you meet me later by the ducks?"

"Damn right. By the ducks. I'll even bring my own roll."

144

19

THE TWO WOMEN stood side by side in the middle of the shop. Maude, the proprietress of the store, was a short, rather dumpy woman in her late sixties with a round, chubby face set off by a halo of white curls. Sarah, the tall, bony woman beside her, looked to be a stern figure of New England Puritan rectitude, which in many ways she was. Yet somehow it was Maude who was the dominant figure in their relationship and had been since they were children.

Sarah was fingering a large platter in the middle of the table. Maude was watching her hand playing nervously over the porcelain surface.

"I don't know, Maude, I just don't know. I told you how Arthur gets."

"But it's such a lovely piece. When you find ones like this, they always seem to have chips. That's why I was so surprised to find one that's perfect."

"Oh, you know I like it; I don't have any secrets from you. It's just that, well, I think Arthur is still upset at me about the chafing dish last week."

"I know Arthur is a cross to bear. I do think it's nice for him, though, that he has someone like you to show him the better things in life."

"That's shameless flattery, Maude, and you know it."

"No, really. Heaven knows Ed had a coarse streak, God rest his soul. I think it's a man's nature. That's why they need us, Sarah, to show them the finer things."

Maude watched her friend fluttering around the large platter a moment longer, then decided to move in for the kill.

"You know what will happen if you don't get it? One of those big-shot dealers from New York City will snap it right up, and the next time you see it, it won't be thirty dollars, it will be seventy-five. *If* I'm lucky enough to find another one, that is."

Sarah sighed. She had no defenses against this argument. It was no longer a simple matter of a rather pretty platter of a somewhat questionable vintage, but the moral imperative of saving an endangered objet d'art from the corrupt rapacity of one of the "big-shot dealers." Sarah had never actually been to New York City. In fact, she rarely traveled farther than a fifty-mile radius from her home in North Adams, Massachusetts. But she never heard the words "New York City" without experiencing a small thrill of fear.

"I suppose I'd better have it then, hadn't I?"

"Good for you, Sarah. Oh, it will look so nice on your sideboard. Just the thing. I'm sure Arthur will *love* it."

After wrapping the platter, Maude invited her friend out to the kitchen for a cup of tea. She hesitated a moment, remembering a large, rather ugly blue pitcher that would be "just perfect" in the middle of the newly acquired platter, but decided not to press her advantage. Arthur was not, unfortunately, quite as predict-

146

able as his wife, and occasionally objects were returned to Maude with great suddenness and finality.

"I swear, Maude, I don't know how you manage it all, I truly don't. To think, when you started this ten years ago a number of us—well, not me, of course, I know you better—but a number of the others didn't think you'd ever make a go of it."

"Oh, it just takes a sharp eye and a keen mind, I always say. And knowing what people want. Now, I knew when I found that platter. I said, 'That's for Sarah.' Just like that. Some people, though, it's not so easy. I remember, a man came in a month or a month and a half ago. He was one of these sharp ones."

She leaned forward, touching the back of her friend's hand.

" 'New York City,' I said to myself."

"Really?"

"Oh, I can tell. Said he was keen on pictures. Well! I had one, you know, up in the guest room. Dark old thing in a big black frame. I got it, oh, back just after the war. I didn't like it much, never had it in the shop. But I had a feeling about this one as soon as I saw him. I thought, 'I just wonder. I just wonder if he's as smart as he thinks he is.' So I went and got it and brought it down. Well!"

"Oh, Maude, tell me."

"He had a yen, I could tell that. Never looked at my other things, didn't even notice my nice Currier and Ives. Quick as a wink, he asked me the price."

"What did you tell him?" Sarah was now breathless with eager expectancy.

"I thought about that hankering. He didn't know I knew about it, of course, but I could feel it. So I came right out with it, plain as day. I said, 'That's a very old and rare picture. Five hundred dollars.' "

"Maude, you didn't!"

"That's what I said. 'Five hundred dollars, not a

147

penny less.' Then he looked at me, he looked at the painting, he looked back at me. Never said a word. You know what he did then?"

"Tell me."

"He took out his wallet, and wrote out a check for every bit of it, five hundred dollars to the cent. Then he picked up the picture and walked right out the door."

"Gracious, Maude. You certainly are a shrewd one."

"A sharp eye and a keen mind, I always say."

That night, shortly after midnight, Sarah woke up suddenly, aroused by the sharp, staccato barks from the terrier across the street. she sat up in bed, bolt upright, her eyes wide and staring. Then at the window she saw the flames across the street. The barks became more desperate, then resolved into a long, continuous, keening howl, and then stopped. Sarah screamed.

It could not have been more than twelve or fourteen minutes between the time Arthur called the fire department and the time they arrived at Maude's Antiques. By then, however, the fire was out of control. The frigid northeast wind that had been steadily intensifying during the evening, swirling down over the Berkshires and gusting in irregular, circular patterns across the long valley below, fanned the flames and whipped them from side to side like waves in a choppy sea. There was nothing to do but wet down the surrounding trees and houses and hope to check the spread. The antique store and attached house, both wooden frame structures, collapsed within an hour.

In two hours the fire was almost spent, and the firemen could get close enough to the house for the first time to train their hoses on the gaunt and blackened wreck.

Halfway between North Adams and Springfield, Elton Ross's black Lincoln pulled off onto the shoulder of the road and stopped. Ross resisted the impulse to collapse, and maintained his grip on the wheel while he waited for the dizziness to pass.

There was no one chasing him and no real reason to expect anyone to, yet he flinched every time his rearview mirror caught the headlights of an approaching car.

She had had to die. He repeated this to himself, halfbelieving that the false implication of inevitability, of fate even, somehow exculpated him.

She had had to die. She could identify the panel, she could tie it to Giardino, she was the last link. He forced his mind to go over it once again.

The woman would be found in her store, a broken kerosene lamp beside her. Why not? She'd heard a noise, perhaps her dog barking, and had gone to investigate. She'd taken a kerosene lantern rather than a flashlight—again, why not?

She'd had to be struck from the front. That part was necessary; it had to look as if she'd tripped and hit her head. An accident, perhaps a burglar. No reason to suspect anything more complicated.

No reason, then, for this terror.

If Giardino had told the truth, there were only three of them who had seen the painting: Giardino himself, Weinstock, and the woman in the antique store. And if Giardino had lied?

He could not have lied.

Ross remembered Giardino, flattened against the wall, pleading for his life.

He began to feel dizzy again. He shook his head to clear it, but he couldn't dislodge the image of Giardino's face. Now there was another face, another image: an old woman, a truncated scream, flames, blood.

Ross slammed his fist against the corner of the dashboard, and the sudden, sharp pain pulled him back from the demons of his imagination. The brief crisis left

149

him exhausted, and he could feel his exhaustion permeating his body like a narcotic. But sleep was another trap, and Ross preferred his waking demons to those that visited him in his dreams.

He started the car, edged it onto the highway, and moved off into the night.

20

THE NEXT FOUR DAYS seemed, to all the people working on the case, rather aimless and fragmented. A great deal of energy was expended to very little effect. Hatcher holed up in various libraries, finding out what he could about Van Dyck, the portraits of Henrietta Maria, and the history of the Stuart England. Sheila spent most of her time running back and forth between Micheline, who was still recovering from Weinstock's death and still prone to violent hysterics, and the studious figure of Hatcher, hunched over his books. The afternoon meetings along the banks of the Charles River became a ritual, and were several times followed by dinner and lovemaking.

O'Rourke and Callahan seemed to fare little better. O'Rourke had studied the list of names suggested by Dr. Sabin and devised elaborately devious ways of checking up on them without exerting too much pressure or telegraphing his intentions. Some of these schemes did not sit too well with Callahan. One that he found particularly rankling involved a brief charade as waiter and busboy at the oldest and most fashionable men's club in Boston, the St. Swithin on Newbury Street.

On the outside, the St. Swithin Club was not particularly imposing. It was a simple, three-story brownstone resembling its neighbors. It had no sign. Instead, there was a small brass plaque above the bell. When the bell was rung, a tall, formidable figure in livery would open the door a crack, cock an eyebrow at the person on the other side of the threshold, and then either open the door wide with a smile as well-worn, highly polished, and mechanical as the brass knocker on the door, or ask him in a chilly and accusatory voice what his business was. In spite of O'Rourke's preparations, when Callahan arrived he was accorded the latter treatment. It was not an auspicious beginning to the assignment.

Several minutes later, Callahan found himself stationed in the main drawing room of the club. He was wearing formal black pants with suspenders that had once belonged to a tuxedo, a white coat, a black bow tie, and gleaming black patent-leather shoes. The white coat was too small and chafed uncomfortably at his armpits. He carried a small silver tray, which reminded him unpleasantly of several summers spent as a waiter during his adolescence. He felt idotic and cursed O'Rourke roundly under his breath.

A less jaundiced eye than Callahan's would have recognized that the room in which he found himself standing was indeed quite elegant, a rich if overblown example of the Tudor Revival, with intricately carved oak beams and panels, leaded windows, and a huge limestone fireplace at one end of the room. The fireplace was particularly ornate, with gables, crockets, and finials borrowed from some English cathedral. Over the mantel was a large portrait of the club's founder, whose expression of smug pomposity seemed borrowed from the doorman downstairs.

Callahan's subject was sitting in a large, leather-covered wing chair in front of the fireplace. His name was T. Huntington Dodd the Third. Most of the people at his firm called him T.H. Old friends called him Biff or Hunty. One of his ex-wives had called him Doodles, but she hadn't lasted very long, so it hadn't become a serious problem. Many other people called him many other things, but he always referred to himself simply as "Huntington." He was seventy years old, and very rich.

He sat morosely in his chair, his hands linked across his ample stomach, and his long legs, crossed at the ankles, stuck out in front of him. He had been sitting that way for perhaps fifteen minutes when, without turning his head, he raised his right hand languidly and waggled a couple of fingers. Callahan went over to him. They were the only people in the room.

"Teddy, get me a manhat—oh. You're not Teddy. Where's Teddy?"

"I'm afraid he's sick, sir. I'm filling in."

"Oh. Then get Williams. He knows how I like my manhattans. Get two of them."

"Right away, sir."

Dodd was just finishing the second manhattan when a dapper little man in a blue pinstripe suit entered the room, strode across the floor, and shook Dodd's hand. Dodd did not get up, but immediately waggled his fingers for Callahan. Callahan was becoming interested. Dodd was clearly upset about something, and the arrival of a second party raised the specter of a possible conspiracy. The snatches of conversation he could overhear between the two men did not, however, increase his professional curiosity.

"Rog? Damn good of you to come."

"Any time, Biff. We go back a long way."

"We do, by God. I had to speak to you. It's about Marjorie."

"Ah. The little woman, eh?"

"Goddamned little round-heeled minx, is what she is. You, there. Dry martini with a twist, eh Rog? And another manhattan for me, and tell Williams not so light on the bourbon."

When Callahan returned with the drinks, the liquor was beginning to tell on Dodd. After handing the two men their glasses, Callahan stationed himself behind Dodd's chair. He did not worry about arousing any suspicion, since it was already clear that his services would be needed early and often.

"Anyway, she's gone."

"She'll be back. She's been gone before, she'll come back. Knows which side her bread's buttered on, as Freddy always says."

"Majorie's not like Freddy. Freddy's solid, salt of the earth. Damn fine woman you've got in Freddy. Why didn't I marry a woman like that?"

"Oh, we've had some bumpy times, too, Biff. Some very bumpy times. But she certainly has the breeding, the fiber."

"This time it's different with Marjorie. This time she's really gone. I want you to draw up the papers."

"Pretty drastic step, Biff. Does she know where she stands if she walks out? I mean financially?"

Dodd sighed and jiggled his drink. He looked more morose than ever.

"She says she doesn't care. She says she loves him."

"My God. It's that ski instructor from Gstaad, is it?"

"Heiss? Hell, no. That was nothing, just a weekend. It's that goddamned interior decorator. I didn't even think about him. I mean, my God, I was sure he was a pansy. He looked like a pansy; wavy blond hair and everything. You can't tell the difference anymore."

He lapsed into a moody silence, then waggled his fingers for another drink. By the time Callahan returned, Dodd was beginning to founder in self-pity.

154

"I mean, how do you know anything about women? I gave Marjorie everything. What the hell do they want?"

"That's what Freud said. He didn't know what women wanted, either."

"You see? I mean, Christ, Freud studied them all his life, and if he didn't know what it was they wanted, how am I supposed to know? She didn't understand me at all, that was another thing. She didn't understand about the art, for instance. Thought it was just a bunch of ugly brown paintings. Well, she won't get any of them. Probably get the yacht, though. Oh, it's all so boring."

"Got to pull yourself together, Biff."

"I don't know. I'd got used to her, that's the problem."

From behind the chair, Callahan heard a series of wet sniffing sounds and realized, with horror, that Dodd was beginning to break down. He felt slightly ill.

The man called Rog repeated, in a somewhat firmer tone, his instructions to Dodd to pull himself together. Then Callahan heard Dodd blow his nose with a loud, mucous honk. When he spoke again, his voice was clear, but sad.

"She was such a pretty little thing."

When Callahan arrived back at the station he immediately went slamming into O'Rourke's office. He was furious.

"Some suspect you gave me. Some killer. All that guy Dodd ever killed was maybe eight million bottles of good bourbon. Some bloated slob of a dirty old Boston richo who's blubbering all over the place because his twenty-five-year-old high-mileage honey of a wife, who's gone down for everybody on the Eastern seaboard at least once already has finally picked some guy to skip out on him with, and I have to waste a whole afternoon dressed up in a fucking monkey-suit pouring drinks into him. You got any other great ideas?"

155

"Finished?"

"No. What's for tomorrow? I stick a ruby in my god-damn navel and take a job as a belly dancer in a gay discotheque?"

"Finished yet?"

"Maybe. For the time being."

"Okay. He was on the list. He's the biggest collector of Old Master paintings in New England, so he was on the list."

"Swell. Take him off it."

"Okay. Anyway, you get the next two days off. It's my turn to play games."

"Games. Some games."

The next day, at twenty past nine in the morning, O'Rourke arrived in uniform at the Boston Museum. Stopping at the turnstile, he debated whether to produce his badge, mumble something about "official business" and breeze through, or pay the suggested two dollars and go first class. He considered the two dollars blackmail, especially since he wasn't planning on seeing any art. He finally compromised, gave the girl at the desk a dollar, and passed through the turnstile blushing hotly. He decided that, by God, if he was going to pay, he *would* see some pictures. He'd see the Impressionists.

Following the instructions of one of the guards, a wizened old gentleman who seemed about as alert as the mummy in the case beside him, O'Rourke finally made his way to the director's office. Once there, the captain eased around the secretary's desk, told her that he would announce himself, and knocked on Ross's door. He could feel the stony gaze of the secretary following him across the room.

Ross opened the door and seemed only mildly surprised to find a policeman standing behind it.

"Yes?"

"Mr. Ross? I'm Captain O'Rourke, Seventh Precinct.

156

I'd like to speak to you about the murder of Samuel Weinstock."

Reconstructing the scene later in his office, O'Rourke could not be absolutely sure whether or not he had imagined it. But he seemed to sense a slight stiffening, like a tic, and perhaps a small loss of color in Ross's face.

"What do you—why are you—" At that moment the telephone on Ross's desk buzzed. He said, "Excuse me," to O'Rourke, went over, pushed a button, and spoke in low tones for several minutes. From the snatches of conversation, O'Rourke gathered that it concerned the typeface for the catalogue of some show or other that was about to open at the Museum. During those few minutes, the policeman knew, any advantage he might have held would be lost.

He was right. When Ross returned, he was quite self-possessed.

"Now, Captain. What can I do for you?"

"I'm investigating the murder of an art dealer, Samuel Weinstock." Here O'Rourke hesitated for a moment, watching Ross. Ross stared back at him, his gaze calm, slightly bored if anything.

"I'm trying to contact anyone who might have known him, or dealt with him."

"I see. I read about the murder, of course. Horrible thing. I'm afraid I never met the man myself, but I believe the name did ring a bell. If you would care to take a seat, I'd be glad to check my files. The Museum may have had some dealing with him in the past. It shouldn't take long."

O'Rourke sat down, feeling suddenly quite foolish. He stuck a piece of gum in his mouth and toyed with his cap while he looked around the office. It seemed very elegantly and efficiently arranged to him, and made him yearn for the cheerful chaos of his little cubicle at the precinct.

157

When Ross returned, he was smiling and carrying a gray folder.

"Success. It seems we bought two small American pictures from him in 1972. Nothing important. Still, they would probably remember him in the American department, and they might be able to tell you something useful. Let me call Miss Frohlich, the head of the department."

It took O'Rourke three quarters of an hour to escape the grasp of Miss Frohlich, an angry, nervous little old lady who insisted on haranguing O'Rourke at length about how Weinstock had tried to foist a bad picture off on the Museum, and then generalized her theme to include all dealers everywhere.

"Crooks, Mr. O'Rourke, all crooks. Of course, that's why we have people like you to uphold the law."

Sensing that he was about to be enlisted in a crusade for the moral rearmament of the art business, O'Rourke gently disengaged himself from the Department of American Paintings and wended his way to the Impressionist gallery. At this point, the peaceful, green lily ponds of Giverny and the shimmering sea off the coast of Normandy looked very beautiful indeed to him. While he looked at the pictures, he recalled the stiffening he had sensed in Ross at first, and decided to leave him on the list.

Malcolm Robinson also stayed on the list, though for different reasons.

Robinson's Gallery, located on Newbury Street not far from the St. Swithin Club, was as sharp a contrast to Weinstock's gallery as Ross's office was to O'Rourke's. Much larger than Weinstock's, Robinson's Gallery seemed almost bare by comparison. O'Rourke saw only about fifteen works of art in the whole place, whereas Weinstock's seemed to have thousands. Each painting on the wall had an elaborate frame, and each one had a small printed label next to it and a hidden spotlight to illuminate it. It took O'Rourke a minute to understand the intended effect. Each picture was being presented to the viewer as an incomparably rare and precious object, like a gem in an ornate gold mount.

Robinson himself was a tall, flaccid-looking man in his early fifties. His thinning black hair was slicked back, he wore heavy glasses with gold frames, and his pink cheeks reminded O'Rourke of a baby's bottom. His face looked smooth all over, as if it had been polished. He had almost no discernable chin. He blinked a lot. O'Rourke disliked him on sight, which was unusual for him.

"Captain O'Rourke, sorry to keep you waiting. I understand you wish to speak to me about that terrible Weinstock business."

"I'm in charge of the investigation, yes."

"A terrible, terrible business. I knew Sammy Weinstock very well, of course. We've had a number of dealings over the years."

"My main question is whether you might know anyone who would have had a motive to kill him."

Robinson put his hands behind his back and rocked back and forth on his heels for a bit, his lips working in and out. He seemed to be preparing a speech.

"Captain O'Rourke, I know one shouldn't speak ill of the dead, but perhaps I should be frank with you."

"Please."

"Sammy Weinstock wasn't . . . well, how should I say it? I'm afraid Mr. Weinstock wasn't one of the better sort of dealers."

"Oh?"

"Of course, I don't mean to imply that he was totally crooked, or anything. It's just that there was something perhaps a little unsavory about him. One always suspected that he was rather too interested in the financial aspect, rather than the aesthetic aspect. One never felt one could entirely trust him."

"I see."

"You must understand about this business. Many dealers, and I would count myself among them, see our role as essentially custodial. We form a link, so to speak, in the great cultural chain stretching back across the centuries. We try to obtain the artifacts of the great periods of history and place them, for a time, in the safekeeping of those few among us cultivated enough to truly appreciate them. I'm afraid Mr. Weinstock did not view his profession in this way."

"You mean he was just trying to make a buck."

"To put it crudely. I, for one, frequently felt that his dealings were not entirely aboveboard. I would not be surprised to hear that he had enemies."

"Would you consider yourself one of his enemies?"

"Me? Good Lord, no! In fact, I sold him a picture just two weeks ago. I always felt rather sympathetic towards him. It can't be easy for a man of his background and training to survive long in a business this . . . well, sophisticated."

"Who do you suppose his enemies were, then?"

"Oh, I shouldn't like to hazard a guess. If you look around a bit, though, I'm sure you'll find them. The art world is rather small and insular."

"I see. Well, thank you very much, Mr. Robinson. If any names occur to you, be sure to call me. O'Rourke, Seventh Precinct. I'll write the number down for you."

By the time he returned to the station house, O'Rourke had concluded that he didn't like the art world much, if at all. Callahan, however, felt profoundly satisfied just from watching O'Rourke's expression as he trudged into his office. He looked like he'd had a very tough day.

21

"CAN'T I THROW NAPKINS over them, or something? Honestly, Amos, it's a little hard to compete."

Hatcher was sitting cross-legged, surrounded by books, on the floor of Sheila's apartment. Two good color reproductions of Van Dyck's protraits of Henrietta Maria were tacked up on a bookcase, and Hatcher was studying them intently. In one, the half-length portrait, the Queen was wearing a dazzling golden taffeta gown ornamented with elaborate lace cuffs and collar, and heavy ropes of pearls falling in loops across the bodice made an accord with the pastel glow of her flesh. In the other, a full-length portrait, the Queen stood majestically on a classical portico, a dwarf holding a monkey posed next to her. Here she was dressed in a gown of deep lapis lazuli blue, and behind her stretched a soft, romantic twilit sky that looked as if it had been painted by Titian. The face in both pictures was exquisitely beautiful, and in both it was animated by a delightfully piquant half-smile.

"You think you've got problems. How about Queen

Elizabeth? There are four portraits of Henrietta at Windsor Castle. Five, including a double portrait with King Charles, and every time Elizabeth sees one, she must feel like a cheap imitation. The point is that no one could conceivably be half as regal as Van Dyck's royal portraits, which is precisely why Van Dyck was such a successful court portraitist."

"I think I like Holbein better. His portraits of Henry the Eighth make him look like a thug, but at least he was telling the truth."

"From what I've read, you wouldn't like Van Dyck at all. Seems he was a narcissistic little fop who went mincing around London in fancy silk clothes. Still, I have to admit that Henrietta Maria is getting to me a little."

"Watch it, Hatcher."

"God's sake, Sheila. I mean the woman herself, not Van Dyck's fantasy. History says she was extremely short and quite plain, but tough and classy. In fact, if King Charles had had half as much spine as she did he probably wouldn't have got his head lopped off."

"Tell me about her."

"Well, let's see. She was very Latin, for one thing."

"You mean, like Micheline? Hot-blooded, proud, that sort of thing?"

"Very. Quick-tempered, passionate, willful. She was fiifteen when she became Queen of England. She came across the Channel to be greeted by all kinds of fanfare and hoopla, took one look at England, and decided she hated it."

"Poor Charley."

"True. She didn't like him much, either."

"What happened?"

"Well, apparently she refused to learn English, wouldn't associate with anyone but her French retinue, and treated her husband with obvious contempt."

162

"Sounds like de Gaulle in London during the war. Then what happened?"

"There was a big row, and Charles finally decided he'd had enough. So he threw all of her French attendants out of England. Strangely enough, that seemed to help. Henrietta apparently resigned herself to the job of being Queen of England, and even fell in love with Charles. From the time she was about eighteen until he was executed they were inseparable, and she was devastated by his death."

"That's a nice story. Now tell me about Van Dyck and the portraits."

"Okay. Van Dyck came to England for the second time, as court portraitist, in 1632. As usual, he was pissing in Rubens's footsteps: Rubens had been knighted by Charles in 1630. Anyway, the royal portraits begin in 1632 and continue until the artist's death in 1641. If we throw in the double portraits and school pieces, there are approximately twelve versions of Henrietta Maria that I can trace. Quite likely there are even more, since they would have been sent all over Europe as gifts. Many so-called Van Dyck portraits of the English period are in fact shop work, but a royal commission would be more likely to be autograph."

"Where are they now?"

"Most of them, of course, are in England. But there is one in Washington, and others in Vienna, Florence, Dresden, and Munich."

"How about size? Aren't most of them life-size, or over?"

"Many of them, but not all. This brings me to the best part of my whole, elaborate theory, by the way, but first I need another cup of coffee."

"What a tease. Why don't I make some for both of us? Espresso?"

"Espresso, fine."

While Sheila prepared the coffee, Hatcher picked up the books and stacked them against the wall. The relationship that had been forming between them was a curious alternation between violent passion and a sort of relaxed domesticity. Nothing between them was determined or defined. Sometimes they would meet in the afternoon, sometimes not; sometimes dine together, sometimes not; sometimes sleep together, sometimes not. Since both their lives were being shaped by intense outside pressures, they had tacitly agreed to maintain the arbitrary, casual tempo with which their affair had begun. They came to view their times together as a sort of temporary haven, and instinctively made no claims or conditions either on it or each other. For both of them it was like a beautiful found object.

Sheila put the tray on the table and sat down.

"Here's the coffee. Let's have the theory."

"The long form or the short form?"

"The long form. That's good espresso."

"I suppose I should start by mentioning something about the English. The English, especially the upper classes and royalty, have always been artistically illiterate. There are exceptions like Ruskin and Clark, but for the most part the British are functionally blind when it comes to art. Charles the First was one of the major exceptions. He commissioned Rubens and Van Dyck, brought Orazio Gentileschi over from Italy, and bought masterpieces by great baroque painters like Reni, Caravaggio, and even Rembrandt."

"Is that why he was executed?"

Hatcher grinned. "Part of the reason, doubtless. Anyway, having commissioned works by one of the two most famous artists in Europe—Rubens—he decided he wanted one by the second, Bernini. In 1636 he ordered Bernini to do a portrait bust of him in marble. Bernini refused to come to England. I suppose by that time kings and queens came to him, not vice versa. So Van Dyck was commissioned to paint a portrait to send to Bernini in Italy. This was the famous *Charles I in Three Positions,* a triple portrait with Charles shown full-face, left profile, and right profile. Van Dyck was particularly sensitive about his reputation in Rome, so he pulled out all the stops here. The triple portrait is one of his finest works."

"I know the painting. I remember that Charles looks rather sad. All three of him."

"Melancholy was supposed to reflect a noble and sensitive soul. It was The Look. Of course, everyone reads the expression as one of tragic premonition."

"Did Bernini ever complete the sculpture?"

"He did indeed, and it was a huge success. The Queen was delighted with the bust of Charles. So delighted, in fact, that she demanded a companion bust of herself. But instead of a triple portrait, Van Dyck—or the Queen—decided to have three individual portraits done instead."

"Aha! And only two of them are known."

"Precisely. Two of them are now in the Royal Collection, the frontal view and the study of Henrietta's left profile. That leaves the right profile portrait unaccounted for."

"You think the stolen painting might be the lost profile portrait?"

Hatcher could feel Sheila stiffen and come alert.

"That *was* my theory until sometime this afternoon, anyway. If you promise not to chuck me out in the cold, I'll tell you the rest of my ideas. They're not nearly as enjoyable as what I've been telling you so far."

"Is there something wrong, some flaw?"

"Several flaws. Too many flaws. First, the inscription. Why just 'Henriette'—why not 'Henriette Marie' or, more likely, 'Henriette Marie, Reine d'Angleterre'?"

"But after the civil war, she wouldn't have been Queen."

"I thought of that. But if the British took away her crown, the French certainly would have emphasized it, and that's a French inscription. There are bigger problems. One that you already noticed: the size. The portraits Van Dyck did for Bernini were small, but not nearly that small."

"The size did bother me, but then I thought of the oil sketches of Rubens. They're often that small or smaller, and all the ones I've seen are on wood."

"Wood. That's another problem. I'm sure we're looking for a wooden panel, and Van Dyck seems to have given up painting on the damn stuff after coming to England. At least he stops using it for portraits. Then there's the problem of the frame itself. It would be dandy for a Dutch or Flemish burgher, but not for the Queen of England. I can explain all these discrepancies, rationalize everything, but I am fairly well convinced that the whole theory is simply a mirage."

"Poor Amos. What now?"

"Back to the books. The 'Henriette' could refer to the sitter, or a collector, anything. I still haven't checked out the seal. But there's something that's bothering me even more. More than the identification of the picture, more than everything else. This is the second crime in a row I've had to deal with that made absolutely no sense to me. And that's what's driving me crazy."

"Come out to the kitchen and tell me about it while I make up some more coffee."

"I won't bore you?"

Sheila laughed. "You really *are* crazy. Of course you won't bore me."

"Well, then. Art crimes—art thefts—generally follow more or less rigid patterns. The motive is almost invariably money, and the trick to catching the thief usually lies in anticipating where he'll go to fence the goods. Here the possibilities are fairly limited, and I'm generally successful simply because I understand the patterns of disposal. The first question, who did it, should automatically be linked to the second, what's going to happen to the art now? What's the next move? That's what I don't understand about this."

"I don't follow you."

"All right. Murder is the rarest sort of art-related crime, and it is almost always the result of the thief's being surprised in the middle of a job and panicking. Murder is counterproductive for several reasons. One, it destroys the option of holding the art for ransom. Two, it makes the work virtually impossible to fence if it is known at all. Three, it eliminates the statute of limitations from consideration. Four, valuable art objects are simply not that difficult to steal, so murder is not only dangerous but unnecessary. A work of art obtained through murder is devalued, perhaps even worthless, and if money isn't the motive here, then what is? That's the question that has both O'Rourke and me up a wall."

"You said there was another case bothering you."

"Yes. This involves a Greek pot stolen from an Italian excavation. Now, the problem here is the importance of the work. It's not just a pot, but a pot decorated by Exekias, the greatest Greek vase painter. It's *too* good, in a way; no reputable dealer would touch it. Do you remember reading about the recent break-in at the Pitti Palace? What did they steal, Titians and Raphaels and Botticellis? Hell, no. They were professionals. They stole paintings they thought they could move, works by minor northern artists like Cornelis van Poelenburgh and Pieter de Molyn that Italians wouldn't care about and probably couldn't identify. That's the problem with the Exekias. Anyone who knows anything about the field will immediately recognize its importance. It's so hot that fifty years in a bank vault wouldn't begin to cool it off. So I'm facing the same question: what's going to happen to it now?"

"What's the connection between the cases?"

"Absolutely nothing. Superstition. I have the feeling that if I were bright enough to figure out one of them, I'd be bright enough to figure out the other. That's all. Two art thefts without any simple, plausible motive."

"You're tired. Maybe you should go to bed."

"Maybe I should. Like a back rub?"

"If you've got one just like the last one."

"Sure. Don't forget the Bunker Hill Monument."

22

THE COUNT-DUKE Amos de Hatcher surveyed his gallery. It had just been completed for him by François Mansart, and the Count-Duke was pleased. It formed a long wing attached to the back of his château, and the towering walls of the Grand Gallery where the Count-Duke now stood were hung, top to bottom in the baroque manner, with masterpieces. The ceiling of the gallery was a long barrel vault of glass supported by a cast-iron frame. On the whole, the Count-Duke felt it was M. Eiffel's masterpiece, much nicer than that vulgar tower.

Aha! He would have a party to celebrate his new gallery. He would invite everybody: Mansart, Eiffel, Titian—whose magnificent equestrian portrait of the Count-Duke had just been unveiled—and King Charles and Queen Henrietta Maria and, of course, Louis XIV and Van Dyck and Bernini and . . .

Just then he felt a series of tremors. My God, the foundations . . . the tremors grew in intensity—

"Amos!"

Hatcher raised an eyelid, painfully, and became vaguely aware that Sheila was shaking him by the shoulder.

"Amos, wake up. I want to talk to you."

"Mpf . . ."

"I have an idea. I want to tell you something."

"Stop! I'm awake. What time is it?"

"I don't know. I think about six."

"Six! Sheila, that's unnatural. No normal people have ideas at six o'clock in the morning. What 'idea'?"

"Nope. First some coffee. I want you awake. By chance, there's a fresh cup waiting for you on the table."

"Lucky me. Oh, what a diabolical trick. You want me, I take it, to actually get up. At six."

"Right. Six in the morning. Up, bright eyes."

"Bright eyes nothing. They're both alizarin crimson, and you know it. Ooooh, I thought you were my friend."

By the time he finished the cup of coffee, Sheila was pleased to discover Hatcher looking more or less awake. Color was beginning to return to his cheeks, and his neck appeared capable of supporting his head all by itself. He certainly seemed to be a night person, as he had claimed. Sheila was a morning person. She took one more look at Hatcher, and decided to chance it.

"I was thinking about France, and French chauvinism, and what the French do to artists' names. They call Guido Reni 'Guide,' Primaticcio becomes 'Le Primatice,' and so on. With Dutch and Flemish artists, though, they frequently change the whole name to its French equivalent. Jacob de Gheyn becomes 'Jacques de Gheyn,' and Ambrosius Boschaert becomes 'Ambroise Dubois.' So, what's the *Dutch* form of 'Henri'?"

"I don't know. Hendrick, I suppose."

"Exactly. Hendrick. So the equivalent for 'Henriette' in Holland would be—"

"My God. Hendrickje! Hendrickje Stoffels."

"Precisely. Hendrickje Stoffels, Rembrandt's second wife."

"Good Lord! Henriette, Hendrickje. It would have to be, wouldn't it? And Hendrickje is just Hendrickje, the way Saskia is just Saskia. And the frame—the frame's perfect. It's just got to be right, it fits. Everything. Sheila, you doll, you great luscious sexy genius. Give me a kiss; I forgive you all."

"Very kind. What are you doing, by the way?"

Amos, who already had on his shirt, was hopping up and down, trying to find his left pantleg with his foot.

"Got to get over to the Fogg Library and check it out."

"At six in the morning?"

"Oh. I forgot. What time do you think it opens?"

"Eight-thirty, nine, probably. If I make us some breakfast, do you suppose you could remain stationary long enough to eat it? Stop pacing, Amos, you're making me exhausted."

"Pacing's good for you. Helps the circulation. Some people jog, I pace. Hendrickje, Hendrickje, Hendrickje, why didn't I think of you, you big beautiful momma?"

"Honestly, Amos, do you know what time it is?"

"My line. You don't happen to have the new Bredius catalogue, do you? Or the Rosenberg?"

"It's not there. I checked."

"That doesn't make any difference. I wouldn't expect it. Oh, Hendrickje, Hendrickje, my love."

"Fickle. Last night, your heart belonged to Henrietta Maria."

After breakfast, Sheila went back to bed. Hatcher was still wound up, so he decided to take a walk. He put on a scarf and cap he had bought the day before in Harvard Square and stepped out into a windy, snowy day.

He felt marvelous, invigorated rather than depressed

171

by the winter weather. He decided to walk along the banks of the Charles. After five minutes or so, he spied a small flotilla of ducks banded together in the lee of a dock. He took a piece of bread he had purloined from Sheila's apartment out of his pocket, tore off a couple of pieces, and tossed them to the ducks. One of them opened its eyes, looked at Hatcher noncommittally for a moment, then turned its head around, rested it in the furrow between its folded wings, and went back to sleep.

Just like Sheila, thought Hatcher.

When the doors of the Fogg opened at eight-thirty, Hatcher was standing impatiently on the steps. There was another wait for the library to open, which Hatcher spent nervously stalking up and down a corridor lined with minimalist pictures of the sixties. He fervently prayed that no one was giving a Rembrandt seminar that semester.

Apparently no one was, because when Hatcher finally got to the Dutch art section of the stacks the collection of Rembrandt material was virtually intact. He found a nearby table and began to carry armloads of books over to it. He hoped no librarian was watching him. After ten minutes the table looked like a medieval fortress, with turrets and towers of books lined up like a defensive wall. Then he set to work.

As he had expected, the search was not easy. He decided that the best pattern would be to work backward chronologically, starting with the most recent publications. Then when he had exhausted the monographs, he would begin working on the periodicals. He dreaded the periodicals.

It took him five hours to find what he was looking for. It was a medium-sized book of grainy black-and-white plates published in Stuttgart and Berlin in 1921: *Rembrandt—Verschollene Gemälde,* Rembrandt's Lost Paintings.

The plate he was searching for was not in the main body of the book, but in one of the appendices. And it was not a photograph of a painting, but of a print, an early nineteenth-century mezzotint. *Hendrickje Standing in a Doorway*, formerly in a private collection in Schwandorf. Hatcher wondered where Schwandorf was. The comment in the text simply noted that the painting had been lost since the end of the nineteenth century. The author of the book declined, on the basis of the mezzotint, to make any judgments concerning the authenticity of the work, but remarked that the composition seemed "derived from the famous Berlin portrait (cf. Bode, 1907, pl. 437)."

It was a small notation at the bottom of the plate that made Hatcher's heart pound. It read *Auf Holz, H. 30, 4; B. 28, 7.* The painting was on a wooden panel. The metrical dimensions, given in height and width, exactly corresponded to the interior dimensions of the empty frame sitting on the bed at the Holiday Inn.

Hatcher went up to the lobby of the Fogg Museum, where he made several telephone calls. The first was to Sheila, who was at Micheline's gallery, the second was to O'Rourke, and the third was to Sabin. They were all very brief. Hatcher considered making a fourth call, and decided to wait on it. Then he returned to the stacks.

He spent the rest of the afternoon in research, but he never found another reference to the picture. The last place he checked, the huge old nineteenth-century portfolios of engravings, left his hands black with dirt and his clothes covered with tiny flakes of crumbled leather. Before he gave up, he did one last thing. He looked through the recent monographs for the best reproduction he could find of the Berlin *Hendrickje*, and when he found it, he compared it with the little mezzotint.

This was an exercise in frustration. Some reproductive engravers of the nineteenth century were virtuosi, and their prints were absolutely faithful transcriptions of the original works. Unfortunately, the mezzotint was the work of a hack. Rembrandt's painting, if it was a Rembrandt, was overlaid, in the engraved version, by the sort of smarmy sentimentality that disfigured so much nineteenth-century academic painting. The printmaker's version of Hendrickje made her impossibly lithe and girlish, and showed her looking out at the viewer with a coquettish smile. Hatcher cursed the shade of the anonymous engraver.

He took the book upstairs and made a photocopy of the mezzotint before returning it, along with the rest of the books, to its place on the shelves. It was still snowing when he left the Fogg. He was famished by this time, so he looked around for the nearest quick, cheap restaurant.

He still felt marvelous.

23

HATCHER QUICKLY BOLTED a cheeseburger, a glass of milk, and a cup of coffee and left, glad to trade the neon glare and bustle of the restaurant for the icy weather outside. The faces on the street appeared purposeful and determined. They were largely those of students and teachers, and most of them looked ferociously intelligent and rather grim. Hatcher, feeling playful and frisky, had to restrain himself from tossing snowballs at signs, throwing himself down in the snow and "making an angel," or doing something else equally juvenile and idiotic. He was suddenly glad to be free of the cloistered, academic world where everyone felt such desperate pressure to be thought bright.

The snow had tapered off, and was now drifting down slowly, drowsily through the dark winter sky like tiny flecks of mica, making everything below sparkle and glint and flicker. Hatcher thought suddenly of Christmas, and skiing in the mountains, and Sheila. It took a mighty effort of will to remind himself that he was on a chase, and that his quarry had stolen a valuable work of art and brutally murdered two people in the process.

When he arrived back at his room he immediately called Sheila.

Sheila sounded sniffly when she answered the phone.

"What's wrong?"

"It's Sam again. Crazy Sam. You know what he did?"

"Tell me."

"He—" Here she broke off, her voice trailing away.

"Sheila?"

"Okay, sorry. I got a call from the lawyers today. He left me—my God, I never knew—anyway, all this money. Almost sixty-five thousand dollars. I can do anything now. Stay, go back to school. Do you know what that means? And the Weinstock Gallery is Miche's, with the proviso that she keep me on if I want. Of course, she would anyway. Sam was so disorganized, I was amazed he even wrote a will."

"That's marvelous. It means you're free, at least for a while. I guess you and Miche were his family, really."

"I suppose. God, I miss him, though. Where are you, Amos? Do you have a copy of the mezzotint?"

"A photocopy. It's mediocre, but so is the print. It doesn't look like much, I want to warn you now, but it's what I was hoping for. Dear, I have some calls to make here. Do you suppose we could meet at the Trattoria Toscana, say about eight-thirty?"

"Fine. Mediocre or not, I'm wild to see that print."

"You should be; it's really your discovery. And, by the way, could you make the reservation?"

"What're you up to?"

"I'll tell you when I see you. Don't worry if I'm a little late."

The first two calls were to Logan Airport and to O'Rourke. Hatcher couldn't reach O'Rourke, but got Callahan instead and gave him elaborate instructions to

176

pass on to his partner. Hatcher could sense Callahan's curiosity and the effort it cost him to conceal it. Torn between his desire for an explanation and his unwillingness to give Hatcher any sort of satisfaction, he let pride finally win out, and he pretended over the phone that he either knew exactly what Hatcher was doing, or didn't care in the slightest.

The third call took much longer to complete, since it was transatlantic. It was finally put through, however, and Hatcher was pleased to find that the voice on the other end, with its slight trace of an accent, was still as strong as he remembered it, even over the cable.

It was three quarters of an hour later when Hatcher arrived at the restaurant carrying a pad of paper. Sheila was sitting at a corner table, softly illuminated from the light of a candle stuck in a Chianti bottle. She looked fresh and happy and very pretty to Hatcher, who leaned over and kissed her.

"Good Lord, Sheila, if that's what you look like by candlelight, you must be positively lethal under a full moon."

"I am. I grow fangs and bay at it. Here, show me the picture."

Hatcher sat down, opened up the pad, and slid out the photocopy. Sheila looked at it for a moment, then made a face.

"I know, it's pretty bad. Most nineteenth-century graphic reproductions are. Ever seen any of the prints of Raphael's Madonnas, with their sappy smiles and big, soulful, cowlike eyes? It'll probably take Raphael's reputation another fifty years to recover from them. I found a nineteenth-century print after the *Night Watch* today that looked exactly like a production number from a Gilbert and Sullivan operetta, only funnier. This doesn't tell us what the painting looks like, only that it exists."

"If the painting resembles the print, then we'd better go back to Henrietta Maria."

"It won't."

They had another grand Italian meal with *fettuccine Alfredo, bistecca alla fiorentina*, salad, wine, and an almost indecently rich, liquor-soaked cake with chocolate and candied fruits called *zuccotta*. During the meal Hatcher told Sheila a number of stories about cases he had worked on at one time or another, some hilarious and some hair-raising. Finally barely able to move, they tottered back to Sheila's apartment.

They were midway through a second cup of espresso when Hatcher got around to the question.

"Sheila, do you suppose I could talk you into taking a little trip with me?"

"I thought you were supposed to be solving a crime."

"I am. This is part of it."

"Where?"

"Amsterdam."

"Amsterdam, *Holland?*"

"I think that's the only one, unless they've given Manhattan back to the Dutch."

"Well, I don't know . . . I mean, when?"

"Tomorrow. Flight seven ninety-three, scheduled to depart Logan at twelve-fifty-five. I've already got the tickets, by the way, so you don't have to worry about that. I assume you've got a passport."

"I do, but my God—are you being serious?"

"Of course. There's a man named Bauer who works at the Hague who ought to see the frame and the print. Also there is a man I have to see about the Greek pot."

"Franz Bauer? I thought he was dead."

"Far from it. He's an old man, and not well, but he still works ten hours a day at the Rijksbureau and he'll be expecting us on Monday. I considered some other things, the Witt photo archives in London, for example, but I think Bauer is the best bet. He's been working on

178

Rembrandt for forty years, and if anyone can tell us anything about that print, he's the man. Oh, and by the way, I've cleared it with the IAAD. You are officially a consultant on the case, so your trip will be paid, as well as a flat per diem rate of fifty dollars. I tried to squeeze them for more, but couldn't. We'll have Sunday free but otherwise it won't be any vacation, I'm afraid. There's a lot of running around to be done. Have you been to Holland, by the way?"

"No, but just a minute—"

"You haven't? Really? Terrific, you'll love it. You won't get any tulip fields this time of year, but you won't get all the tourists, either. I'd pack some warm clothes if I were you."

"Just one small second, you silver-tongued devil. How long is this little junket figuring to take? I don't think I ought to just walk out . . ."

"I spoke to Micheline about it. She likes the idea. There isn't much for you to do here, at least for the moment, and I think she's realizing that she has to be alone with it sooner or later. It might as well be sooner. Also, I don't think we'll be gone all that long: a minimum of five days, a maximum of ten. I realize I haven't given you any notice on this, but I have the feeling that time is becoming an important factor."

"Have you spoken to O'Rourke?"

"Yes. He agrees. I doubt if another murder is likely, but it's a possibility."

"All right, then. Anything. I'd do anything at all to help get that bastard."

"Good. I'd better get back to the Holiday Inn. There are some other things to do. Why don't I come by for you at ten, and we can take a cab to Logan."

"Okay. Good night, Lover, and thanks for the gorgeous meal."

"Good night, Gorgeous, and thanks for the lovely company. See you tomorrow."

24

TWO DAYS LATER, Hatcher awoke to find Sheila in front of the window overlooking a canal in Amsterdam. She was standing very still and was smiling softly. Hatcher wished he had a camera.

"We must be in the right place. If you had a pearl earring you'd be a perfect Vermeer."

"Good morning, dear. Oh, I love this town. Are there many ducks on the canals?"

"Millions of them. Swans, too."

"I was just remembering the telegram Robert Benchley sent to Dorothy Parker from Venice: 'Streets full of water. Please advise.' What's the name of our canal?"

"The Leidsegracht. *Gracht* means canal. Don't worry about pronouncing it correctly; nobody can except the Dutch. It's one of those little, everyday words like the French *rue* that marks you as a foreigner as soon as you say it."

"Can you speak Dutch?"

"A little. Badly. I speak several languages, all of them badly, but my Dutch is perhaps the worst. It doesn't make much difference, really, since the Dutch usually speak perfect English."

"Come here and look. Isn't it beautiful?"

Hatcher threw on his bathrobe and went over by the window. It was the first real view they had had of the city. The flight had been delayed as well as bumpy, so they were both comatose when they fell into bed shortly after midnight the night before.

The view from the window was indeed beautiful. The canal held only a few small barges laden with produce, and veils of mist, like steam, were rising off the surface of the water. The sky was overcast, and the brick facades on the other side of the canal were a dark russet color set off against the gray stone and gleaming white of the doorways and windows.

"I love the gables. Every house has a slightly different kind, doesn't it?"

"There are just a few basic types: neck gable, step gable, and so on, but you're right, there are endless variations. Since all the houses are approximately the same size and material, the gable is the only place to express individuality. Most of the houses across there are seventeenth-century, by the way, but there are a few that are earlier. There are plenty of places in Holland where you can still feel like you're stepping straight into a baroque painting. The town square of Haarlem, most of Delft, bits and pieces of Amsterdam. Later I'll take you to the Rembrandt House. It's original except for the upper stories. Almost next door there is a view down the canal towards the Montelbaans Tower, which is still exactly the way Rembrandt drew it three hundred years ago. Even the red-light district, the *Rosse Buurt*, hasn't changed much in the last three centuries."

"The funny part is that it doesn't feel like an old city.

It's nothing like Florence or Venice, where you feel like you're walking around in a museum."

"The Dutch have a genius for adaptation. People come, people go, Amsterdam remains. The Spaniards were here in the sixteenth century, the Germans were here in the forties, now it's hippies and junkies and porno parlors, and in ten years it will be something else. Who knows, probably Arabs. The Amsterdammers will figure out how to make a neat profit from all of them; then, when there's no more profit to be made, ease them out. No problem. Amsterdam is called 'the Venice of the North,' which is ridiculous, because except for the canals the two cities are diametric opposites. Venice is essentially a dying Renaissance city. Amsterdam has managed to become a modern city without destroying its past. And it's thriving. Nothing works in Venice; everything works in Amsterdam."

"So show me. But first, feed me."

After a huge breakfast of boiled eggs, rolls, cheese, and thinly sliced ham washed down with coffee, the two set off for the Rijksmuseum. When they reached the point at the end of the gravel walk where the great museum loomed before them in all its majesty, Sheila was overcome with admiration and wonderment.

"My God, it's Harvard's Memorial Hall to the tenth power. I've never seen such a grandiose example of architectural bad taste in my life."

"Isn't it marvelous? The Dutch are very proud of it. The architect, a certain Cuypers, also designed the central train station in exactly the same style, with the result that the station looks like a museum, while the museum looks more or less like a train station. You'll forgive them, though, when you see what's inside."

When they arrived at the *Night Watch*, it was walled off behind large sheets of transparent Lucite.

"Are they worried that some other maniac will slash it again?"

"Perhaps, but that's not the reason it's sealed off. When it was repaired and the full restoration completed, it was varnished with a new synthetic resin that can develop a milky bloom from swirling air currents while it's wet, so they had to seal it off hermetically. When the varnish is dry, they'll take down the partitions."

Hatcher enjoyed watching Sheila scrutinizing the painting.

"Something's wrong with the composition. I think the little girl in blue is marvelous, and there are some incredible passages, but I much prefer *The Jewish Bride*. There's something show-offy here, as if he was trying to prove he could out-Hals Hals. I like the van der Helst militia piece better. Isn't that wicked?"

"Very wicked. Everyone knows the *Night Watch* is Rembrandt's masterpiece."

"My other dirty secret is that I don't like the *Anatomy Lesson* much either. Or the *Syndics of the Cloth Guild*. But the late portraits of Titus and Hendrickje have me in tears. Maybe it's just group portraits; they look so much like fraternity composites. The class of fifty-seven always looks like the class of fifty-seven, even when it's the class of 1657 and painted by Rembrandt."

Hatcher discovered, during the next few hours, that a trip to a museum with Sheila was both delightful and enlightening. Although he had spent a great deal more time studying Dutch art than she had, her perceptions were always acute and frequently witty as well as original. She announced at one point that she thought Dirck Hals was greatly underrated simply because he was Frans's kid brother, and would have been much more famous if his last name had been Smith. She spent fifteen minutes studying two almost identical cityscapes, one by Jan van der Heyden and the other by Job Berckheyde, and then proclaimed that in her opinion van der Heyden was a "magician" and Berckheyde was a "bum." Some artists she thought overrated: de Hooch and Maes; while others such as Hobbema and Metsu seemed to her distinctly better than their reputations. She was quite voluble as well as being an attentive listener. The only times she was rendered speechless were in front of some of the late Rembrandts and Vermeer's *Woman in Blue*, which held her silent and hypnotized for a long time.

The rest of the afternoon was spent on an elaborate walking tour of Amsterdam. Sheila proved to be an indefatigable sightseer, which was lucky since Hatcher turned out to be a merciless tour guide. They saw the stately classical facades along the Prinsengracht, visited the Rembrandt House and the Six Collection and the old Amsterdam Town Hall, now the Royal Palace, saw the Old Church (begun 1306) and the New Church (begun 1414) and the tiny, jewellike little courtyard of the Begijnhof. Finally they wended their way along the canal called the Oudezijds Voorburgwal ("This district is of bad repute," states the guide book; "Live Sex Show, Real Focky-Focky" state the endless signs) and came to a tiny restaurant called the Hong Do, where they rewarded themselves with a twenty-course Indonesian *rijsttafel* that included food of every conceivable color, flavor, and texture.

An hour later, at the hotel, Sheila found Hatcher staring at heavily creased and worn scraps of paper which appeared to be simply lists of names. When he realized Sheila was watching him, he folded them up and replaced them in his wallet, then swung round in his chair to face her.

"I'm afraid tomorrow we have to get to work. I'd better get up early. I want to catch the first available flight out of Schiphol. I'll call you from Zurich. Can you take care of the errand at the Hague? I'll give you a letter for Bauer."

185

"Of course. How long will you be gone?"

"I hope just a couple of days. A week, at the most. I may just be chasing shadows, but I have a feeling that if I can find the man I'm looking for things will begin to fall into place."

"Want to tell me?"

"It's nothing yet, really, just a hunch. Maybe it's just a coincidence; two crimes, two thefts, and neither one of them makes any sense. Until you put them together. Then, maybe they begin to. Or maybe they just seem to, like the business with Henrietta Maria."

25

IT WAS IN MID-AFTERNOON the following day when Sheila, armed with the frame and photocopy, found her way to the office of Franz Bauer in the Bureau for Art Historical Studies in the Hague. Somewhat timidly she knocked at the door.

The figure that opened the door was nothing like her expectations. Partly from the volume of his scholarship, partly from the vigorous, occasionally acerbic qualities of his writing style she had imagined a tall, powerful person with a brusque manner. Bauer was, in fact, rather small and physically frail. He seemed genuinely glad to be interrupted at his labors.

"Miss Woods? I am so pleased to meet you. Please come in. Amos told me you had some things to show me. Here, let me take your parcel."

The office was small but high-ceilinged, and resembled an antiquarian bookstore. Volumes lay everywhere, and shelves of books ran floor to ceiling on three walls, interrupted only by a large oak filing cabinet that looked thirty or forty years old.

"You will perhaps join me in a small glass of sherry? I'm afraid that it is one of the few pleasures my doctor still allows me. In fact, he insists on it."

Looking around the office, noticing the stacks of papers, scholarly journals, folders, notes, letters, and the general blizzard of paper, Sheila smiled. Sam Weinstock would have approved of Dr. Bauer's office.

"I must apologize for the chaotic state of things. You see, I am trying to finish my Rembrandt researches. I find I have enough energy now to take the books down from the shelves, but never enough to put them back."

Sheila laughed.

"I'm afraid my apartment suffers the same fate. I've always considered a mania for neatness a most suspicious characteristic in people. Maybe we are both rationalizing."

"Well, we are certainly not Dutch. They are the neatest people in the world. Except, perhaps, the Swiss."

Bauer handed Sheila a tiny glass of cut crystal (the "small glass of sherry" had not been a euphemism) and filled it from a decanter. He gestured to a chair beside the desk and held it for her, and then brought her package over and set it down on the table.

"Would you care to show me what you have brought now?"

Sheila extracted the pad of paper from the bag and slid the copy of the print out from where Hatcher had secreted it. Bauer looked at it for a moment, and then smiled.

"I believe I can help you."

He got up from his chair and went over to the oak cabinet; when he returned a minute later, he was carrying an envelope. Sitting down at his desk, he pulled a photograph from the envelope and set it down next to the photocopy. Sheila gasped.

"*Voilà!* There, I think, is your painting."

"Good Lord. It's so similar, yet so different. Then you know about the panel?"

"Unfortunately, I know no more about it than the photograph you see in front of you. And, of course, the terrible mezzotint of it which you have also discovered."

"Where was it? Where did you get this photograph?"

"The photograph, to the best of my knowledge, is unique, and I have never seen, nor have I met anyone who has seen, the original work. The photograph I found loose, stuck in a copy of the 1928 version of *Rembrandts Gemälde* from the library of Klaus Hassler which I acquired just after his death in 1947."

Bauer turned over the photograph.

"As you see, there is no indication where the painting was when Hassler saw it, or if he saw it, or even where he obtained the photograph. Just the three words scribbled here: *vielleicht echt—Krofta*. Have you heard of Milan Krofta, by the way?"

"I'm afraid not."

"Well. Krofta was a brilliant young scholar at the University of Prague. Like so many others, he did not survive the war. The bomb which took his life also eliminated years of research. So. Krofta was brilliant, as I say, but very conservative. He would never comment on a picture unless he had seen it, and would never accept an attribution unless he was certain of it beyond the smallest shadow of doubt. The words *vielleicht echt*—'perhaps genuine'—are as close as Krofta would come to endorsing a picture other than with absolute certainty.

"As you may imagine, I was excited by the discovery of the photograph and tried to track the picture down myself with no success. Bode and Valentiner both mention it in footnotes, and both dismiss it out of hand. Whether either one of them ever saw the original or not I do not know.

"Now, there are good reasons to doubt the authenticity of the picture. If you would excuse me for a moment . . ."

Bauer went to his cabinet again, and returned with a black-and-white photograph of the portrait of Hendrickje in Berlin.

"So. You see, they are quite similar. It would be easy to assume that the picture in the photograph was a copy. But this is not so. They are close, but different. The pose, the mood, they are not the same. Now it is an axiom that Rembrandt did not paint replicas of his own work, and that he never made a preliminary oil sketch for a painting. But, as I say, I do not feel it is either a replica or an oil sketch."

"Do you think it is by Rembrandt?"

"That is difficult. In the old days, a connoisseur like myself was treated like a magician or a witch doctor who had only to wave a wand over a painting and its author's name would miraculously appear. Now, I think the days of the magic wand are over, although many of my colleagues still pretend they have one. I have a feeling. But I must tell you that it is a feeling only. Let me show you one more work."

The third time Bauer returned from the cabinet, he brought with him a photograph of another portrait of Hendrickje.

"You see, the Metropolitan picture of 1660 is unfinished. Already Hendrickje is sick. She is dying. I imagine that Rembrandt could not bring himself to complete it. One can feel the tragedy, the sense of mortality. These are the things I can't escape in the photograph of the panel. My opinion is that the lost panel should be dated close to 1660 with the Metropolitan picture, not 1658 with the Berlin picture."

"Why would Rembrandt repeat the pose of the Berlin picture, then?"

"My answer to that is entirely hypothetical. You see,

he knew she was dying. He'd watched Saskia die, and his children. He was no stranger to death. Yet he wanted to deny it, to evade it, to recapture Hendrickje as she had been two years before: vital, sensual, radiant. But if you look at the ravaged form in the lost panel you can see, I think, that death is just beyond the threshold. In the end, it seems, he could not bring himself to avoid the truth."

He stopped speaking. With his eyes half-closed, he traced the outline of Hendrickje's face on the photograph before him with his index finger.

"Yes, I believe this painting is by Rembrandt."

26

"IT IS MY TURN to be astonished. The frame you discovered is certainly the same one that is shown in the photograph."

Bauer laid the frame on the desk carefully next to the photograph and bent forward to examine it.

"I think we can do a little better than 'Holland or Flanders, seventeenth century.' This frame was, I believe, made in Amsterdam about the middle of the century, certainly not much before 1640, nor much after 1660."

He turned it over.

"The treatment of the corners—this is curious. This zigging and zagging. 'Herringbone' I think is the word, is it not? This is interesting. I have seen it before, on Rembrandt paintings of that period. If you will excuse me for another moment, I should like to find something else."

When he returned this time he held two photographs. One was a portrait of a man in a lace collar and wide-brimmed hat. The face in the portrait was similar to

Rembrandt's own, though distinctly more handsome. The sitter appeared intelligent and acute, yet kindly, and had responded to the artist's scrutiny with a warm smile of friendship. It was clearly signed and dated in the lower right-hand corner: *Rembrandt, 1640*. The second photograph was of a drawing of a landscape. Strong washes and a delicate, wiry network of lines described a vast landscape vista under a stormy sky. In the foreground, a single figure was shown plodding wearily along.

"The man in the portrait is Herman Doomer. Doomer was a famous and successful cabinetmaker and framemaker in Amsterdam. The drawing is by his son, Lambert Doomer, who was apparently a student of Rembrandt's some time after 1640. He was a marvelous draftsman, as you can see, but he appears to have done very few paintings, and the ones we have are far less interesting than the drawings. We can detect from the drawings that Lambert Doomer traveled widely, but unfortunately we know very little else about his life. I have the idea, you see, that he continued his father's career, that he was likewise a framemaker. Many of Rembrandt's frames have this herringbone pattern at the joint. It is my notion that this is the signature of the Doomer shop."

He paused, running his hands across the frame, feeling the wave-patterns on the front panels with his fingers.

"Like so much else, I'm afraid this must remain a conjecture. There are no records, no signatures. The Dutch in the Golden Age loved art, but only to look at, not to record in words. Even with Rembrandt, what do we have? Seven letters, a few legal records, a lot of hearsay and fairy tales."

Bauer closed his eyes and continued to stroke the wooden frame.

"I love these old frames, the look and touch of the

194

wood. Ebony was rare and prized in Holland then. The sailors brought it back from India and Ceylon. You see, even on a frame like this it is not solid, but only a thin veneer. The French, too, understood the beauty of this marvelous material. Even today a French cabinetmaker is called an *ébéniste*."

Bauer laid the frame back down and went over to a shelf beside the filing cabinet. There was a violin case lying there which he carried back to the desk. His movements were stiff and labored, and Sheila could sense that the interview was tiring him, yet she could not bring herself to try to break away. He opened the case, removed the violin, and handed it to her.

"This is surely my most valuable possession. It is by Nicolò Amati, the teacher of the great Stradivarius. When I was young, I played it all the time. I even considered at one time becoming a concert violinist. Luckily I had not the talent. Now, you see, my joints no longer allow me to play at all. Yet I look at the violin almost daily, and it is a continual joy to me as a work of art. The flame of the wood, the curve of the scroll, the carving of the pegs—these are things I barely noticed when I thought of the violin merely as an instrument of music. So, you see, old age has its compensations. The pleasures of life are smaller, perhaps, but they are no less intense. But I must be boring you."

"Please. Not in the least. I'm only sorry that Amos could not come with me."

"Ah, Amos. I taught the history of art in the United States for thirty years, and he was one of my finest students. Did he tell you that? I was saddened that he left the world of scholarship, but I suppose it is rather like the priesthood. One must have a sense of vocation. It must be a calling."

"He told me you were his favorite teacher, yes. But I'm not sure he has left the world of scholarship. Most of his work seems to take place in libraries."

195

"May I hope to see you both, then? Please tell Amos that if he can visit the Hague I will expect you both to come to my apartment for *Glühwein* and fondue. It will be like my old seminar parties."

"I'm sure he would love to, and I certainly would. Thank you; and thank you for your help."

"I was delighted to meet you. Tell Amos that I hope he finds the painting. To steal such a thing is a terrible crime, but to shed blood over it: that, I think, is quite obscene."

When Sheila left, Bauer's study was shrouded in shadow. The old man was seated at his desk, illuminated softly by the oblique rays of the late afternoon sun filtered through the Venetian blinds. Bauer's eyes were half-closed, and his expression had the bemused quality of one whose thoughts are solitary and wise, like the old Jewish scholars in Rembrandt's canvases.

27

AS THE BUS eased down the snow-covered roads leading from the airport to the Zurich *Hauptbahnhof*, Hatcher let his mind wander back and forth between Holland and Switzerland. He recalled Hemingway's characterization of the latter: "a small, steep country, much more up-and-down than sideways." Physically, the two countries could hardly have formed a sharper contrast. The flat expanse of the Dutch countryside was almost entirely "sideways." But the monotonous dunes and polders of Holland had inspired some of the greatest landscape painters in the world: van Goyen, Ruisdael, Cuyp, and Rembrandt, a few among many. Yet Switzerland, with the most dramatic topography in Europe, had inspired whom? A small number of foreigners such as Brueghel, Turner, and Caspar David Friedrich had drawn and painted the Alps with great drama and eloquence, but Hatcher found that he had a hard time recalling a single landscape painting by a Swiss artist before the Romantic period.

Wait. There was one, *The Miraculous Draught of*

Fishes, by the fifteenth-century painter Conrad Witz. Christ was depicted striding across the surface of Lake Geneva, the town of Geneva itself represented with microscopic fidelity in the background. Was this a stroke of genius, Hatcher wondered, or just a complete absence of imagination? Later, of course, there were great Swiss artists such as Holbein. In the twentieth century, Giacometti and Kleè and Hodler. Who else? Nobody much that Hatcher could think of.

Maybe the sheer spectacle of Switzerland made artists despair. Or maybe, as Harry Lime nastily implied in the movie *The Third Man*, the greatest product of the Swiss creative imagination over centuries of time really was the cuckoo clock.

As Hatcher began to catch glimpses of the spires of the Grossmünster and Fraumünster, he found himself wondering at the curious blandness of Swiss cities. Even the churches dating back to the twelfth century seemed to belong to the nineteenth century instead. There was a strange lack of historical resonance, of patina. Hatcher tried to imagine Huldreich Zwingli in the pulpit of the Grossmünster, dramatically crying out against the abuses in the Church, or, later, when the Reformer was cut down leading his troops at the battle of Kappel. Such a frenzy of passion seemed to Hatcher an anomaly in the peaceful, smug, cozy city spreading before him. This wasn't a city for dreamers or martyrs, but for anonymous, purposeful little men adding up neat columns of figures.

Zurich is one of the prettiest large cities in the world, at least on the surface. All the dirty little secrets of graft, theft, political swindles, and mass violence are kept tidily locked away in vaults below the spotless, picturesque exterior.

Because of his job, Hatcher knew Zurich well. It was one of the main clearing houses for smuggled goods, and Hatcher was all too well aware that the stolen art hidden away in the vaults could have furnished a medium-sized museum. Several times already Hatcher had followed the intricate movement of a stolen masterpiece only to be halted by the prim, curt replies of some Zurich gnome.

We do not disclose that information. We are not at liberty to ask. That question is illegal; please refer to the code of civil law, Zurich Canton, articles 423, 426 and 518. Please do not pursue your inquiries. Please leave. Bitte schön. Viel' Dank. Auf Wiedersehen.

From the Bahnhof Hatcher went immediately to a small hotel along the Limmat Quai. He always stayed there when he was in Zurich on a job, because it placed him close to the Kunsthaus, the Art Museum, and only a block away from the Zürichsee, where he would rent a boat and sail for hours on the huge lake.

As soon as he checked into the hotel, Hatcher placed a call to an old friend of his named Karl Seefeld. Seefeld, a reporter on the *Züricher Zeitung,* was known to his friends as *Karl der Rose*—"Pink Karl." This was both a pun on the teutonic form of Charlemagne's name, Karl der Grosse, and a reference to Seefeld's political views, which were to the left of everybody else's on the newspaper. Seefeld was very interested in exposing some of the gamier aspects of Zurich's financial manipulations, and naturally had many enemies. He had done a series of articles on stolen art in Switzerland for which Hatcher had provided much of the background material, and the two men had also collaborated in tracking down an art ring that specialized in phony Paul Klee watercolors.

"Karl Seefeld *hier.*"

"Karl, Amos Hatcher. *Wie geht's?*"

"*Ach, Amos, der Detektiv, der berühmte Bluthund.* How are you, my old friend? What brings the famous bloodhound to Zurich? No more Klees, I hope."

"No, thank God. I leave Klee to you. I'm trying to

find someone. An old acquaintance of yours, Sarkes Manoukian."

"Manoukian? The big fish, eh? *Das ist schwer*, Amos, very difficult. Manoukian, he keeps down the head. Two, three months, no one sees him. I tell you though his contact: Jakob Glauber, Glauber Galerie, Löwenstrasse. He knows. He knows, but I don't think he will tell."

"Is there any reason that you know of why Manoukian is keeping out of sight?"

"No, that is the problem. Something feels strange. Last week we have a big, big scandal. *Antiquitäten:* Greek, Etruscan, everything. They catch eight people, but Manoukian is not in Zurich, maybe not even in Switzerland. But Glauber knows."

"Okay. Thanks, Karl. If I can get anything out of Glauber I'll be in touch with you."

Hatcher dropped off his bag at the desk and walked down to the bus stop near the Münster Bridge. The temperature was several degrees below freezing, and the sharp wind was kicking up choppy waves on the river and lake. Hatcher had noticed in the newspaper that a cold winter was expected, and he wondered if the lake would freeze over. He had been there one furious winter in the early sixties when this had happened, transforming the Zürichsee into the world's most spectacular skating rink.

It was mid-afternoon when he got to the Glauber Galerie in the Löwenstrasse. It was a small gallery. The window was faced with an elegant wrought-iron grill, and the shelf behind it held only one work of art. This was a carved wooden statue of Saint Christopher. He carried the tiny Christ Child on his shoulders, and the cloak he wore billowed out to the side in a bewildering array of little hooks, tubes, and folds. Hatcher didn't know much about German late-Gothic sculpture, but the piece looked very fine to him.

On the other side of the shelf was a bronze plaque which read *Glauber Galerie—seit 1886* and carried a small armorial seal.

Hatcher considered simply walking in off the street, then decided against it. It would merely be a repetition of his fruitless interviews with Zurich bank officials. He decided, instead, to go to the Kunsthaus and consider the situation from different angles. Hatcher did most of his work in libraries, but most of his thinking in museums.

In a small, temporary room of Italian Renaissance paintings Hatcher found what he needed. It took him just a couple of minutes more to reconnoiter; then he left the museum and went straight back to his room in the hotel. When he got there he immediately placed a telephone call.

"Ja, Glauber Galerie."

"Herr Glauber?"

"Ein Moment, bitte."

When Glauber came to the phone, his voice sounded clipped and curt.

"Hier spricht Herr Glauber. Wer sind Sie, bitte?"

"Herr Glauber, I am a friend of Sarkes Manoukian. I have been unable to reach him on a rather important business matter. I've been told that you could tell me where to find him."

There was a moment's pause before Glauber replied.

"You will excuse me, please. I do not know any such person."

Which Hatcher had expected.

"Herr Glauber, I must congratulate you. I am placing this call from the Kunsthaus, and I have been admiring the superb Giovanni Bellini *Madonna* you so generously placed on loan. It is such a perfect example of early Bellini, and in such perfect condition, too. Does it not frighten you what might happen to it without a Plexiglas hood? I mean, after the tragedy of the

Night Watch? To think what some madman could do to your *Madonna* with just a small penknife, or even just an ordinary nail file . . ."

After another minute's conversation, Hatcher hung up the phone. It was a pity that he had to pay for the room without using it, but he needed to move quickly. He picked up his bag, still unopened at the foot of the bed, and carried it down to the desk in the lobby. Twenty minutes later he was boarding a train.

28

HATCHER DECIDED to spend the night in Chur, and the next morning got a cab to take him the eight or so miles up to Churwalden. Chur was a city considerably smaller and less interesting than Zurich, and Churwalden was barely more than a village. It had a hotel, of course. In Hatcher's experience, every Swiss village had a hotel before it had anything else, just as every habitable area in America seemed to have a gas station before it had anything else. But there was nothing in Churwalden of any note besides farms and a meat-curing factory. Churwalden was just a place on the way to other, more interesting places, such as St. Moritz. It was a curious spot to look for Sarkes Manoukian.

Nevertheless, it was the place where Manoukian was said to be. At nine-thirty, after Hatcher had checked into the hotel, he entered the restaurant and immediately spotted Manoukian sitting at a corner table. Although the two had never met, Hatcher knew Manoukian's reputation, and had no trouble recognizing the heavyset, swarthy figure with the comically improbable eyebrows.

Manoukian looked bored. He was picking away at a tiny breakfast: a single egg, a piece of toast, a small wedge of cheese, and a slice of meat. He drank his coffee from a demitasse, and periodically dabbed at his mouth with a corner of the large linen napkin he held in his lap. He seemed, to Hatcher, like the cross between some depraved Levantine flesh-peedler and a dandified Edwardian aesthete.

Hatcher went over to the table. Aside from the inevitable waiter, they seemed to be the only people in the room.

"Mr. Manoukian?"

Manoukian's gaze turned toward Hatcher. Without any obvious change, Manoukian's expression of boredom was gone, replaced with another which Hatcher found difficult to identify. Danger, perhaps. But the voice, when Sarkes Manoukian spoke, was silky smooth.

"I'm afraid you have the advantage over me."

Not much of one, thought Hatcher. And it probably won't last long.

"My name is Amos Hatcher. Let me give you my card."

While Hatcher took the business card from his wallet and handed it to Manoukian, he noticed that the air of boredom had returned. He could not tell if it was real or feigned. Manoukian read the card slowly, tilting it back and forth in the light. The card simply identified Hatcher as an investigator for the International Association of Art Dealers.

Manoukian had not extended his hand or asked Hatcher to sit down, so he still stood before Manoukian's table. Manoukian offhandedly returned Hatcher's card, and again patted his fleshy mouth with the napkin. He still didn't say anything, but cocked one eyebrow at the tall man in front of him.

"I think we have a common interest, Mr. Manoukian." Manoukian smiled.

"None of my interests are common, Mr. Hatcher. Nevertheless, please sit down."

"I believe we share an interest in Greek pots."

"Ah yes, Greek pots. They are indeed an interest of mine. But I'm afraid you have been misled. I would expect that Churwalden is rather lacking in Greek pots. It does, on the other hand, have a large number of cows. Are you also interested in cows, Mr. Hatcher?"

It was Hatcher's turn to smile.

"Only in Dutch paintings. I love Aelbert Cuyp's cows, for example. But I'm afraid horses bore me stiff, except Leonardo's and Gericault's. And some of the Greek horses. I love the Metropolitan horse, for instance, even if it is a fake. Do you like horses, Mr. Manoukian?"

"Again, I'm afraid you are misinformed. The Greek horse in the Metropolitan is good. As I have always maintained. Laboratory tests have recently confirmed my judgment. Do we have any other 'common interests,' as you say?"

"Exekias. Another fine artist for horses. But I don't have to tell you that, do I? Exekias has recently become, I understand, something of a passion of yours. A business interest, of course, as well."

"Ah yes, Exekias. A sublime artist. But we shouldn't discuss such things over breakfast, should we? Tell me, Mr. Hatcher, are you staying at the hotel?"

"As a matter of fact, I am."

"A pleasant coincidence. What room, if I may ask?"

"Room forty-two."

"I see. Why don't you stay here and have breakfast? I have some small matters to attend to. I could arrange to come and see you at—say, eleven?"

"Eleven would be fine. I'll be waiting for you. Room forty-two."

Hatcher followed the dealer's suggestion and stayed for breakfast. Along with eggs and coffee, he ordered a platter of *bündnerfleisch*, the specialty of the canton. This was uncooked, air-cured beef cut paper-thin, and its flavor resembled that of the best Italian prosciutto. Since it was uncooked, it could not be exported. Even here in Graubünden Canton, where it was made and processed, *bündnerfleisch* was enormously expensive. Still, Hatcher concluded that it was a justifiable luxury. He did not expect the coming interview with Manoukian to be much of a pleasure.

In the hotel corridor near Hatcher's door he passed a small, thin man with olive skin and sunglasses who was fumbling with a map. He looked like an Arab tourist. Hatcher debated whether to ask the man if he could be of help, decided against it, and opened his door. He had just turned the knob with his left hand and dropped his key in his coat pocket with his right when he felt someone suddenly grab his right wrist, turn it sharply, and jerk it back up between his shoulder blades.

Hatcher felt a powerful stab of pain in his back, and at the same moment felt himself involuntarily being drawn up on his toes. Instinctively he realized that if he dropped back down on his heels he would dislocate his shoulder with the weight of his body.

"Quiet. Go inside." The man spoke in a coarse whisper, almost a croak, and Hatcher could smell a strong odor of garlic.

Tiptoeing grotesquely, Hatcher entered the room propelled by a slight pressure on his twisted arm. He was breathing in short gasps, and had to suppress an impulse to scream from pain. His vision was becoming blurred. He felt a throbbing in his temples and bile in the back of his throat.

"Enough, Mehmet." Hatcher had been no more

206

aware of Manoukian's entering the room than he had been earlier of the small man's coming up behind him. The pressure on his arm stopped suddenly, but in its stead came a feeling of total exhaustion. Hatcher half-fell, half-fainted against the wall and slid to the floor. His right arm dropped to his side, useless and numb. The pain was no longer so sharp, and as he stared at Manoukian his retinal image began to come slowly back into focus.

Manoukian now had a small black pistol, but his face held the same expression of boredom Hatcher had seen in the restaurant.

"Talk, Hatcher. Everything you know about the Exekias. How you know, who else knows, everything. And quickly."

Hatcher was still gasping for breath. He felt slightly dizzy, and his mouth was dry. When he spoke, his voice was rasping.

"Nothing . . . till now. Didn't . . . know anything. Guessed."

"How did you guess?"

Hatcher waited for his breathing to return to normal. He was beginning to feel rage overtaking his fear.

"How the hell . . . do you think? How many people could have done it? You think a small-time thug could have done it? Someone like him, some dirty little cutthroat scab like your friend Mehmet there?"

"Don't forget your situation, Hatcher."

"Fuck you. Don't forget *your* situation. I didn't have any idea who stole the pot. I just had a list of names, that's all. You just told me. Now we both know, don't we, Manoukian? So don't forget *your* goddamn situation."

"Tell me about the names. What names?"

"You know them. Everyone knows them. Do you think that Roberto Anselmo hasn't got the same list? First, Baring-Gould in London. Pierre Renaud, Paris.

Bertelli and Scarpia in Rome. You. Demetriou in Athens. How many crooks are there who can handle something that big?"

"I suppose you just went down the list then, Mr. Hatcher?"

"Just went down the list. Baring-Gould was my first name. He was in Turkey when it was stolen."

"How do you know?"

"I asked him. I just asked him, and he told me. I didn't hire some piece of shit to tear his arm off."

"I warn you, Hatcher."

Manoukian handed his gun to Mehmet, who stood impassively next to the door. Hatcher wondered, in a moment of blind panic, if he had gone too far.

"We shall see. Stay here and don't move. I should return within the hour."

Then Manoukian left the room. Hatcher sat where he had fallen, leaning against the wall. His shirt was damp with sweat. He didn't much like the idea of being left alone with Mehmet, and found himself profoundly hoping that the Turk's command of English wasn't fluent and idiomatic. The guard's face, however, was quite expressionless. He did not speak to Hatcher, or even look at him. He apparently assumed that Hatcher was not fool enough to try to do anything, so he stood languidly by the door picking his teeth, waiting for Manoukian to return and give him his next order.

Neither man had moved or spoken, when Manoukian entered the room three quarters of an hour later. The dealer seemed in high spirits when he returned. He almost bounced through the door, reclaimed the gun from Mehmet, and put it in his pocket.

"Well, Mr. Hatcher, John Baring-Gould sends you his regards. I am very glad to discover that you were telling the truth about your little list. You see, if there had been any real evidence it might have posed something of a problem. Now, I am glad to say, we can be friends."

"Terrific. Your enemies must lead hard lives."

"A sense of humor. I have always admired that in you Americans."

Sarkes Manoukian giggled for a moment. Then he looked hard at Hatcher, his face serious.

"The Exekias. The Exekias is one of the most beautiful pots in the world, Hatcher. But, alas, I do not have it. This you must believe. I am retired at present, a retired gentleman-scholar. An admirable occupation, is it not? I am now devoting myself to the life of the mind. I have not, of course, entirely abandoned the life of the senses."

As he said this, he leered openly at the Turk, who was still standing impassively, close to the door. Hatcher smiled. Mehmet was, it seemed, a man of varied talents and accomplishments.

"Now, where was I? Ah, the Exekias. I was quite certain until this morning that my name could in no way be associated with the unfortunate disappearance of that distinguished object. I am glad to have been reassured on that score. Our encounter was, as they say, a shot in the dark. I do not, you understand, believe that I am in any way vulnerable in that matter. Indeed, I have only a small anxiety. Since you have been honest and forthcoming with me, I shall be equally so with you."

Manoukian took a small gold cigarette case from his pocket. He opened it, offered Hatcher his choice of pastel-colored cigarettes, which Hatcher declined, and took one himself.

"My anxiety concerns Signor Anselmo. I rather enjoy Switzerland, you see; it is a safe, clean, pretty little country, and it understands that a certain respect should be accorded the very rich. Nevertheless, I periodically find it unbelievably dull. For boredom, of course, there is always Italy. Italy is my antidote, my narcotic, my love. Should Signor Anselmo suspect that I am a principal in the episode of the Exekias krater, I'm afraid my access to Italy might be severely curtailed. Perhaps even terminated."

"You don't want me to tell Anselmo that you took it, in other words."

"I should put it rather more strongly than that. You have already encountered Mehmet, who is one of my friends. A man in my position must have friends. I have many friends, in many parts of the world."

"And if I tell Anselmo, I can expect to meet lots more of them. Is that it?"

"Precisely, Mr. Hatcher. Well, I'm afraid I must go. Before I do, however, let me give you a small suggestion. Have you ever been to Boston, Massachusetts?"

"Yes, many times. What about Boston?"

"A charming city. An excellent place, I am told, to study the works of Exekias. The little-known works, that is. I'm afraid I can't be any more specific. You understand."

"I understand. Why are you telling me this?"

Manoukian smiled broadly, disclosing a gold canine tooth, and shrugged.

"A quid pro quo. You forget, I am an ex-businessman. Favors, even small ones, should be rewarded. Also, I seem to have spoiled your trip to Churwalden."

Manoukian gestured to Mehmet, who opened the door and held it for his master.

"Shaking your hand might cause you some discomfort at the moment, so I shall forgo that ritual. Nevertheless, I must say that I have greatly enjoyed meeting a man of your intelligence. It is not often that I am so neatly tricked. Good-bye, Mr. Hatcher."

The door closed behind him. Hatcher stayed where

he was for a minute or so, then slowly got up. His right arm was throbbing and his shoulder was tender and painful, so he decided to take a hot bath before going back to Chur. It occurred to him later as he lay in the tub that he had spent in the neighborhood of sixty American dollars for hotel rooms in Zurich and Churwalden, and all he'd got for his money was one hot bath. Fifteen minutes later, still in the tub, Hatcher concluded that it was worth it.

29

THE WEATHER WAS GRAY and chilly when Hatcher stepped out of the Amsterdam train station. Hatcher didn't mind, being gray and chilly himself. It was seven-thirty in the morning. Hatcher had gone from Chur back to Zurich only to find the airport socked in by a near-blizzard which forced him to take the overnight train to Amsterdam. In the daytime, the trip would have been spectacular: from Zurich to Basel, then up through Germany following the Rhine valley. But at night, with a shoulder that registered the slightest movement with a sharp, painful twinge, the journey was something of a horror.

At Zurich, Hatcher had bought himself a souvenir scarf that he could fashion into a sling for his arm. There hadn't been any plain ones, so he had had to settle for a red, yellow, and black one with a huge belligerent-looking bear charging forward on its hind legs, surrounded by the coats of arms of the various Swiss cantons. The scarf made him look ridiculous, but it also made him a bit more comfortable. The problem was not

213

just his shoulder. Mehmet had apparently given Hatcher's arm an affectionate half-twist at some point, just enough to strain several ligaments in his elbow severely.

Hatcher caught the first tram he could find that went near the hotel on the Leidsegracht, and discovered, on the way, that he was desperately anxious to see Sheila again. It had recently occurred to him that he was falling in love with her. Since he had boarded the plane in Zurich, the image of Sheila standing by the windows gazing out over the rooftops of Amsterdam that first morning had come back to him again and again, like an *idée fixe*.

He was enormously relieved, at the hotel, when she opened the door of the room and flung her arms around him.

"Amos, Amos, I'm so glad . . ." She drew back, noticing the sling. "What happened to you?"

"Nothing serious. I just got my arm twisted, to coin a phrase. By a Turk. How are you? What success did you have with Bauer?"

"Amos, your arm! Is it really all right?"

"Really. Just strained a little. The Turk apparently thought my elbow and shoulder were universal joints. Tell me about Bauer, and you, and then I'll give you my story."

"Promise?"

"Of course."

"Well, you were right. Rembrandt, or damn close. Bauer had a photograph. I got a copy of it from him yesterday. Look, darling."

Sheila went over to the bed and picked up a copy of the photo. Hatcher looked at it, turned it over, and whistled softly.

"That's it. The frame clinches it. What did Bauer say?"

"He said he thinks it's Rembrandt, although he

214

couldn't be absolutely certain without seeing the painting."

"God. Where did he find this photo?"

"It was stuck in a book owned by a scholar Bauer knew. The only indication of where it came from was an inscription on the back giving the opinion of a Czech scholar named Krofta. Krofta thought it might be right. Heard of him?"

"Yes. Milan Krofta. He had an amazing eye, apparently. Didn't write a lot, though. It looks good to me, from the photograph. Not much like the mezzotint, though, is it?"

"Nothing at all. You were dead right there. Can we go back to the Hague? Dr. Bauer's a charming man. He invited us for a little party. Amos, he'd love to see you again."

"I know, I'd love to see him. We haven't got time, though. It's beginning to crack open. I got my hands on another large chunk of it yesterday in Switzerland."

"What happened?"

"I twisted a couple of arms myself. I was right about the stolen Greek pot; the two cases *are* linked. I don't know who has it, but it's in Boston. That bit of information came from the original thief, a man named Manoukian, who apparently fenced it and skipped off to Switzerland. It may have cost me my serve and backhand for the next six months or so, but it was worth it. If he'd given me the name of the man he fenced it to, I would have thrown in my left arm for nothing."

"Poor baby. Can I rub it?"

"No time. We've got to get out to Schiphol and grab the first plane back. I've got a strong idea who did it: who has the pot, and the panel, and two murders on his head. It's tricky, though. We still don't have any solid proof of anything."

215

"Can you tell me? Amos, tell me who you suspect."

"Not yet. Soon, though, probably in the next ten days. When I'm sure I'm right. If you're packed, let's go down and look for a cab. I'll tell you the rest of the story about my trip to Switzerland on the way to the airport."

They found a taxi quickly, and, as the spaces between the canals became wider and wider and the canals finally stopped altogether, Hatcher told Sheila the story of his trip. At first she asked frequent questions, then toward the end became more and more quiet. Hatcher wondered if something were wrong.

"I think it's rotten, that's all."

"What?"

"I think it's a stinking trick not to tell me who you suspect, and why. I'm not Callahan, for Christ's sake. I thought we were partners in this thing. I didn't come all the way to Europe to be treated like somebody's research assistant."

"Sheila——"

"I'm not through. Either you don't trust me, or . . . there's something you haven't told me, or . . ."

"Sheila? Sheila, please, dammit, stop. You're right."

"What?"

"You're right. Absolutely. When we get to Schiphol, I'll give you my theory, everything. It's just that I'm not absolutely certain, and——"

"And you don't want to look like a damned fool, is that it?"

"Yes, more or less."

"Do you think you have to be perfect, or omniscient, or something? For me? God, Amos, you probably don't even have to be reasonably bright. I love you, you idiot."

"Do you? Then kiss me. Kiss me all the way to the airport."

"It's too bumpy. We wouldn't have any teeth left by

the time we got there. Wait till we get back to Boston, though."

A few minutes later, the taxi pulled up in front of the main terminal. Hatcher sent Sheila ahead to the restaurant while he checked the flights and made the arrangements. Over the years he had got to know several KLM officials pretty well, so he was able to secure tickets on a mid-afternoon flight to Logan with a minimum of difficulty. Then he quickly made his way to the restaurant. He'd had no real meal since the breakfast at Churwalden, and he was beginning to feel light-headed.

At the end of the meal, over coffee, Hatcher got the list of names Dr. Sabin had suggested to O'Rourke out of his wallet. By this time it was warped, crumpled, and torn, and Hatcher tried to smooth it out by rubbing it back and forth against the edge of the table. Then he put it in the middle of the table, facing Sheila.

"This is the list of names Sabin gave O'Rourke. It has nothing to do with any crime per se, it's simply a list of people Sabin thought capable of recognizing an obscure painting by a major northern baroque artist on sight. Some of the names on the list I know, some O'Rourke—or Sabin—described to me. I'll tell you what I know about each person on the list, and at the end of it you can tell me if any one stands out."

"I thought *you* were going to tell *me* . . ."

"I know, I will. I just want to see if you reach the same conclusion independently."

"In case you haven't noticed, independence has never been one of my problems."

"I've noticed. Okay, let's start at the top."

After Hatcher had run through the list of names, Sheila frowned, pursed her lips, and tapped on the Formica absentmindedly with a pencil. Then she gave one strong final tap on the list of names.

"Ross. It has to be Ross."

"I agree. Want to say why?"

"He's the only one on the list with that kind of range. The second thing is the money. If he bought the Exekias krater from Manoukian, he must have paid a huge amount for it. Even stolen, and we don't know if Ross even knew that. The third thing is what you hinted before. If the two crimes are connected, the second could have been a cover-up for the first. I don't quite understand how or why, though."

"I don't either. There's still a lot I don't understand. But I'm almost certain Ross is the one. Do you know anything about him?"

"Not much. He's supposed to be ice-cold and smart as hell. That part certainly fits. Can we get him now?"

"Not yet. I think we're close, though. I mentioned ten days. It may be longer, maybe a month. But we're in the end-game now."

Hatcher pushed back his chair and painfully rose to his feet. Now that he'd satisfied his hunger, he suddenly felt the cumulative exhaustion of twenty-eight hours without sleep. He put his good arm around Sheila, who impulsively kissed him, and the two of them staggered off to find the departure gate.

30

NIGHT WAS THE WORST TIME. Ross would lie flat on his back on the bed and force his eyes closed, praying that the Nembutals, Seconals, or Scotch—one of them, or all of them—would somehow carry him through a dreamless sleep to daybreak. But the nightmare returned again and again, leaving him pallid and shaken when the sun finally rose.

Ironically, it always began like the dream he had had many times before, a marvelous fantasy of omnipotent triumph. A Walter Mitty dream.

It began with Ross standing in an Alpine valley, gazing up at a great tower of rock rising thousands of feet above him. He stood there for a moment, then put on his backpack, checked his ice ax, rope, pitons, and crampons. Then he turned his back sharply on the curious band of tourists and spectators watching from the hotels, and walked proudly forward toward the foot of the wall.

As in the old dream, the first part of the climb was smooth and effortless. Ross moved up the near-vertical face of the Alp with an easy, swinging rhythm, negotiating the rock pillars, the tricky diagonal traverses, and ice fields flawlessly. As he gained height, he felt the same old sense of exhilaration. The people below seemed puny and laughable, the denizens of some inferior realm.

As he moved inexorably upward he felt himself becoming stronger and more alert, his senses keener, his climbing faster and more assured. He could leap crevasses, devise elaborate rope slings that swung his body out over the void and brought it back safely to the rock. He could skip acrobatically from shelf to shelf and crack to crack.

In the denouement of the earlier dream, Ross had emerged from under a ledge and looked up to see a dazzling mantle of snow leading up to the summit ridge. Now when he looked up, he saw instead an ominous gray cloud.

This was always the beginning of the nightmare.

The nightmare took many forms. But it always began with the sensation of a sharp pang, like a chill, passing over Ross the moment he saw the cloud.

In one variation, Ross became lost on the face of the mountain. He suddenly found himself standing on a narrow ledge with several cracks leading diagonally upward from it, but he could no longer remember the proper route. He decided to explore each of them until he found the correct one.

But they all proved to be false leads. Some ended in sharp overhangs or treacherous cornices, some in crevasses, and some of them merely petered out. After what seemed to be hours of frustrated experiments Ross returned to the original ledge, bone-tired and defeated. With his last reserves of energy he hammered a piton into a crack over his head and attached a rope harness to it to hold him on his perch overnight.

The night brought a savage storm with violent winds,

freezing rain, and snow. Ross fought the elements for as long as he could, slapping his arms against his sides and banging his feet against the rock to maintain circulation. Then slowly, as he weakened, the cold began to engulf him. First his feet became numb, and then his hands. Icicles began to grow from his gloves and boots.

When dawn broke on the mountain Ross was dead; dead, but still sentient. He could feel himself hanging from his ropes, swinging slowly back and forth like a marionette on a string. His head had slumped forward on his chest, and through glazed eyes he could make out the antlike figures below gesticulating, pointing, and swarming around the telescopes on the hotel terraces.

Other variations of the nightmare were no better. In one, the peak of the mountain seemed to recede from Ross, like the water from Tantalus. Hour after hour, pitch after pitch, Ross struggled upward toward the exit cracks heading to the summit. Each time he seemed about to reach his goal a huge shelf of rock appeared, blocking his path.

He could feel his strength ebbing. His hands and feet became awkward and heavy, his movements clumsy and lurching. At last he found himself just below a promontory jutting out from the face. A perch, perhaps. If he could just reach it . . .

As he came closer, he saw gray strands of rope curling down from the rock, fluttering in the wind. When he finally dragged himself onto the horizontal shelf of rock, he was shocked to find that the ropes were attached to a body. It was another mountaineer who had seemingly fallen from somewhere near the summit, his body smashing against the stone spur.

The corpse was not at all decomposed. Apparently it had been mummified by the cold, dry air. With a sense of foreboding, Ross raised the hood of the parka which had slipped down over the face of the corpse.

It was the face of Harry Giardino.

Other versions of the nightmare held other horrors. In some there were avalanches which dragged Ross, clawing, from his holds, sweeping him down the mountain to be dashed against the rocks below. Sometimes the brittle crust of snow gave way and he was sucked into a crevasse, and sometimes he was hammered off his feet by one of the fusillades of loose rocks that periodically raked the face of the mountain. Again and again, there was the sensation of helplessly falling, falling.

Ross never escaped, in the nightmare. And he always seemed to experience his own death.

Sometimes Ross awoke with his hands locked around the bedpost, and once he'd had to massage them and soak them in hot water to get rid of the cramps. One morning he found his nails splintered and broken, the tips of his fingers bleeding, and the headboard of his bed pitted and slashed.

Ross's bedroom was at the opposite end of the hall from his wife's. If he ever screamed or cried out in his sleep, she never heard it, or at least never mentioned it.

The form of his nightmare struck Ross as curious, since his only mountain-climbing experience was one summer spent in Switzerland as a college student. The few climbs he had done there had been easy ones, and he could recall no moment either of particular danger or fear.

But it was a nicely appropriate metaphor, he decided, for someone who was losing his grip, or reaching the end of his rope.

31

"YOU FIGURE IT WAS ROSS, hey? Good, that makes three of us. You figure it was Ross, I figure it was Ross, she figures it was Ross. I haven't asked Callahan, yet. I think Callahan figures it was Hatcher."

O'Rourke and Callahan were still getting along rather shakily. Callahan hadn't forgiven O'Rourke for the afternoon at the St. Swithin Club, and O'Rourke hadn't forgiven Callahan for not forgiving him.

"I figured maybe it was Ross the day I met him at the Museum. When I told him I was investigating a murder, I could see it hit. Not much, sort of just a little tic. But enough. I put him under surveillance the day you two skipped off to Europe together."

"We were on the job, O'Rourke."

O'Rourke smiled, and gave his gum a couple of extra hard smacks. He hadn't expected Hatcher to rise to that one.

"Yeah, on the job. Anyway, I got him under surveillance."

"No one's shadowing him, I hope."

"Nope. Loose surveillance. Just comings and goings, mostly. Ross leads a regular life. Almost too regular."

"What do you mean?"

"It's almost compulsive. Every day he arrives at the Museum at exactly the same time, leaves at exactly the same time, always follows the same schedule. It's funny. Most people react to pressure by letting go and becoming slobs. Others tighten up, as if they were trying to cover up the internal mess with external structures. Everybody goes one way or the other."

"Captain, I don't want to push, but I'd suggest you drop the surveillance. Our best shot is letting him think he's home free, and I think the worst thing would be letting him know we're watching him."

"I agree. Done."

"Anything on the auctions?"

O'Rourke's face fell. He sighed, took the gum out of his mouth, folded it in paper, and dropped it in the wastepaper basket.

"The auctions. Christ, Hatcher, do you know how many goddamn auctions go on in New England every goddamn day? Do you have any idea how much time we've spent checking out that stuff? Besides which, you should see my office. It's none too tidy on a good day, but recently you can't even move. Walk in the door and you're immediately up to your ass—pardon me, Ma'am—up to your knees in antiques magazines, clippings, auction catalogues, and God knows what all. It isn't doing my reputation any good around the station, either. On top of which, we haven't found anything."

"Sorry, Captain. I'll take care of that detail myself from now on."

"Great. None too soon, either."

"I really *am* sorry. I think it's important."

"What's that all about, Amos?"

"I'll explain in a minute. First, I think we have some moves. Move number one: find out who the president

224

of the Board of Trustees of the Museum is and set up an appointment to see him. I think it would be better at his office, if he has one. That should be as soon as possible. O'Rourke and me, Sheila if she wants to come."

"Could I help?"

"I'm not sure, on this one. Frankly, maybe not. There's plenty of other stuff that has to be done."

"Cutting out clippings. Right?"

"Not just that. Libraries. Someone's going to have to check major libraries in the whole Boston area. Could you do that?"

"Only if I get Callahan to go with me."

Sheila smiled brightly. Hatcher looked annoyed; O'Rourke looked aghast.

"You're a brave woman, Ma'am. Once around the block with Callahan can be something to tell the grandchildren. You haven't seen him drive."

"Good. That's settled then."

After O'Rourke left the Holiday Inn, Sheila swung around in her chair to face Hatcher. She was still angry.

"Anything else I can do, Boss? Sahib? Stack pencils, type, darn socks? A woman's work, like they say . . ."

"Look, dear, if you would just please, quietly stuff it for a moment, I'll be happy to explain."

"How lovely. I just love explanations. Explain me a few explanations, big boy."

"All right. First, about going to see the president of the Board of Trustees of the Museum. I want to break him down, I want him to show us some dirty linen. And he won't, not if you're there. He'll look at you, and sixty years of Wasp macho pride will take over and he'll freeze up like the Great Wall of China."

"I didn't know the Great Wall of China ever froze up. All right, I'll buy that for the time being. It's a nice rationalization, anyway. What is all this about the auctions?"

"I didn't explain about that?"

"Correct. This is correct. You have never, in point of fact, mentioned any auctions."

"Well. My idea is this, about the auctions. Whoever has the painting, Ross presumably, murdered two people to get it. The Greek pot is dirty, but nothing like the Dutch panel. Whoever has the panel has to clean it. Launder it, just like Nixon's campaign money. Think of Ross. Assume he bought the pot, found out it was stolen, and somehow stole the painting to cover up. What good is it to him? It has no past, no provenance, no legitimacy. Even if it can't be tied to the two murders, nevertheless there is no way to avoid speculation connecting the painting with the murdered dealers. Also, what can Ross tell the Board of Trustees—that he found a Rembrandt on his doorstep one morning with a pink bow tied around it? He has to launder it, and he also has to give it a past. No matter how flimsy. The only way to do it is through an auction."

"I don't understand. Wouldn't it be spotted immediately?"

"The painting in Bauer's photograph would almost certainly be spotted, sure. But there's one thing to remember. It's almost impossible to make a mediocre painting look like a Rembrandt, but it's fairly easy to make a Rembrandt look like a mediocre painting. A little overpainting in water-soluble acrylics, a little here, a little there, clumsy, but not too clumsy. Then the whole thing covered with several layers of dark copal varnish, maybe mixed with a little burnt sienna, and what do you get? An ugly, brown baroque mess, school of who-cares, worthless."

"Why not work it through a dealer?"

"No. Too risky. Dealers are trained to spot that sort of thing. You'd spot it. You'd look at it under a black light, you'd start to ask questions. The same thing is true of the big auction houses like Sotheby Parke Bernet, Christie's and so on. What Ross needs is a small auction house somewhere in the country, where he can feel safe that a hoked-up Dutch panel won't be spotted. He'll leave it there under a false name, buy it, photograph it, *then* clean it and present it as a rediscovered masterpiece. I've spent hours working that out, and that's the only way I can see his pulling it off."

"You didn't tell me."

"So you're mad."

"A little hurt."

"Will you hold me?"

"No. That's not the answer."

"If you hold me, just hold me in your arms quietly, I'll try to tell you the answer."

"All right. Dammit."

"Look, the problem is I'm a fairly medium-average sort of guy, kind of funny-looking, bald, middle-aged, God knows not rich or ever liable to be rich. But the thing is I'm in love with you. No, don't say anything, not yet. And so I have to try to be clever. Which I can be, reasonably so, anyway. One of the ways I like to show my cleverness is by pulling rabbits out of hats, and now you come along and every time I pull one out you get mad—"

"Amos—"

"No, wait. You get mad because I didn't let you see me trying to stuff the little bugger up my sleeve when I was offstage, and—"

"Amos. What you said about 'Wasp macho pride'?"

"Yes. All right. I suppose it is that. Partly, anyway."

"Amos, oh Amos. Please make love to me now."

32

AT PRECISELY the appointed time, Walker Richards's door swung open to admit Hatcher and O'Rourke.

"Gentlemen, please come in. Miss Palmetier, I won't be taking any phone calls this morning. If there are urgent messages, please refer them to Bill. I'll be available between two and four this afternoon, and anything else should keep till then."

Richards's law firm was situated near the top of one of the newest and tallest buildings on State Street. His office, on the corner of the floor, had two large ribbon windows that gave him a stunning view over the harbor. O'Rourke and Hatcher both found themselves gaping.

"Spectacular, isn't it? On the left you can see down toward Marblehead and Lynn, and on the right the South Shore, toward Quincy, Hingham, and so on. That view has done me a great deal of good in the last couple of years, although I'm afraid it hasn't helped my law practice any. But you came about a more serious matter."

"I'm afraid so. I'm investigating a murder. Two murders, in fact. Mr. Hatcher here is a private detective who is officially connected with the case. We have some questions we'd like to ask you, but first I must be certain that our visit, and our questions, remain absolutely secret."

"Discretion is the keystone of legal ethics, Captain. I will mention this to no one."

"Thank you, sir. First, then, we would like to know if the Museum has recently made any major purchases. If so, were they made on or with the recommendation of Elton Ross?"

"I'm afraid that, too, is an area for discretion. The meetings of the Board of Trustees, especially those regarding acquisitions or potential acquisitions, are sensitive matters. Are we speaking of some kind of financial chicanery—mismanagement, embezzlement, something of that sort?"

"The crime is murder."

"In that case, the issue is clear. Please, gentlemen, sit down."

For a moment Richards went to the window. His back was turned and his hands, clasped behind it, kept flexing and relaxing spasmodically. Then the tall man sighed and turned to face the pair across the desk.

"Perhaps I can tell you what you want to know, although God knows I hate to do it. Approximately four months ago, Elton Ross convened an extraordinary session of the Board of Trustees. This in itself is unusual. It was midsummer, and many members were on vacation. They came, though, from Maine, Sweden, the Costa Brava, everywhere. This says something about Ross, about the nature of the man. He communicated a kind of vivid excitement, a force, like an electromagnetic field. Can you understand that?"

"I think I can."

"Very well. His message to the trustees was essentially very simple. There was a work of art of the utmost importance and magnitude, a work which would dwarf the most significant acquisitions that had been made by any museum, anywhere, for years. Boston must have it. He, Ross, must have it. But it had to be acquired in total secrecy. Not even the board itself could know the identity of this extraordinary object. Our function was simply to support Mr. Ross in his unholy mission. And of course, to finance it. To give him, in effect, a blank check. A blank check that could be filled in to a sum not exceeding, but perhaps closely approximating, one million dollars."

"Good Lord."

"Do you see the absurdity of the situation? He was asking not merely for the money, you understand, but for the self-destruction of the Board of Trustees as a responsible governing body. It was a political maneuver, a virtual coup d'etat. And it was successful. Against my protest, against all sober judgment, the board complied. It gave him his check, and no one, myself included, yet has the faintest idea what Ross did with the money."

"It must have been some meeting."

"Oh yes, it was quite an extraordinary performance, I assure you. Ross was obsessed, relentless, like some modern Cagliostro or Svengali. A virtuoso performance. And now, now I find myself wondering if this marvelous work of art ever even existed. You see why I asked you if the subject of our meeting was embezzlement?"

"I see. Has the Board of Trustees met since that time?"

"No, indeed. Ross has twice been approached about a meeting and twice refused. I have been forced to issue a deadline: December twelfth, two weeks from now. I suspect that shortly before that date or shortly thereafter, either Elton Ross or myself will have terminated his association with the Museum."

"I doubt that Mr. Ross will be a problem for you much longer."

"You mentioned murder. Is Ross a suspect in the death of that art dealer?"

"Do you really want to know? Would it surprise you?"

"I think the answer to both questions is no. Is there anything further I can tell you?"

O'Rourke looked at Hatcher.

"I don't believe so. Thank you very much for your time, Mr. Richards."

"Don't mention it."

When Hatcher and O'Rourke left, Richards was standing in front of the window. He was gazing far out to sea.

33

"I THINK WHAT Richards said was substantially correct. Ross wanted the pot, but he also wanted to make damn sure that the triumph was his, and his alone. And he apparently thought that if he could get carte blanche on the pot, he would have a virtual dictatorship over Museum acquisitions in the future. At least that was Richards's conclusion. Everything went smoothly until he discovered he'd been taken by Manoukian. What did he have then? A hot pot, which was worthless to him, and a canceled check for something like a million dollars."

"How did he find out about the panel?"

"Blind luck, I'd imagine. Either Giardino or Weinstock must have taken it to the Museum. Wait: it must have been Giardino, since Ross went after him first. The chance appearance of the panel must have seemed to Ross his only possible escape. Of course, if anyone could have identified the picture, the whole scheme was worthless. So Ross became a multiple murderer as well as a thief."

"Can't you get him now?"

"Sure. O'Rourke could haul him in on suspicion. Maybe even get a search warrant, who knows? But he wouldn't find anything, and we still don't have the evidence to hold him. If O'Rourke grabbed him and then had to let him go, he'd find a way to destroy both the pot and the painting, and then we'd have nothing."

"What about Manoukian?"

"He wouldn't talk. In fact, we couldn't even get him out of Switzerland. We don't have enough proof to support a case for extradition or deportation."

"This is ridiculous. You've solved the crimes. You have the means, the motive, everything, and you still can't touch him?"

"Evidence. It's absurd, I know, but we don't have any real evidence. 'Hard evidence,' as they say. That's why I asked you to run around to all those damned libraries. How is that coming, by the way?"

"Nothing yet. I still think Callahan's sweet. Oh, by the way, he's not that dumb, either. He worked out a plan. We call first and make an appointment. Rather, Callahan calls. He puts his voice down an octave and tells the librarians that this is a very serious, very confidential matter. The librarians love it, of course. They probably think we're with the CIA or possibly the KGB. Anyway, they pull all the cards for us and sort them before we arrive."

"How many have you checked?"

"Most of the Boston and Cambridge ones. The Boston Public, that took an hour and a half. The Fogg, B.U., Cambridge Public, a couple of others. The Museum, of course."

"He wouldn't have used that. Most of the others are probably also too close to home. The Fogg, for example. Too obvious. But he needed the books, unless he has a really extraordinary library himself."

"He lives in Lincoln, so tomorrow we're going to

start there. Lincoln, Lexington, Belmont. Brandeis University seems a good bet. Amos, what makes you think Ross would use his own name on the checkout cards?"

"Less dangerous, on the whole. Ross is a public figure. He could easily be spotted in a library. If he used a false name and was caught . . ."

"Of course. He'd look like a horse's ass. Everyone would remember and wonder."

"Yes."

"What are you doing tomorrow, by the way?"

'Same thing I did today. Wade through newspapers, magazines, classifieds, auction pamphlets. I can sympathize with O'Rourke about that now. Six hours of it and you're ready for a padded cell. It's like the Chinese water torture, or two or three hours of Ravel's *Bolero*."

"Some secretaries spend their lives doing work like that, Amos."

"I know. Some scholars do, too. Maybe that's why you're not a secretary and I'm not a scholar."

"Or vice versa."

"Of course. Or vice versa."

The next afternoon Hatcher was in his motel room, sitting cross-legged in the middle of the floor, surrounded by stacks of magazines, when Sheila's call came through.

"Amos? Sheila. We've got it."

"Sheila, where are you?"

"Wellesley. Wellesley College. The art history library. We found six cards with Ross's name on them. Also, the librarian remembers him. It's not usually a lending library, so he had to get special permission."

"Great. Rembrandt, the pot, or both?"

"Both. The cards are dated, and the dates fit. Three one time, three the other, and both times he only kept the books out overnight."

"Right. That's all he'd need. What are they?"

"Let's see. The Greek pots, first of all . . . uh, something called *Greek Vase Painting,* by Arias and Hirmer . . ."

"Terrific."

"Then two volumes of some corpus . . . let's see . . ."

"Corpus Vasorum Antiquorum?"

"Right. How did you—"

"Which cities? Which collections?"

"Let me see. One's Berlin, I think, and the other's Munich."

"Perfect. What about Rembrandt?"

"First, *Rembrandt Paintings.* That's the recent book by Gerson."

"Good. Funny Ross didn't have it already. What else?"

"Two old monographs. One by Bode, the other by Valentiner."

"Excellent. One more thing. Could you get all the cards photocopied?"

"I've already done it. Three copies of each."

"Then fly back to me. Boy, do you get a great meal tonight!"

"What about Callahan?"

"Callahan? Callahan gets a handshake. Does that make me a sexist pig?"

"Probably. I'll have to think about it. 'Bye, Lover."

When Sheila came into Hatcher's room she found him hunched over a catalogue. He was motionless, totally absorbed, and he didn't even glance up when she came through the door.

"Sheila? I've found the painting. Come and look."

She went over and took the magazine, then seemed to freeze. She didn't say anything for about a minute. Hatcher handed her the copy of the photograph they had obtained from Bauer, and her eyes flicked back and forth between the photograph and the plate in the catalogue.

"It's incredible."

"Isn't it? It's an almost perfect job. The more you look at it, the better it gets."

Sheila put the two reproductions side by side on the table. The reproduction in the catalogue was entitled *Girl in a Window* and attributed to the School of Murillo. The changes that had been made in the picture made it look, curiously, much more like the mezzotint engraving than the picture in Bauer's photograph.

The most dramatic change was in the face. The mouth was now set in a smile that looked like something between a grimace and a leer, and the eyes had been exaggerated so that they seemed to bug idiotically out of their sockets. The costume had been changed slightly also, so that the woman's shoulders and arms were now bare. The pearls and other jewelry were gone, and there was a large flower in the sitter's hair. It was clumsily painted; it might have been either a rose or a carnation, and it was annoyingly obtrusive and cute. There was a large handkerchief in her left hand, which upset the balance of the composition, and the surfaces had been glazed over to cover any traces of the powerful brushwork that was there before. Hatcher had been right about the tinted varnish. The picture was now covered with a dark, muddy film.

"It looks like a portrait of one of the whores down in the Combat Zone, only uglier."

"I agree. Would you want this picture?"

"I can hardly bear to look at it. No one with any taste at all would touch it with a barge pole."

"Can you tell it's been tampered with?"

"I don't know. Have you got a loupe?"

Hatcher rummaged around in his bag, then came back with a lens in a leather slipcase. Sheila bent over the plate in the catalogue and examined it closely, from side to side and corner to corner.

"No. Not from the photograph. Maybe if I examined

the original carefully I could spot it. But of course I wouldn't. I'd take one look and go right past it. Spanish baroque painting anyplace outside of Madrid or Seville can be pretty clumsy and naive, so I'd probably accept it as original."

"Exactly."

"Another thing: 'School of Murillo.' Murillo is about the hardest baroque artist to sell. Both his reputation and his prices are still way down. We had one at the gallery. Beautiful picture, too, and it sat around for years. School pieces are a dime a dozen, and so are copies, fakes, manner pictures, the lot. So I'd imagine that the speculative value of something like that would be just about zero."

"And you'd never suspect there was anything else under all that bad overpainting and mucky varnish?"

"Not in a million years. I wouldn't even take the trouble to clean it. Where is it, Amos?"

"Ever heard of Bartlett's Auction Barn in Falmouth, Massachusetts?"

"No. Is that where he's got it?"

"Yes. The auction's next Tuesday. We'll be there, in force."

"Will Ross, do you think?"

"Maybe. I hope so. Or maybe he'll send someone. Either way, we'll get him when he picks it up."

"Oh, I almost forgot. Does it say who the owner of the panel is supposed to be?"

"There's a note in the catalogue. It just says 'Property of a Gentleman.' "

"The final touch."

34

THE AFTERNOON BEFORE the auction, Sheila and Hatcher hired a car and drove down to the Cape, arriving at West Falmouth shortly after seven. The weather, which had warmed up briefly, was turning sour again.

It had been Hatcher's idea to come down the day before. Part of it was the weather; they were getting reports of a possible nor'easter, and Hatcher wanted to be very sure that they weren't snowed in at Boston. Part of it was nerves. They had spent several hours with Callahan and O'Rourke rehearsing the scenario for the auction, but there really wasn't that much to it and they all found they were repeating themselves after the first half hour.

O'Rourke had had several pictures taken of Ross through a telephoto lens when he was under surveillance: Ross entering the Museum, Ross leaving the Museum, Ross grabbing for his hat on a gusty afternon, Ross fumbling for his car keys. Hatcher had examined all of them closely, and had quickly become bored with them. None of them told him any of the things he wanted to know about Ross at all, except that he looked more or less the way Hatcher had imagined him.

Other than that, there was nothing to do. Nothing but wait. Hatcher couldn't tell whether it was the inactivity or the anticipation, but he found that both he and Sheila were lapsing into periods of morose silence, and snapping at each other over nothing. The trip to West Falmouth was at least an escape from the claustrophobic atmosphere that was suffocating them in Boston.

Choosing to remain as inconspicuous as possible, they decided to stay at the most anonymous-looking spot they could find, and eventually settled on the Piney Knoll Motel. The Piney Knoll was about as nondescript as could have reasonably been expected, even in a motel: simply a row of little white cottages with green trim linked by a boardwalk. Sheila announced delightedly that it looked just like the motel in Alfred Hitchcock's *Psycho*, and spent several minutes elaborating the fantasy of Tony Perkins bursting into their cabin grinning maniacally and waving a bread knife. Hatcher enjoyed the joke, but later, when she decided she needed a shower, Sheila was deadly serious when she stationed Hatcher directly in front of the bathroom door. Nerves, Hatcher decided. But he stood there nevertheless, as solemn as a statue.

The next morning broke gray and cold. Sheila and Hatcher were out of the motel by eight. They decided to get over to Falmouth as quickly as possible, locate the auction house, and then look around for breakfast. Hatcher wanted to be at Bartlett's as close to the opening time of nine as he could. The auction was scheduled to begin at eleven, but they wanted to allow plenty of time to reconnoiter.

They passed Bartlett's Auction Barn twice before they found it. The sign was small and discreet, almost prim, and the neat Gothic letters formed an amusing

240

contrast to the neon exuberance of the sign announcing Phil's Steak House thirty yards or so farther on.

The auction barn was set well back off the highway, and was screened from it by a row of pines. Hatcher swung the car onto the sandy driveway, past the cordon of pines, and pulled into a parking area in front of Bartlett's. Both the parking area and the auction house were larger than Hatcher had expected, and he was also somewhat surprised to find that Bartlett's Auction Barn had, in fact, once been a barn. It was a plain, no-nonsense clapboard building with a hipped roof, which sported an elegant gilded weathervane in the form of a running horse. It was painted white instead of red, but otherwise gave the impression that it had not changed much in seventy-five years or so.

Sheila was charmed.

"What a nice oasis. I don't have the feeling the people at Sotheby Parke Bernet have a whole lot to worry about, though."

"I wouldn't be too sure. But one or two of them will probably be here, so you can ask them."

"What? For a little country auction?"

"We'll see about that 'little country auction.' Let's get some breakfast first, though."

They walked back through the driveway, and found a diner a couple of blocks down the highway. There they had a breakfast that seemed to consist largely of papier-mâché boiled in grease, and both of them needed a couple of cups of coffee to get rid of the taste. That left them with the problem of getting rid of the taste of the coffee, which was black and bitter and seemed to have been mixed with several teaspoons of charcoal granules.

"Like Nelson Algren said, never eat at a place called Mom's."

"It's not; it's called Charley's."

"Same thing."

"This is the off-season, Amos."

"That's lucky. I was about to suggest that they give Cape Cod back to the Indians. If they'd take it."

"Sure they'd take it. They could sell it to the Arabs."

"Only if they threw in Nantucket and Martha's Vineyard, I bet."

Several minutes later they were back at Bartlett's. The interior of the auction house was quite different from what Sheila, at least, had expected, and it reminded her of Hatcher's earlier remark about the Parke Bernet people.

The large central hall of the barn had been neatly sub-divided, with a space for the auction itself and a somewhat larger room, to the left, where the objects could be viewed beforehand. They were met at the door by a rather severe-looking young woman standing next to a table with a pile of catalogues and a stack of bidding cards. Hatcher took two of these, writing his and Sheila's name in a book, and noting the numbers on the cards. He hesitated for a moment over whether or not to use a pseudonym, then decided against it. He put Sheila's address down for both of them.

The auction room was simple and undecorated. Rows of collapsible wooden chairs were lined up facing a dais set on a platform at the back of the room, and to the left of the dais stood a heavy oak table with an easel on it. The space was punctuated by three massive wooden posts which directed one's eye up to the elaborate wooden truss supporting the roof.

If the effect of the auction room was New England rural, the viewing room next to it was decorated in a Madison Avenue mode. It had a modern ceiling with expensive track lights, a parquet floor, and paneled walls covered with monk's cloth for hanging things. Sheila had the curious feeling that Bartlett's Auction Barn was composed of two very different places, rather like Micheline's antique store.

242

The amount of material was impressive, and so was the range of quality. There was furniture of just about every vintage and condition: chairs, tables, cabinets, grandfather clocks, player pianos, love seats, desks, even a small wooden box with holes in the top and one open side that was identified in the catalogue as a seventeenth-century footwarmer. There was also a row of tables lined up against one wall stacked with every imaginable kind of plate, platter, cup, tureen, glass, and mug, and the opposite wall was crowded with every conceivable type of hanging decoration, from paintings to tapestries to a large black silk banner with orange trim that proclaimed: 'Princeton, Class of '29."

The pictures were as diverse as the furniture. There were a number of handsome, anonymous eighteenth-century American portraits, several strong marine paintings, and a large American Impressionist nude that made Sheila wish that Weinstock were with them. There were not as many European pictures as American, but there were several late nineteenth-century French and English academic paintings whose dazzling technique and sentimentalized eroticism had again become fashionable. Amos and Sheila were surprised to find that one of them was estimated in the catalogue at between twelve and fifteen thousand dollars.

Some of the paintings were dreadful, however, and when they found their panel they were only mildly surprised. The halftone illustration in the catalogue could indicate the formal distortions that had been introduced into the composition, but not the tawdriness of the color. All the areas of flesh had been tinted an awful shade of orange, and the flower in the hair was shocking pink. The background was now opaque rather than transparent, a uniform, milky greenish-brown that set off the hideous orange of the flesh tones.

The frame around it was a cast plaster neo-Victorian monstrosity. It was painted with bronze powder which had turned brown, and someone had tried to cover up the chips and broken corners with another metallic paint of a slightly different shade. As a result, the frame looked mottled and leprous. It had once been decorated with little plaster rosettes, but in time most of these had fallen off.

Since they didn't want to draw attention either to the painting or to themselves, Sheila and Amos quickly moved on, feigning an interest in some Victorian stoneware on a table in one corner. Periodically they glanced surreptitiously across the room, but no one seemed even to notice the panel. There was an anonymous American still life next to it, a small canvas with a simple arrangement of peaches and strawberries, that was drawing a good deal of interest. Scrutinizing the other people around her, Sheila realized that while a number of them were casual collectors simply browsing around, a number of others were dealers who knew exactly what they were looking for, and looked as if they were already mentally calculating profit margins.

Ten minutes later they decided they'd had enough. They were both becoming tense with anticipation. Although they didn't really expect Ross to appear, the chance that he might kept them both edgy. They found a fried-chicken restaurant on the highway with coffee a bit more palatable than Charley's, and spent half an hour or so trying to understand the mysterious metamorphosis of last year's junk into this year's Rare Americana.

They waited until it was nearly time for the auction before going back. Sure enough, Callahan was sitting in an unmarked car directly across the parking area from the entrance to the gallery. He was wearing a blue work shirt, slacks, and tinted sunglasses, and he was drumming idly on the steering wheel with his fingers as he watched the entrance. They walked past him without making a sign.

"Subtle, isn't he? He looks exactly like the wheel-man in every film about a bank robbery that's ever been made. All he needs is a violin case on the seat next to him."

When they entered the gallery, most of the rickety-looking wooden chairs were occupied. O'Rourke was seated far to the left in the back row, close to the door. He was wearing brown slacks, a chlorophyll green shirt open at the neck, and a brown sports coat. He was sitting in his accustomed pose of Neanderthal stupidity, with his arms hanging down at his side like dead weights and his jaw working up and down, mouth open.

"I like O'Rourke a little better, but not much. He looks like a bouncer in a tough South Boston saloon."

"He always looks like a bouncer in a South Boston saloon. Even when he's in uniform."

The last two remarks were whispered. The auctioneer was standing at a wooden lectern, tapping the microphone with his fingers to test it. There were perhaps two hundred seats in the house, and the auctioneer seemed pleased with the turnout, occasionally smiling at familiar faces.

Sheila stayed in the back row, at the opposite end from O'Rourke, and Hatcher edged his way up to the front row and sat down just as the auctioneer began to speak. He was a nervous, slight man, with a voice that sounded as though it had been to all the right schools.

"Good morning, welcome to Bartlett's December auction. Today we'll be offering for your consideration fine furniture, Americana, decorative items, objets d'art, and paintings of various schools. I hope you all have numbered cards if you intend to bid. If you don't, you may obtain one from Miss Hamilton."

He pointed to the woman who had previously been standing at the door; she flashed a brief, rather pained smile and held up a stack of cards. Several people got up and went over to her.

245

"As most of you know, the final price on any bid is an aggregate of the hammer price plus ten percent, as well as state and local taxes. If you wish to leave before the end of the auction with an item that you've purchased, please speak to Miss Courtney, whose office is through this door on my right. A detailed account of terms of payment and guarantees may be found on page three of the catalogue."

The auctioneer opened a notebook, cleared his throat, and waited for the people getting cards to return to their seats.

"Item number one."

Two beefy characters appeared at the side door pushing a dolly on which a huge oak rolltop desk was placed. They carted it neatly to the front of the room and swung it around toward the audience.

"I think we'll start this at seven hundred . . . do I hear seven hundred? . . . Good, seven, near the post. Do I hear seven fifty? Seven fifty then, eight hundred in front to my right . . ."

The litany continued briskly for a minute or so, then went more slowly, the hammer finally falling at eleven hundred dollars. Hatcher could feel himself tensing. The panel was coming up soon; it was listed as number eight in the catalogue. He shifted nervously in his seat, and it creaked loudly beneath him. Without thinking, he rolled his catalogue in a tight coil, and when he unrolled it he noticed dark stains where his hands had been. He reached down and absentmindedly wiped his palms on the coat he'd hung on the back of the chair.

"The catalogue should note that the mate to this is in the Winterthur Museum. . . . Perhaps we should start this at two hundred dollars . . ."

35

"NUMBER EIGHT, *Girl at a Window*—School of Murillo. What should I ask to start the bidding? Shall we say two hundred? One fifty, then? Good, one fifty at the back . . . now, one seventy-five . . ."

Hatcher's heart was racing. The plan was for Sheila to open the bidding and stay in until it reached four hundred dollars, and to bid fast, accelerating the pace, to allow Hatcher to spot the other bidders quickly. It took a powerful effort of the will to keep him from swinging around in his chair with the first few bids, but he forced himself to wait to avoid being too obvious.

"Two twenty-five in the middle. Do I hear two fifty? Two fifty at the back of the room, now two seventy-five in the middle, back to you at three hundred . . ."

By the time the bidding reached three hundred dollars, it was clear that the only people still in it were "the lady in the back row," which Hatcher assumed meant Sheila, and a mysterious "gentleman in the middle." Finally Hatcher turned around in his chair, grabbed his coat, and stood up. He went to the aisle on his left, turned, and slowly walked to the back of the room.

A quick glance proved that the "gentleman in the middle," whoever he was, was not Ross. He was a bald, middle-aged man in a tan leisure suit. He was staring down at the catalogue in his lap, and periodically signaling his bid by languidly raising his right hand and wagging his fingers. He looked as bored as Callahan and O'Rourke.

By the time Hatcher reached the back of the room, the bidding had gone to four hundred dollars. Sheila put her hand down just as Hatcher slid into the seat next to her, and with the next bid the painting went to the man in the tan leisure suit. Sheila leaned over to whisper to Hatcher.

"Not Ross?"

"No, not Ross. He must have sent a stooge to get it for him."

"What happens now?"

"We follow him, and when he hands it over to Ross we grab both of them."

"Relieved or disappointed?"

Hatcher smiled.

"A little of both, I guess. I don't know why, but Ross frightens me."

"Sure you know why. He's frightening. He's frightening as hell."

They sat through the rest of the auction because there was nothing else to do and because they wanted to keep an eye on the character in the tan suit. But they increasingly felt a maddening combination of nervous excitement and profound boredom, like people waiting in the dentist's office.

After what was in fact two hours but felt like several weeks, the last item had been sold. Most of the people had gone. The two grips who had been moving articles from the viewing room to the sales room were now busy stacking chairs, and the successful bidders had gone back to pick up their new possessions.

But the man in the tan suit still sat where he'd been sitting during the auction. Apparently he had no inclination to go claim his prize. O'Rourke was still at the back of the room, and he was watching Hatcher. Sheila was watching him too, and it was clear that he was becoming more and more upset. Finally he got up.

"Something's all wrong. Wait for me here, will you?"

Hatcher went over to the man in the leisure suit. He spoke to him for a few minutes, and the man alternately smirked and looked sheepish. Then Hatcher broke away and went over to the auctioneer, who was standing at the lectern reviewing the sale. Hatcher looked furious, and the auctioneer seemed bewildered. He listened to Hatcher for a while, shrugged, then went through a door at the back of the room leading to the offices and storerooms. He emerged a minute later with a couple of pieces of paper. Hatcher took them, made some notes on the back of his catalogue, turned on his heel, and went back to Sheila.

The auctioneer was also upset by this time, and called after Hatcher.

"There's nothing irregular in that, you know. It happens all the time."

Hatcher wasn't listening to him. He was white-faced and seething. When he got to Sheila, he grabbed her roughly by the shoulder and propelled her toward the entrance.

"We've been had. Let's get O'Rourke and get the hell out of here."

In front of the auction barn Hatcher swore and savagely kicked the dust in front of him. While O'Rourke tried to calm him down, Sheila got Callahan and suggested that they have a conference at the fried-chicken restaurant. When they squeezed into the booth, Hatcher was more controlled but still livid.

"Ross was there."

"What? He couldn't have been."

"He was there, goddammit!"

"How? I was next to the door, Callahan was across from the entrance . . ."

"He never went near the front entrance. He was out at the back. He called and arranged it with the auctioneer early this morning. He told him that he wanted the painting, and that he would have someone bidding on it for him in the audience. He said that somebody else would be in the audience, and that he didn't want the other person to know what he was buying. Anyway, as soon as it was sold it was taken out to Ross, who was parked by the loading platform. Ross paid cash, signed a receipt with a phony signature, and took off."

"The auctioneer probably thought Ross was a dealer. Dealers are always playing little games, little tricks, and none of them wants any of the others to know what he's doing."

"Exactly. This sort of thing happens a lot."

"What about the bidder, the man in the tan suit?"

"He's a bartender from Quincy. He never saw Ross before this morning. Ross grabbed him, told him what he wanted done, and promised him two hundred easy dollars—one down, one later."

"Could he describe Ross?"

"Not closely enough to do us any good. Ross was wearing a ski cap and sunglasses, and kept his hand over his mouth most of the time."

"Well, where did the panel come from? Who's the owner supposed to be?"

Hatcher put his auction catalogue upside down on the table, and read his notes in a sarcastic voice.

" 'H. K. Wilmott, 202 South Street, Pawtucket, Rhode Island.' "

"Well, at least that's—"

"Forget it. There's no such person, no such place."

250

"How about the signature on the receipt?"

"An illegible scrawl, not nearly enough for a graphologist."

"I could put out an APB . . ."

"Forget that too. He's probably home by now. Besides, what could you hold him on? What have you got? Possession of stolen property, at the very most, and what the hell good is that?"

O'Rourke tapped the saucer several times with his spoon, and sighed.

"Neat. How did he get it here?"

"Sent it. Everything else was done by telephone. The only people who saw Ross were the stooge who bid for him and the woman who took the painting out to him, and probably neither one of them could make a positive identification."

They paid the bill and left. When they got outside, Hatcher put his hand on Sheila's shoulder.

"I want you to take Callahan back with you in the car. I'm going with O'Rourke."

"Now just a second—"

"Sheila!"

His voice sounded like an angry snarl. He'd never spoken that way to Sheila before, and it frightened her.

"Okay. All right, Amos."

36

THEY WERE TWENTY MILES north of Falmouth now, heading for Boston. Hatcher's left leg was doubled up and his left foot was placed on the seat. His right hand was clenched in a fist which he tapped rhythmically on the dashboard. The tapping was not hard, but determined.

Hatcher looked straight ahead. O'Rourke thought he seemed coiled. Like a spring, or maybe a snake.

Neither man had spoken since the ride began.

It had begun to snow. The flakes were tiny, and there was as yet no accumulation on the road. The cars ahead threw up swirling white eddies in their wakes. O'Rourke had lived in Boston all his life, and he recognized the pattern. The snow would gradually get heavier, and it might last for days.

When Hatcher finally spoke, his voice was surprisingly gentle and without any inflection whatsoever.

"I'm going to go after him."

O'Rourke waited for a moment before he spoke.

253

"Look. Why not just wait until he produces the picture. He has to produce it, and fast. Why not—"

"Listen, Mike. I'm going after him. He'll have it all rigged, just like he had the auction rigged. He's been miles ahead of us, all the way. You know damn well—"

"Okay. But you're not going alone."

"God, no. I'm not mad. But I'm going in first. I go first, then you and Callahan . . ."

"Maybe. But we'll have to think it out. Plan it."

Hatcher hesitated a moment before he spoke.

"No. I'm going after him tonight."

"You crazy, Amos? We won't even be back in Boston until half-past seven, at least."

"Plenty of time. It has to be done this way. We both know that. Thinking's bullshit, planning's bullshit. The only way we'll ever get him is to go after him, flat out, with everything we've got. It doesn't make any difference whether it's tonight, tomorrow, or eight years from now, it's still got to be done. And this is still the only way to do it. I want to do it tonight because I'm ready to do it tonight and I'm not sure I'll be ready tomorrow, or the next day, or ever again. So I'm doing it tonight, with or without anybody else."

"Okay. Then it's tonight. What about Sheila?"

"Sheila's out of this. Sheila stays in Boston."

"She's not going to like that."

"I know."

The snow had become much heavier by the time they got to Boston. The first stop was Sheila's apartment. The last glimpse Hatcher had of her made him very sad. She was standing forlornly in the snow by a street-lamp, crying softly.

It was quarter past eight when they got to the station, and quarter of nine when they got to Hatcher's room in the Holiday Inn.

Hatcher had already put the photographs in the envelope. He was sitting on the bed with his shirt off.

O'Rourke had a large surveyor's map of Lincoln township, and was pointing out a route to Hatcher with his finger.

"There's a little hill here, see, and then there's a level patch for a hundred yards or so. Then there's a much steeper hill . . ."

"Mike, how do you know all this detail?"

O'Rourke smiled.

"I thought it through myself this way, so I drove out that way just to check it. A couple, maybe three times."

"That's what I suspected. Go on."

"Okay, a little hill followed by a big hill. There's a sign for lights maybe halfway up the hill, and then another sign that says 'No Left Turn.' That's key—can you remember that?"

"Sure. No left turn."

"Reason it's key, see, is that that's where you're gonna want to go, but you can't. At the top of the hill, at the lights, is the street you want. You have to go right. A hundred yards or so down the street is a little turnaround, not really a traffic circle. Use it, then go back the other way. You'll come to the same lights where you turned right before. This time you go through them, passing Mike's Garage on your right. Got that?"

"Mike's Garage, on the right."

"The place you want is about three hundred yards from the garage, again on the right. There'll be a long stone wall, ending with a short brick wall. That's the driveway. You'll see a small sign that just says 'Ross.' There's a long driveway, maybe a hundred yards even, but it only goes to one place, so don't worry about it. Ross's place is big, a kind of low, modern number of brick and fieldstone. And a lot of glass. Got that?"

"Got it."

"Also, they have spotlights. If they turn one on, don't let it spook you. Okay?"

"I won't."

"Remember. We'll be right behind you."

"I hope to God you will."

It took O'Rourke another twenty minutes to get Hatcher properly wired.

"This one here, the one we got taped to your chest?"

"Yes? What about it?"

"The adhesive tape's probably going to itch like crazy. For heaven's sake, don't scratch it. First, if you do you call attention to it. Second, we'll pick it up in the car. Magnified. Last guy we wired up scratched the tape, and my hearing hasn't been any too good since. Okay?"

"Okay."

"Good. Now this other one, the one that looks like a ballpoint pen?"

"Yes."

"The way this works, see, it's just like a real pen. You've got to push in the knob at the top until you hear a click, just like a pen. Don't do that until you get to the front door. That activates it. Now, there's a thin wire that I've run down through the lining of your jacket to the pocket. This end is attached to a box hidden inside this pack of Marlboros. Do you ever smoke?"

"Not cigarettes."

"Good. Dangerous habit. Reach for one tonight, and it might be an even more dangerous habit. That's all. Just remember to push the knob when you get to the front door."

"Okay, Mike. Now I want a gun, and a shoulder holster."

"Forget it. It wouldn't help you, and it might get you killed. Callahan and me, we're the ones that get to play with guns."

"All right. But be there. Just give me twenty minutes—"

"Like hell I will. You get ten minutes, and we're coming in. Whether you've got anything, or nothing at all, you got just ten minutes."

"Okay. When?"

"Show me your watch. You say nine-twenty-two. Okay, just a minute, nine-twenty-uh-two. The second hands are close, just ten seconds off. That should do it. I want you going through the door at exactly ten-forty-five by your watch. That should give you plenty of leeway, but we'd better get moving. Ten-forty-five exactly, got it? Okay, let's go."

The two men were in the parking lot. Hatcher was in the driver's seat, with his hand on the wheel, and O'Rourke was talking to him through the open window.

"One more thing, Mike. Tonight, when you follow me out, you do the driving, okay?"

O'Rourke roared.

"Of course. Are you kidding? I don't want *anybody* getting killed tonight."

Hatcher shook O'Rourke's hand, rolled up the window, and drove off.

37

THE SNOW WAS HEAVY by the time Hatcher got the unmarked police car onto Fresh Pond Parkway, and was
even heavier when he got past the rotaries and onto
Route Two. The area in Cambridge was lined with liquor stores, supermarkets, and fast-food restaurants, but
just a few miles beyond, the countryside became much
more open and sparsely populated. It occurred to
Hatcher, with irony, that this morning he was cursing
the vulgarity of just such stretches of plastic businesses
and neon signs, but now that they were falling behind
him, he felt an intense pang of loneliness and isolation.
Maybe they were ugly and tasteless, but such roadside
emporia were nevertheless emblems of human warmth
and community.

The snow under the wheels muffled the sound of the
car, and Hatcher suddenly was overcome by a curious
sense of unreality. He felt totally alone. He left Route
Two, turning the car onto a narrow street. Hatcher suddenly felt quite lost, as if he were in some upside-down,
Alice-in-Wonderland world, as if he'd been hanging on

to the lip of a huge funnel and now, his grip broken, were starting to slide down into the chute, with no way of stopping himself.

Then he realized where he was. The little hill, then a level patch. Good, this must be *the* level patch. Now the big hill. That must be the one ahead. Now, signs. What signs? Ah, a stoplight sign, now there should be—right, the sign that says No Left Turn. "Reason it's key, see, is that that's where you're gonna want to go, but you can't."

Hatcher tried to remember O'Rourke's instructions verbatim, and repeated them to himself like a magic incantation.

". . . a little turnaround, not really a traffic circle . . ." Right, that must be here, this little triangle.

"Mike's Garage," okay so far. Closed up tight. Wonder where Mike is? Probably in bed. Watching TV, screwing his wife, reading a book. Best of luck to you, Mike, thought Hatcher.

Hatcher stopped the car by the side of the road right across from the sign that said "Ross." He checked his watch. Ten-thirty-two, thirteen minutes to go. He turned off the engine, and found himself shocked by the silence, which had suddenly become almost absolute.

All he could hear was the beating of his own heart. He tried to think about things to quiet his nerves.

He thought about Sheila. Then he thought about Amsterdam, and Zurich, and Churwalden. He found these thoughts soothing, so he thought about other places he'd been, places he loved: London, Paris, Venice, Rome, and Florence. When he looked at his watch again, it was exactly ten-thirty-seven.

Six minutes later, when Hatcher stopped his car and stepped out onto the covered walkway leading to the front door of Ross's house, he felt totally calm. He knew no reason for this, nor did he question it. He simply walked to the front door, depressed the knob on the phony ballpoint pen as he'd been instructed to do, and rang the bell. The envelope was in his right hand.

A minute later, the door opened a crack. He could see the heavy chain lock and, behind it, a woman's face.

"Who are you? What do you want? Do you know what time—"

"I'm very sorry to disturb you, Mrs. Ross, but I must speak to your husband. It's a crucial matter; it won't wait. Tell him . . . tell him H. K. Wilmott of Pawtucket, Rhode Island, is here to see him."

"Very well. You'll have to wait here, though."

The door closed. In a minute, Hatcher would hear the chain lock being unfastened, and a few seconds later the door opened.

"Please come in, Mr. Wilmott. My husband says that he's anxious to speak to you. If you want, you can leave your coat and hat on those pegs, and your galoshes on the mat. My husband is in his study, just down at the end of the hall. Now, if you'll excuse me, please . . ."

It seemed to Hatcher that Mrs. Ross must once have been a beautiful woman. She was still a handsome one. But she seemed drawn and spiritless, as if she had sustained some ultimate, debilitating spiritual defeat. As she drifted up the spiral staircase out of sight she reminded Hatcher of Blanche DuBois in *A Streetcar Named Desire,* or Violetta in the last act of *La Traviata.*

Hatcher walked down the hall to Ross's study. Ross was seated at his desk. His elbows were resting on the top of the desk, and he held a pistol in his hands that was pointed at Hatcher's chest.

He looked older than Hatcher had expected, and did not seem angry so much as profoundly sad.

"Close the door behind you, and sit down in that chair in front of the desk. I will shoot you if I have to. 'One false move' is the cliché, I believe."

Hatcher did as he was told. He suddenly had the feeling that he had very few moves, false or otherwise,

261

and wished that O'Rourke had at least given him a gun.

"Now, who are you and what do you want? And don't give me that 'H. K. Wilmott' business again."

"My name isn't important . . ."

"Listen, you stupid bastard . . . All right, then. Take off your jacket. Take it off slowly, and slide it across the desk to me. Slowly."

Be here, O'Rourke.

Hatcher handed Ross his jacket. Keeping his gun trained on Hatcher, Ross removed the wallet from the jacket pocket and dropped it on the desk. He ran his left hand over the jacket, patting it, then handed it back to Hatcher.

Ross checked through the wallet until he found the card he was looking for and then read it aloud.

" 'Amos Hatcher, Investigator, International Association of Art Dealers.' I'm afraid all that means nothing to me, Hatcher. You'd better explain."

Ross's voice was tight and menacing.

"I want to talk about the pot, Ross."

"Pot? What pot?" The director's expression didn't change. Hatcher had the feeling that he was back in Switzerland seated across the table from Sarkes Manoukian and, as before, felt the situation slipping from his control.

Time's up, O'Rourke. Time to come and get me.

"You know, Ross. The Manoukian pot."

"I think I recall the name, Manoukian, Manoukian . . . yes, of course. An excellent man for rugs. I think we got our Bokhara . . ."

"Nope, that's Harry Manoukian, the rug king. And Freddy Manoukian, he's a pants presser in Dorchester, and Big Daddy Manoukian plays left tackle for the Green Bay Packers. I'm talking about Sarkes Manoukian, the art dealer, the man who commissioned the *tombaroli* in Cerveteri to steal the Exekias krater, the

262

man who smuggled it out of Italy and brought it to the States to sell. And sold it to you, Ross."

You're late, O'Rourke. For God's sake.

Ross tensed. His right hand tightened around the pistol, and Hatcher noticed that his knuckles were white. For a moment Hatcher half-expected him to shoot. Then Ross seemed to relax slightly. He gave Hatcher a nasty smile.

"All right, I'll ask you again. Who are you, and what do you want?"

"I work for dealers. I trace stolen art and I try to get it back. That's all."

"Very noble, Mr. Hatcher. I admire you. You must have got to Manoukian. I'll assume that, that you somehow got him to talk. But that won't do you any good, because you don't have the pot and you can't get Manoukian out of Switzerland. A deposition, perhaps, a piece of paper, but not extraditon. And a piece of paper is worthless, since Manoukian is a notorious liar."

Please, Mike.

"I wouldn't be too sure about Manoukian. We can't extradite him, you're right. But maybe we can get him to come voluntarily."

"Never. That's absurd."

"Not entirely. Manoukian lives in Switzerland, but his heart—using the term broadly—lies in Italy."

"The pretty young men hanging around the Piazza di Spagna?"

"Partly, perhaps, but other things as well. If I can convince Roberto Anselmo and the Italian officials that Manoukian was responsible for the theft of the pot, they'll never let him back in their country again."

"So?"

"Unless, of course, Manoukian himself is a principal agent in the recovery of the pot and its restitution to Cerveteri."

"Blackmail, in short. It might even work—if I didn't have this gun, and you hadn't walked in here alone and unarmed."

Alone. Where the hell are you, O'Rourke?

Hatcher felt his fear returning. There wasn't much time left, and he was running out of lines.

"I'm not alone, Ross. And it isn't just the pot. It's the panel, too."

Ross gasped, remembering "H. K. Wilmott." He was visibly shaken, and for the first time his composure cracked.

"So you knew about the panel? How the hell could you?"

"I was there at Bartlett's. With the police. I know all about the panel. And Weinstock, and Giardino. I have something to show you."

Please, O'Rourke, please, please, please.

Hatcher opened the envelope that was lying on his lap, extracted a photograph, and slid it across the table to Ross. Ross glanced at it momentarily, scowled, and glared at Hatcher.

"Where did you get this?"

"From an art historian in the Hague. It's an old photograph, but it's valuable because it shows both the panel *and* its frame. I have another photograph that should also interest you."

Hatcher took the second photograph from the file and handed it to Ross.

"That's Weinstock's body, in the foreground, lying where you killed him. But that's not important. What's important, as evidence, is the fact that you can see the same frame leaning against the bin in the background. The same frame, Ross. I can prove that."

Ross looked at the photograph, then glanced up at Hatcher. There was nothing in his eyes, not even hatred.

My last card, O'Rourke.

"You can't prove anything, Hatcher, not if you're dead. Look behind me, out that window."

Ross swung his right hand, the hand with the pistol, in a vague arc over his head.

"See the fields back there? And the woods? Forty-three acres of land, Hatcher. That's a good deal of land. My land. No one ever walks around it except me, my family, and an occasional dog. The snow piles up in deep drifts that don't disappear until early May, sometimes. Your body won't be found for months, if ever."

Hatcher was looking out the window. Not at the woods, but at the panting figure of O'Rourke, who was fumbling with his parka in the effort to reach his gun.

"All that's over, Ross. All the murders. Look behind you."

O'Rourke stood poised, his feet spread, his automatic free.

"Don't be silly, Hatcher."

Smiling, Ross raised his gun to fire.

At that moment, Hatcher kicked his legs under the chair and jackknifed forward. He tried to spin his body sideways, flinging out his right arm to break his fall.

A muffled explosion and the sound of shattering glass were the last things Hatcher heard before his head struck the corner of the desk.

O'Rourke's shot caught Ross in the shoulder, spinning him around with its impact and sending him sprawling. When he recovered he realized that his body was beneath the level of the sill, safe from another shot through the window. Gritting his teeth against the pain, he tried to train his gun on Hatcher, who was shielded by the heavy mahogany desk. Ross fired twice in a futile rage, which produced nothing but a shower of splinters, and heard, like an echo, O'Rourke's fist beating on the front door.

Ross felt weak and dizzy, and with the last of his strength he managed to raise his gun one more time.

When the last shot was fired O'Rourke had already burst through the door, and was pounding down the hall toward the study. He was horrified by the scene he found there, and for a moment thought that he was too late. Hatcher was lying on the floor bleeding heavily from a head wound, and Ross was wedged between the chair and the desk. There was a small black mark on the side of his head, and blood trickled from the corner of his mouth.

As O'Rourke bent over him, Hatcher began to moan and rock back and forth, rubbing his forehead. O'Rourke was just reaching for the telephone when the spectral figure of Mrs. Ross, standing in the doorway, started to scream.

38

THE CELEBRATION that took place late the following afternoon in Hatcher's hospital room was, in general, a happy one.

Sheila sat on the side of the bed, with her hand on Hatcher's good shoulder. Her face wore the same soft, dreamy expression Hatcher had seen that first morning in Amsterdam.

Hatcher also seemed happy, an impressive feat under the circumstances. His head was bandaged, and he wore a splinted and weighted cast from his right shoulder to his wrist.

Callahan looked more than happy. He looked positively gleeful. Although usually he was terse and taciturn, today they found it almost impossible to shut him up.

Only O'Rourke didn't seem to share in the general merriment. He was hunched over in his chair next to Hatcher's bed. He looked utterly miserable. Periodically he would glare homicidally at Callahan, which didn't seem to bother Callahan at all.

"So there we were, the captain and me, just kinda tooling along. O'Rourke's driving, see? Everything's smooth, everything's cool, we've got time to burn. We're already in Lincoln and just sort of gliding along, then you know what happens?"

"Bastard." That was the first thing O'Rourke had said in fifteen minutes.

"You know what happens then? This itty-bitty little rabbit, this tiny little bit of a thing, goes hippity-hopping right into the middle of the road—"

"You know how many times Callahan's told this story? In the last six hours, how many times?"

"So you know what Mike does? He *whips* the wheel over, WHAP! like that, and then he *slams* on his brakes. Ker-WHAM! Like that."

O'Rourke's upper body seemed to slide several inches closer to the floor. His voice sounded dull, defeated.

"It's a reflex. I brake for animals, I can't help it. Callahan now, Callahan wouldn't brake for his own mother."

Callahan wasn't listening to O'Rourke.

"So what happens then, see, is we go into this terrific skid, just like a kid on a sled: WHOOSH! And we go right off the road. Right off the road, and up over the stone wall . . ."

O'Rourke's voice became even more lugubrious and funereal.

"I brake for animals. I even got a bumper sticker . . ."

Callahan heard that and became even more gleeful.

"You know, he does. A bumper sticker. On a goddamn *police cruiser*, for God's sake. Anyway, there we are stuck up on this stone wall. Two wheels on one side, two wheels on the other, just like some crazy see-saw—"

"Hatcher. You heard about police brutality? You

268

heard about sadistic cops? Take Callahan. Classic case."

"And you know what that little bunny-rabbit's doing? He's sitting right in the middle of the road, laughing his little head off."

O'Rourke, who could take it no more, exploded.

"That's a lie, that's a stinking lie! Rabbits don't laugh, first of all . . . Callahan! Callahan's the one that's laughing like a madman—"

"I wasn't. I was calling for a backup."

O'Rourke sighed. It sounded almost like a moan.

"That's the only part Callahan tells. That's the punch line, about the laughing rabbit, which is a vicious lie. Callahan never mentions how I ran two, three hundred yards maybe, through the snow—"

"Two hundred. At most."

"—through the snow, cross-country, or how I got Ross cleanly, first shot, right through the shoulder—"

"Yeah. He wasn't aiming for the shoulder, though."

"You see, Hatcher? You see? He's a sadist!"

Hatcher, who had been enjoying the scene enormously up to now, decided maybe it was time to intervene.

"Come on, Leo. Enough. Mike saved my life, for God's sake."

"Thank you, Hatcher."

"What the hell, everyone was a hero. Even me, and I was passed out on the floor—"

"Not passed out. Knocked out. Apparently your arm gave out completely when you landed on it, and you knocked yourself cold on the edge of Ross's desk. When you hit the deck like that, you gotta know how to land."

Sheila, incensed at the implication that there was anything Hatcher couldn't do, explained to O'Rourke and Callahan how Hatcher's arm had been twisted and wrenched in Switzerland. There was a strong hint in her explanation that if Hatcher's right arm had been healthy he would have done a cartwheel, a plié, and a double axel, and ended by kicking the gun out of Ross's hand.

When Callahan spoke again, his voice sounded sober.

"I'll make a deal, Mike."

O'Rourke's face clouded over.

"No deals. Not with you."

"You haven't heard it yet. This is the deal, your part. One, I go back to being the driver. Right? Two, no more cracks about my driving. I've been taking crap for years about that, so no more. No more of this 'Mario Andretti' stuff. Right?"

"I don't know about this. What do I get?"

"What you get is, I don't tell the story about the rabbit."

O'Rourke concentrated for a moment. His jaw pumped furiously.

"Blackmail, Leo."

"Right."

O'Rourke concentrated some more.

"Okay."

Callahan jumped up, grinning delightedly. He went over to O'Rourke, slapped him on the back, and stuck out his hand.

"Friends, Mike?"

"Okay." O'Rourke shook Callahan's hand unenthusiastically, without looking up from the floor. Sheila and Hatcher were totally deadpan, but Sheila gave Hatcher's shoulder a firm squeeze.

A bit later, Hatcher asked about Ross.

"Ross is apparently going to be okay. More or less."

"I'm sorry about that. I wish you'd killed him." Sheila's voice was deadly serious.

"I think maybe so does Ross. Like I said, I got him through the shoulder. I still can't figure out how he got the gun up to his head. He must have wanted to do it pretty bad, is all I can figure. Anyway, he did it, but he didn't do it right. The slug missed the brain entirely and exited through his left temple. But it cut the optic nerves. Ross will be permanently blind."

"What about the panel, and the pot?" Sheila still sounded intent.

"The panel was easy. It was in his basement in a little sort of workshop. Sitting right on a table. He was probably working on it when Hatcher rang the bell."

"And the pot?"

O'Rourke grinned.

"You're going to like this. We found the pot in his office at the Museum. It was in a box covered with red and green foil, with a big silk bow. A card, too, which said, 'Don't Open Until Christmas.' The box had little reindeer and Santas stuck all over it."

"That's cute. I was wondering how he planned to get it out of the Museum."

A little while later, Callahan and O'Rourke left. Before they went out the door, though, they left a Christmas present for Sheila and Hatcher. It was a huge bottle of Irish whiskey.

"That was sweet, wasn't it, Amos? Do you like the stuff, by the way?"

"You mean straight? God, no. It tastes just like kerosene. I like Irish coffee, though."

"Swell. We can have Irish coffee for the next year and a half."

They were silent for a bit, just enjoying being together.

"It's funny, Sheila. They think of us as a married couple, and we almost think of them as a married couple. We'll have to get something for them. What do you get for two Boston Irish cops?"

"What about a stuffed rabbit?"

271

Epilogue

THE NEXT DAY, somewhat against his doctor's orders, Hatcher left the hospital and moved into Sheila's apartment.

He was still there a week later. His shoulder and elbow were healing nicely, and it was decided that the cast could be taken off. Sheila made Hatcher a sling. She cut out several pieces of cloth and worked very hard for two days, and finally presented it to Hatcher ceremoniously. It had a bear on it, just like the Zurich scarf, but in place of the bear's face it had Sheila's face. Sheila rampant, in a field of blue.

They talked incessantly during that week, about everything. One of the things they discussed was marriage. Sheila hesitated, not because of Hatcher, but because she was unwilling to give up Boston, or the gallery, or a routine of daily life that she enjoyed. Hatcher respected this and did not press her. He realized that it would be equally hard for him to give up his peripatetic habits or his job. The issue of marriage did not, finally, seem to be particularly significant, so they let it ride.

The disposition of the panel provided a final irony. Ultimate ownership of the painting proved to be a complex legal issue, but on the face of it, it seemed to belong to Micheline, as sole heir to Samuel Weinstock's gallery and estate. Micheline decided without hesitation that it should be donated to the Boston Museum in Weinstock's name. Thus it was taken to the Museum pro tem, pending the outcome of the case. After that, it was presumed by everyone, it would become a permanent part of the collection.

Ross's overpainting, as Hatcher had suspected, proved to be very easy to remove. The heavy varnish underneath it, however, was extremely stubborn. After several days, though, the painting at last resembled Bauer's photograph again.

It was the photograph that gave Hatcher the notion. He discussed it first of all with Walker Richards, who thought it was a splendid idea, and then with the conservator of paintings, who concurred. Hatcher's proposal was that the Museum should fly Franz Bauer to the United States, find him an apartment near the Museum, and appoint him to a temporary position on the curatorial staff. He could oversee the final stages of the cleaning and restoration of the panel, analyze the work, and then publish his conclusions either in the Museum's journal or as a separate booklet.

Hatcher contacted Bauer by phone and received his reply the next day by wire. Dr. Bauer said that he would be delighted to accept the invitation with, however, a single stipulation. This was simply that the museum refrain from making any public announcement referring to the picture as anything other than "Dutch, seventeenth century" until Bauer had had a chance to render an informed scholarly judgment on the matter.

This amused Sheila. "How old-fashioned. Bauer apparently doesn't understand that museums today are ninety percent showbiz, PR, and hype. He probably still thinks of King Tut as an Egyptian pharaoh rather than a media event."

Both Hatcher and Sheila were extremely excited with the notion of Bauer's projected visit, which was scheduled for late February or early March, and Hatcher immediately set about trying to arrange a colloquium of Bauer's former students in his honor. It was in the middle of this that the argument began.

Like most serious domestic disputes, it started innocently enough.

"Have you ever been to Chios, dear?"

"No. Where's that?"

"One of the Greek Islands. It's in the Aegean, just off the coast of Turkey."

"What about it?"

"It's supposed to be lovely. Not at all spoiled, like Mykonos and some of the others."

"I repeat: what about it?"

"Nothing, dear. I just was reading something in the paper, that's all."

At this point it wasn't even an argument. But, several hours later:

"Sheila, do you know what a *kouros* is?"

"I think so, yes. Isn't it an archaic Greek statue of some kind? A man or a woman?"

"Man. A woman's called a *kore*."

"So?"

"I was just reading around in one of your books. I just ran across it."

Sheila was suspicious by this time, but she let it drop. The next morning, though, she noticed that Hatcher seemed preoccupied.

"Penny for your thoughts, Amos."

"A *kouros*."

"What?"

"I was thinking about a *kouros*. I mean, those things are big. Ten feet tall, some of them."

"Amos, what's this all about?"

"Nothing, I was just thinking. If you wanted to move a *kouros*, that would really be an operation. We're talking about a life-size marble figure. Maybe even larger. If you wanted to move it, you'd have to have the right equipment. A forklift, or something."

"Amos—"

"And once you figure out how to move it, where are you going to move it *to?* I mean, Chios is a pretty big island, but it's not *that* big. It must have been done by boat, that's the way I see it."

"Amos—"

"That means there have got to be eight or ten people, right? This thing must have been nicely organized. Once you've got it, what do you do with it? What good is it? That's the second problem."

"Amos!"

"Huh?"

"Amos, dear. You haven't said anything in the last ten minutes that's made any sense at all. Kindly explain what you're talking about."

"What? Oh. I was just flipping through the newspaper the other day, and I came across an item. Just a few lines. It said that a *kouros* was stolen last week—"

"—from the island of Chios—"

"—from the island of Chios, and I was just curious about it. That's all."

"You want to go to Chios. You want to go after it, right?"

"Well, I was thinking . . . I mean, the traffic in stolen antiquities is something fierce."

"So? Look, Amos, you're a free man. You want to go to Chios, go to Chios."

"I checked with the IAAD. They're very concerned about it."

"What's the problem, then?"

"Well, I talked it over with the people at the IAAD.

276

They agreed. It looks complicated, just on the surface. It looks like a ring, an organization. I told them it looked too complex for one person, so they told me to get someone else. An assistant."

That's when the argument began.

"You aren't thinking about me, are you?"

"Well, actually—"

"Amos, do I look like a detective to you?"

"That's it. That's exactly it. You look nothing like a detective at all, that's why—"

"Dear? Thank you, but no. I'm a simple Boston girl, a poor-but-semi-honest art dealer, and I can't just go skipping off to Amsterdam this week, the Aegean the next week—"

"Why not?"

"Why *not*? Are you serious? I have responsibilities, for one thing."

"Repressions. It's your New England background."

"*Repressions?* How can you, of all people—"

Hatcher blushed.

"I don't mean that kind. I mean the work ethic."

"It's not that. I have responsibilities, that's all. I have a gallery to run. Micheline. Friends."

"Ducks."

"That's right, ducks."

The argument continued over the next three days. It seldom became emotional. Rather, it became increasingly complex and subtle. At the end, it was as tortuously convoluted and oblique as a disputation between medieval scholastic theologians. Late in the evening of the third day, Sheila discovered the final, unassailable argument why she could not, under any circumstances, leave Boston and go to Greece with Hatcher.

She leaned over to tap him on the shoulder. Then she stopped herself, sighed, and settled back in her seat.

At that moment they were thirty-eight thousand feet

over the coast of Nova Scotia, and Sheila was having difficulty making herself heard over the sound of the *bouzouki* music from the loudspeaker in the overhead rack.

The Gentlemen of 16 JULY

a work of narrative nonfiction

René Louis Maurice

and the author of
Triple and *Eye of the Needle*

Ken Follett

"A gripping, astonishing story of a remarkable bank theft..."—*Manchester Union Leader*

"A page-turner!"—*New York Daily News*

"A storyteller's dream—and the authors have made the most of it."—*John Barkham Reviews*

"A clear, fast-paced story of a crime that rivals anything in fiction."—*Baton Rouge Sunday Magazine*

☐ 41-655-5 **GENTLEMEN OF 16 JULY** $2.75

Buy it at your local bookstore or use this handy coupon

Clip and mail this page with order